Resnick's Menagerie

MIKE RESNICK

Resnick's

Menagerie

With an Introduction
by Kij Johnson

SILVERBERRY
PRESS

This book is a work of fiction. Except in the appendix, references to real people, events, establishments, organizations, or locales are intended only to provide a sense of authenticity and are used to advance the fictional narrative. All other characters, and all incidents and dialogue, are drawn from the author's imagination and are not to be construed as real.

RESNICK'S MENAGERIE
Introduction by Kij Johnson. All stories © Mike Resnick, as described below, with excerpts from THE HUNTING OF THE SNARK by Lewis Carroll, 1874 on pp. 86–137. All photographs © Mike Resnick.

THE ELEPHANTS ON NEPTUNE © 2000 by Mike Resnick. First appeared in *Asimov's Science Fiction*. THE LAST DOG © 1977 by Mike Resnick. First appeared in *Hunting Dog Magazine*. MALISH © 1991 by Mike Resnick. First appeared in *Horse Fantastic*. ROYAL BLOODLINES © 2010 by Mike Resnick. First appeared in this form in *Running with the Pack*. BARNABY IN EXILE © 1994 by Mike Resnick. First appeared in *Asimov's Science Fiction*. A BETTER MOUSETRAP © 2007 by Mike Resnick. First appeared in *Nature*. HUNTING THE SNARK © 1999 by Mike Resnick. First appeared in *Asimov's Science Fiction*. STALKING THE UNICORN WITH GUN AND CAMERA © 1986 by Mike Resnick. First appeared in *The Magazine of Fantasy and Science Fiction*. STALKING THE VAMPIRE © 2008 by Mike Resnick. First appeared in *Stalkling the Vampire: A Fable of Tonight*. STALKING THE DRAGON © 2009 by Mike Resnick. First appeared in *Stalking the Dragon: A Fable of Tonight*. THE ONE THAT GOT AWAY © 2004 by Mike Resnick. First appeared in *Weird Trails: The Magazine of Supernatural Cowboy Fiction*. BLUE © 1978 by Mike Resnick. First appeared in *Hunting Dog Magazine*. POST TIME IN PINK © 1991 by Mike Resnick. First appeared in *Newer York*. OLD MACDONALD HAD A FARM © 2001 by Mike Resnick. First appeared in *Asimov's Science Fiction*. DARKER THAN YOU WROTE © 1996 by Mike Resnick. First appeared in *The Williamson Effect*. THE BOY WHO CRIED "DRAGON!" © 2005 by Mike Resnick. First appeared in *Young Warriors*. ON SAFARI © 2010 by Mike Resnick. First appeared in *Gateways*. TRAVELS WITH MY CATS © 2004 by Mike Resnick. First appeared in *Asimov's Science Fiction*. LORD OF THE (SHOW) RINGS © 2008 by Mike Resnick. First appeared in *Challenger*.

Cover Art by Borislav Varadinov.   SILVERBERRY PRESS
Interior Illustrations © 2012 by Will Jacques.   P.O. Box 492, Sharon, MA 02067
Book Design by Leonid Korogodski.   http://www.silverberrypress.com

Cataloging-in-Publication data have been applied for.
ISBN   978-0-9843608-8-8
LCCN 2012930368

First Edition September 2012   10 9 8 7 6 5 4 3 2 1

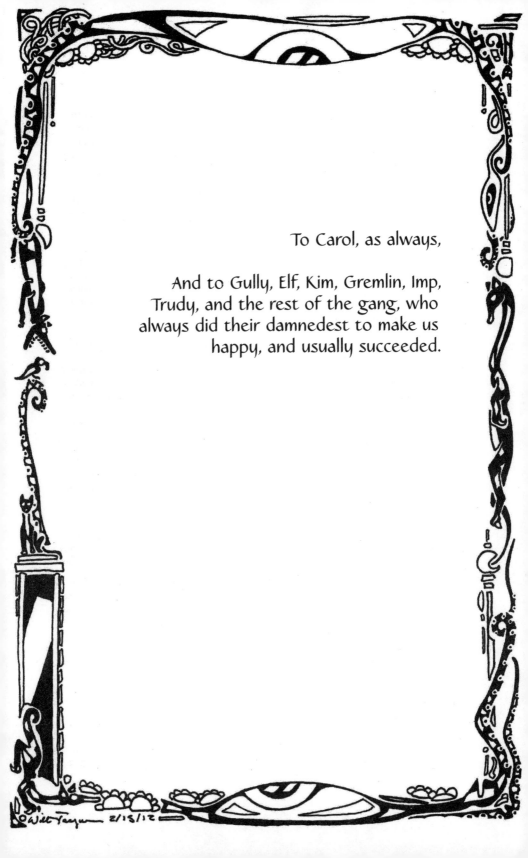

To Carol, as always,

And to Gully, Elf, Kim, Gremlin, Imp, Trudy, and the rest of the gang, who always did their damnedest to make us happy, and usually succeeded.

Introduction

by Kij Johnson

M ike Resnick may be an elephant person.

Lots of people like animals, but some take it up a notch. Cat people (okay, crazy cat people, anyway) have houses crammed with cat-shaped pillows, cat-shaped teapots, and cat-shaped cats. And if you have a horse-person friend, you already know that you will never lack for holiday gift options.

So far, Resnick has written two stories about elephants, included here in his *Menagerie*. Why elephants? This is at least two more than most writers, and so, to my mind, this may make him an elephant person.

Or he might be a dog person, like me. He writes fiction about them with knowledge, affection, and respect. He also has had many, many dogs in real life, as the cofounder, with his wife Carol, of a kennel breeding award-winning collies. I can easily imagine that he has a house filled with collie plush toys, coffee mugs, tea towels, waffle-weave cotton lap-rugs, and quaintly shaped car fresheners.

Or unreal beasties. He writes a lot about them, too.

I thought it might be a good idea to catalog all the animals in *Resnick's Menagerie and* see if there's a clear trend. This is what I got, not counting walk-ons:

- *Bonobos*: 1
- *Cats*: 3
- *Cat-like thingies*: 1
- *Dogs*: 2, plus 3 non-fictional collies, in *Lord of the (Show) Rings.*
- *Horses*: 1
- *Possums*: 1
- *Alien monsters*: 2
- *Were-thingies*: 4
- *Assorted mythological beasts*: 4
- *Mice*: Hundreds, but they're not individuals so much as a collective.
- *Butterballs*: Many, ditto. "Butterballs?" you say. Read on.
- *Elephants*: Lots more than your average short story collection.
- *People.*

Mostly people. People with hearts and hopes and fears. People with funny stories to tell—or sad ones. People who make me laugh—or who break my heart. Some who aren't even human.

Why are Mike's animal stories so affecting? Because all his stories are affecting in one way or another—charming, wry, hilarious, or exciting. But beyond this, I think that he finds satisfaction in writing about animals for the same reasons I do. They are aliens, friends, foes, comic foils, role models, and tools. They reflect what we do well as human beings—or what we do badly. But they are not human and not exactly what we want them to be; they have their own concerns, their own agendas. Mike's animal stories push at the lines between people and not-people, always in interesting ways.

So do some ambling about this marvellous menagerie of Mike's. Look into all the exhibits. There's something for everyone, big and small, monsters and mice. I laughed a lot, bit my nails in a couple of places, and I cried. See if you do, too.

And on your way out don't forget to buy Mike a nice elephant mug. I bet he'll love that.

—Kij Johnson
February 2012

Kij Johnson is the author of *The Fox Woman* and *Fudoki*, the critically acclaimed fantasy novels about kitsune, the Japanese were-foxes. She is hardly new to writing speculative short fiction about animals. To her belong the Hugo and Nebula award-winning *Ponies*, the Hugo- and Nebula-nominated *26 monkeys! Also, the abyss*, the Nebula-nominated *The evolution of trickster stories among the dogs of North Park after the Change*, and *The cat who walked a thousand miles*. You can find out more about her and her writing at *KijJohnson.com*.

Resnick's Menagerie

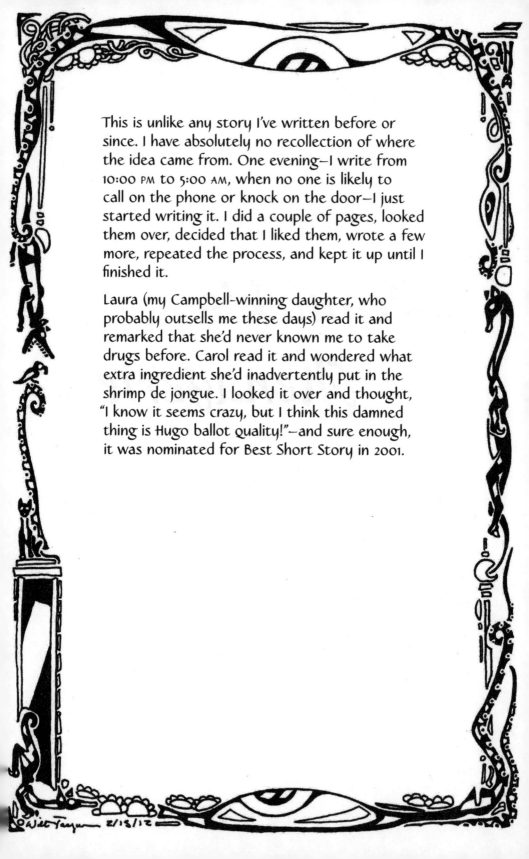

This is unlike any story I've written before or since. I have absolutely no recollection of where the idea came from. One evening—I write from 10:00 PM to 5:00 AM, when no one is likely to call on the phone or knock on the door—I just started writing it. I did a couple of pages, looked them over, decided that I liked them, wrote a few more, repeated the process, and kept it up until I finished it.

Laura (my Campbell-winning daughter, who probably outsells me these days) read it and remarked that she'd never known me to take drugs before. Carol read it and wondered what extra ingredient she'd inadvertently put in the shrimp de jongue. I looked it over and thought, "I know it seems crazy, but I think this damned thing is Hugo ballot quality!"—and sure enough, it was nominated for Best Short Story in 2001.

The Elephants
on Neptune

The elephants on Neptune led an idyllic life.

None ever went hungry or were sick. They had no predators. They never fought a war. There was no prejudice. Their birth rate exactly equaled their death rate. Their skins and bowels were free of parasites.

The herd traveled at a speed that accommodated the youngest and weakest members. No sick or infirm elephant was ever left behind.

They were a remarkable race, the elephants on Neptune. They lived out their lives in peace and tranquility, they never argued among themselves, the old were always gentle with the young. When one was born, the entire herd gathered to celebrate. When one died, the entire herd mourned its passing. There were no animosities, no petty jealousies, no unresolved quarrels.

Only one thing stopped it from being Utopia, and that was the fact that an elephant never forgets.

Not ever.

No matter how hard he tries.

WHEN MEN FINALLY landed on Neptune in 2473 A.D., the elephants were very apprehensive. Still, they approached the spaceship in a spirit of fellowship and goodwill.

The men were a little apprehensive themselves. Every survey of Neptune told them it was a gas giant, and yet they had landed on solid ground. And if their surveys were wrong, who knew what else might be wrong as well?

A tall man stepped out onto the frozen surface. Then another. Then a third. By the time they had all emerged, there were almost as many men as elephants.

"Well, I'll be damned!" said the leader of the men. "You're elephants!"

"And you're men," said the elephants nervously.

"That's right," said the men. "We claim this planet in the name of the United Federation of Earth."

"You're united now?" asked the elephants, feeling much relieved.

"Well, the survivors are," said the men.

"Those are ominous-looking weapons you're carrying," said the elephants, shifting their feet uncomfortably.

"They go with the uniforms," said the men. "Not to worry. Why would we want to harm you? There's always been a deep bond between men and elephants."

That wasn't exactly the way the elephants remembered it.

326 B.C.

ALEXANDER THE GREAT met Porus, King of the Punjab of India, in the Battle of the Jhelum River. Porus had the first military elephants Alexander had ever seen. He studied the situation, then sent his men out at night to fire thousands of arrows into extremely sensitive trunks and underbellies. The elephants went mad with pain and began killing the nearest men they could find, which happened to be their keepers and handlers. After his great victory, Alexander slaughtered the surviving elephants so that he would never have to face them in battle.

THE FIRST CLASH *between the two species of elephants. Ptolemy IV took his African elephants against Antiochus the Great's Indian elephants.*

The elephants on Neptune weren't sure who won the war, but they knew who lost. Not a single elephant on either side survived.

Later that same 217 B.C.

WHILE PTOLEMY WAS *battling in Syria, Hannibal took thirty-seven elephants over the Alps to fight the Romans. Fourteen of them froze to death, but the rest lived just long enough to absorb the enemy's spear thrusts while Hannibal was winning the Battle of Cannae.*

"WE HAVE IMPORTANT things to talk about," said the men. "For example, Neptune's atmosphere is singularly lacking in oxygen. How do you breathe?"

"Through our noses," said the elephants.

"That was a serious question," said the men, fingering their weapons ominously.

"We are incapable of being anything *but* serious," explained the elephants. "Humor requires that someone be the butt of the joke, and we find that too cruel to contemplate."

"All right," said the men, who were vaguely dissatisfied with the answer, perhaps because they didn't understand it. "Let's try another question. What is the mechanism by which we are communicating? You don't wear radio transmitters, and because of our helmets we can't hear any sounds that aren't on our radio bands."

"We communicate through a psychic bond," explained the elephants.

"That's not very scientific," said the men disapprovingly. "Are you sure you don't mean a telepathic bond?"

"No, though it comes to the same thing in the end," answered the elephants. "We know that we sound like we're speaking English to you, except for the man on the left who thinks we're speaking Hebrew."

"And what do we sound like to you?" demanded the men.

"You sound exactly as if you're making gentle rumbling sounds in your stomachs and your bowels."

"That's fascinating," said the men, who privately thought it was a lot more disgusting than fascinating.

"Do you know what's *really* fascinating?" responded the elephants. "The fact that you've got a Jew with you." They saw that the men didn't comprehend, so they continued: "We always felt we were in a race with the Jews to see which of us would be exterminated first. We used to call ourselves the Jews of the animal kingdom." They turned and faced the Jewish spaceman. "Did the Jews think of themselves as the elephants of the human kingdom?"

"Not until you just mentioned it," said the Jewish spaceman, who suddenly found himself agreeing with them.

42 B.C.

THE ROMANS GATHERED *their Jewish prisoners in the arena in Alexandria, then turned fear-crazed elephants loose on them. The spectators began jumping up and down and screaming for blood—and, being contrarians, the elephants attacked the spectators instead of the Jews, proving once and for all that you can't trust a pachyderm.*

When the dust had cleared, the Jews felt the events of the day had reaffirmed their claim to be God's chosen people. They weren't the Romans' chosen people, though. After the soldiers killed the elephants, they put all the Jews to the sword, too.

"IT'S NOT HIS fault he's a Jew any more than it's your fault that you're elephants," said the rest of the men. "We don't hold it against either of you."

"We find that difficult to believe," said the elephants.

"You do?" said the men. "Then consider this: the Indians—that's the good Indians, the ones from India, not the bad Indians from America—worshipped Ganesh, an elephant-headed god."

"We didn't know that," admitted the elephants, who were more impressed than they let on. "Do the Indians still worship Ganesh?"

"Well, we're sure they would if we hadn't killed them all while we were defending the Raj," said the men. "Elephants were no longer in the military by then," they added. "That's something to be grateful for."

THEIR VERY LAST battle came when Tamerlane the Great went to war against Sultan Mahmoud. Tamerlane won by tying branches to buffalos' horns, setting fire to them, and then stampeding the buffalo herd into Mahmoud's elephants, which effectively ended the elephant as a war machine, buffalo being much less expensive to acquire and feed.

All the remaining domesticated elephants were then trained for elephant fighting, which was exactly like cock-fighting, only on a larger scale. Much larger. It became a wildly popular sport for thirty or forty years until they ran out of participants.

"NOT ONLY DID we worship you," continued the men, "but we actually named a country after you—the Ivory Coast. *That* should prove our good intentions."

"You didn't name it after *us*," said the elephants. "You named it after the parts of our bodies that you kept killing us for."

"You're being too critical," said the men. "We could have named it after some local politician with no vowels in his name."

"Speaking of the Ivory Coast," said the elephants, "did you know that the first alien visitors to Earth landed there in 1883?"

"What did they look like?"

"They had ivory exoskeletons," answered the elephants. "They took one look at the carnage and left."

"Are you sure you're not making this all up?" asked the men.

"Why would we lie to you at this late date?"

"Maybe its your nature," suggested the men.

"Oh, no," said the elephants. "Our nature is that we always tell the truth. Our tragedy is that we always remember it."

The men decided that it was time to break for dinner, answer calls of nature, and check in with Mission Control to report what they'd found. They all walked back to the ship, except for one man, who lingered behind.

All of the elephants left too, except for one lone bull. "I intuit that you have a question to ask," he said.

"Yes," replied the man. "You have such an acute sense of smell, how did anyone ever sneak up on you during the hunt?"

"The greatest elephant hunters were the Wanderobo of Kenya and Uganda. They would rub our dung all over their bodies to hide their own scent, and would then silently approach us."

"Ah," said the man, nodding his head. "It makes sense."

"Perhaps," conceded the elephant. Then he added, with all the dignity he could muster, "But if the tables were turned, I would sooner die that cover myself with *your* shit."

He turned away and set off to rejoin his comrades.

NEPTUNE IS UNIQUE among all the worlds in the galaxy. It alone recognizes the truism that change is inevitable, and acts upon it in ways that seem very little removed from magic.

For reasons the elephants couldn't fathom or explain, Neptune encourages metamorphosis. Not merely adaptation, although no one could deny that they adapted to the atmosphere and the climate and the fluctuating surface of the planet and the lack of acacia trees—but *metamorphosis*. The elephants understood at a gut level that Neptune had somehow imparted to them the ability to evolve at will, though they had been careful never to abuse this gift.

And since they were elephants, and hence incapable of carrying a grudge, they thought it was a pity that the men couldn't evolve to the point where they could leave their bulky spacesuits and awkward helmets behind, and walk free and unencumbered across this most perfect of planets.

THE ELEPHANTS WERE waiting when the men emerged from their ship and strode across Neptune's surface to meet them.

"This is very curious," said the leader.

"What is?" asked the elephants.

The leader stared at them, frowning. "You seem smaller."

"We were just going to say that you seemed larger," replied the elephants.

"This is almost as silly as the conversation I just had with Mission Control," said the leader. "They say there aren't any elephants on Neptune."

"What do they think we are?" asked the elephants.

"Hallucinations or space monsters," answered the leader. "If you're hallucinations, we're supposed to ignore you."

He seemed to be waiting for the elephants to ask what the men were supposed to do if they were space monsters, but elephants can be as stubborn as men when they want to be, and that was a question they had no intention of asking.

The men stared at the elephants in silence for almost five minutes. The elephants stared back.

Finally the leader spoke again.

"Would you excuse me for a moment?" he said. "I suddenly have an urge to eat some greens."

He turned and marched back to the ship without another word.

The rest of the men shuffled their feet uncomfortably for another few seconds.

"Is something wrong?" asked the elephants.

"Are we getting bigger or are you getting smaller?" replied the men.

"Yes," answered the elephants.

"I FEEL MUCH better now," said the leader, rejoining his men and facing the elephants.

"You look better," agreed the elephants. "More handsome, somehow."

"Do you really think so?" asked the leader, obviously flattered.

THE ELEPHANTS ON NEPTUNE   21

"You are the finest specimen of your race we've ever seen," said the elephants truthfully. "We especially like your ears."

"You do?" he asked, flapping them slightly. "No one's ever mentioned them before."

"Doubtless an oversight," said the elephants.

"Speaking of ears," said the leader, "are you African elephants or Indian? I thought this morning you were African—they're the ones with the bigger ears, right?—but now I'm not sure."

"We're Neptunian elephants," they answered.

"Oh."

They exchanged pleasantries for another hour, and then the men looked up at the sky.

"Where did the sun go?" they asked.

"It's night," explained the elephants. "Our day is only fourteen hours long. We get seven hours of sunlight and seven of darkness."

"The sun wasn't all that bright anyway," said one of the men with a shrug that set his ears flapping wildly.

"We have very poor eyesight, so we hardly notice," said the elephants. "We depend on our senses of smell and hearing."

The men seemed very uneasy. Finally they turned to their leader.

"May we be excused for a few moments, sir?" they asked.

"Why?"

"Suddenly we're starving," said the men.

"And I gotta use the john," said one of them.

"So do I," said a second one.

"Me too," echoed another.

"Do you men feel all right?" asked the leader, his enormous nose wrinkled in concern.

"I feel great!" said the nearest man. "I could eat a horse!"

The other men all made faces.

"Well, a small forest, anyway," he amended.

"Permission granted," said the leader. The men began walking rapidly back to the ship. "And bring me a couple of heads of lettuce, and maybe an apple or two," he called after them.

"You can join them if you wish," said the elephants, who were coming to the conclusion that eating a horse wasn't half as disgusting a notion as they had thought it would be.

"No, my job is to make contact with aliens," explained the leader. "Although when you get right down to it, you're not as alien as we'd expected."

"You're every bit as human as *we* expected," replied the elephants.

"I'll take that as a great compliment," said the leader. "But then, I would expect nothing less from traditional friends such as yourselves."

"Traditional friends?" repeated the elephants, who had thought nothing a man said could still surprise them.

"Certainly. Even after you stopped being our partners in war, we've always had a special relationship with you."

"You have?"

"Sure. Look how P.T. Barnum made an international superstar out of the original Jumbo. That animal lived like a king—or at least he did until he was accidentally run over by a locomotive."

"We don't want to appear cynical," said the elephants, "but how do you *accidentally* run over a seven-ton animal?"

"You do it," said the leader, his face glowing with pride, "by inventing the locomotive in the first place. Whatever else we may be, you must admit we're a race that can boast of magnificent accomplishments: the internal combustion engine, splitting the atom, reaching the planets, curing cancer." He paused. "I don't mean to denigrate you, but truly, what have you got to equal that?"

"We live our lives free of sin," responded the elephants simply. "We respect each other's beliefs, we don't harm our environment, and we have never made war on other elephants."

"And you'd put that up against the heart transplant, the silicon chip, and the three-dimensional television screen?" asked the leader with just a touch of condescension.

"Our aspirations are different from yours," said the elephants. "But we are as proud of our heroes as you are of yours."

"You have heroes?" said the leader, unable to hide his surprise.

"Certainly." The elephants rattled off their roll of honor: "The Kilimanjaro Elephant. Selemundi. Ahmed of Marsabit. And the Magnificent Seven of Krueger Park: Mafunyane, Shingwedzi, Kambaki, Joao, Dzombo, Ndlulamithi, and Phelwane."

"Are they here on Neptune?" asked the leader as his men began returning from the ship.

"No," said the elephants. "You killed them all."

"We must have had a reason," insisted the men.

"They were there," said the elephants. "And they carried magnificent ivory."

"See?" said the men. "We *knew* we had a reason."

The elephants didn't like that answer much, but they were too polite to say so, and the two species exchanged views and white lies all through the brief Neptunian night. When the sun rose again, the men voiced their surprise.

"Look at you!" they said. "What's happening?"

"We got tired of walking on all fours," said the elephants. "We decided it's more comfortable to stand upright."

"And where are your trunks?" demanded the men.

"They got in the way."

"Well, if that isn't the damnedest thing!" said the men. Then they looked at each other. "On second thought, *this* is the damnedest thing! We're bursting out of our helmets!"

"And our ears are flapping," said the leader.

"And our noses are getting longer," said another man.

"This is most disconcerting," said the leader. He paused. "On the other hand, I don't feel nearly as much animosity toward you as I did yesterday. I wonder why?"

"Beats us," said the elephants, who were becoming annoyed with the whining quality of his voice.

"It's true, though," continued the leader. "Today I feel like every elephant in the universe is my friend."

"Too bad you didn't feel that way when it would have made a difference," said the elephants irritably. "Did you know you killed sixteen million of us in the 20ᵗʰ Century alone?"

"But we made amends," noted the men. "We set up game parks to preserve you."

"True," acknowledged the elephants. "But in the process you took away most of our habitat. Then you decided to cull us so we wouldn't exhaust the park's food supply." They paused dramatically. "That was when Earth received its second alien visitation. The aliens examined the theory of preserving by culling, decided that Earth was an insane asylum, and made arrangements to drop all their incurables off in the future."

Tears rolled down the men's bulky cheeks. "We feel just terrible about that," they wept. A few of them dabbed at their eyes with short, stubby fingers that seemed to be growing together.

"Maybe we should go back to the ship and consider all this," said the men's leader, looking around futilely for something large enough in which to blow his nose. "Besides, I have to use the facilities."

"Sounds good to me," said one of the men. "I got dibs on the cabbage."

"Guys?" said another. "I know it sounds silly, but it's much more comfortable to walk on all fours."

The elephants waited until the men were all on the ship, and then went about their business, which struck them as odd, because before the men came they didn't *have* any business.

"You know," said one of the elephants. "I've got a sudden taste for a hamburger."

"I want a beer," said a second. Then: "I wonder if there's a football game on the subspace radio?"

"It's really curious," remarked a third. "I have this urge to cheat on my wife—and I'm not even married."

Vaguely disturbed without knowing why, they soon fell into a restless, dreamless sleep.

SHERLOCK HOLMES ONCE *said that after you eliminate the impossible, what remains, however improbable, must be the truth.*

Joseph Conrad said that truth is a flower in whose neighborhood others must wither.

Walt Whitman suggested that whatever satisfied the soul was truth.

Neptune would have driven all three of them berserk.

"TRUTH IS A *dream, unless my dream is true," said George Santayana.*
He was just crazy enough to have made it on Neptune.

"WE'VE BEEN WONDERING," said the men when the two groups met in the morning. "Whatever happened to Earth's last elephant?"

"His name was Jamal," answered the elephants. "Someone shot him."

"Is he on display somewhere?"

"His right ear, which resembles the outline of the continent of Africa, has a map painted on it and is in the Presidential Mansion in Kenya. They turned his left ear over—and you'd be surprised how many left ears were thrown away over the centuries before someone somewhere thought of turning them over—and another map was painted, which now hangs in a museum in Bombay. His feet were turned into a matched set of barstools, and currently grace the Aces High Show Lounge in Dallas, Texas. His scrotum serves as a tobacco pouch for an elderly Scottish politician. One tusk is on display at the British Museum. The other bears a scrimshaw and resides in a store window in Beijing. His tail has been turned into a fly swatter, and is the proud possession of one of the last *vaqueros* in Argentina."

"We had no idea," said the men, honestly appalled.

"Jamal's very last words before he died were, 'I forgive you,'" continued the elephants. "He was promptly transported to a sphere higher than any man can ever aspire to."

The men looked up and scanned the sky. "Can we see it from here?" they asked.

"We doubt it."

The men looked back at the elephants—except that they had evolved yet again. In fact, they had eliminated every physical feature for which they had ever been hunted. Tusks, ears, feet, tails, even scrotums, all had undergone enormous change. The elephants looked exactly like human beings, right down to their spacesuits and helmets.

The men, on the other hand, had burst out of their space-suits (which had fallen away in shreds and tatters), sprouted tusks, and found themselves conversing by making rumbling noises in their bellies.

"This is very annoying," said the men who were no longer men. "Now that we seem to have become elephants," they continued, "perhaps you can tell us what elephants *do?*"

"Well," said the elephants who were no longer elephants, "in our spare time, we create new ethical systems based on selflessness, forgiveness, and family values. And we try to syn-thesize the work of Kant, Descartes, Spinoza, Thomas Aquinas and Bishop Barkley into something far more sophisticated and logical, while never forgetting to incorporate emotional and aesthetic values at each stage."

"Well, we suppose that's pretty interesting," said the new elephants without much enthusiasm. "Can we do anything else?"

"Oh, yes," the new spacemen assured them, pulling out their .550 Nitro Expresses and .475 Holland & Holland Magnums and taking aim. "You can die."

"This can't be happening! You yourselves were elephants yesterday!"

"True. But we're men now."

"But why kill us?" demanded the elephants.

"Force of habit," said the men as they pulled their triggers.

Then, with nothing left to kill, the men who used to be elephants boarded their ship and went out into space, boldly searching for new life forms.

NEPTUNE HAS SEEN many species come and go. Microbes have been spontaneously generated nine times over the eons. It has been visited by aliens thirty-seven different times. It has seen forty-three wars, five of them atomic, and the creation of 1,026 religions, none of which possessed any universal truths. More of the vast tapestry of galactic history has been played out on Neptune's foreboding surface than on any other world in Sol's system.

Planets cannot offer opinions, of course, but if they could, Neptune would almost certainly say that the most interesting creatures it ever hosted were the elephants, whose gentle ways and unique perspectives remain fresh and clear in its memory. It mourns the fact that they became extinct by their own hand. Kind of.

A problem would arise when you asked whether Neptune was referring to the old-new elephants who began life as killers, or the new-old ones who ended life as killers.

Neptune just hates questions like that.

Elephants at the Chobe National Park, Botswana. From the personal photo collection of Mike Resnick.

Carol and I moved to Cincinnati in 1976, when we bought the second-largest luxury boarding and grooming kennel in America. It had a huge, well-furnished meeting room that we rented out to various dog and cat clubs six nights a week, but one night was reserved for the local science fiction writers group. Maybe meeting in a kennel inspired them to write dog stories, and I remember that one night I got really annoyed at the similarity and predictability of the stories and remarked that I was sick and tired of stories in which the alien animal of the far future always turned out to be a cute Bassett puppy or a dog with psi powers, and couldn't anyone write about a real dog?

So naturally I was challenged to do so, and I wrote *The Last Dog*. Back then none of the magazine editors knew my name, and it got form rejects from all of them (which meant it never got past the slush pile to the editor), so—at a time when the digests were paying three to four cents a word—I reluctantly sold it to *Hunting Dog Magazine* for a quarter a word. A few months later it won me my first fiction award of any kind, the American Dog Writers Award for Best Short Fiction of 1977.

The Last Dog

The Dog—old, mangy, his vertebrae forming little ridges beneath the slack skin that covered his gaunt body—trotted through the deserted streets, nose to the ground. He was missing half an ear and most of his tail, and caked blood covered his neck like a scarf. He may have been gold once, or light brown, but now he looked like an old red brick, even down to the straw and mud that clung to those few portions of his body which still retained any hair at all.

Since he had no true perception of the passage of time, he had no idea when he had last eaten—except that it had been a long time ago. A broken radiator in an automobile graveyard had provided water for the past week and kept him in the area long after the last of the rusty, translucent liquid was gone.

He was panting now, his breath coming in a never-ending series of short spurts and gasps. His sides ached, his eyes watered, and every now and then he would trip over the rubble of the decayed and ruined buildings that lined the tortuously fragmented street. The toes of his feet were covered by sores and calluses, and both his dew claws had long since been torn off.

He continued trotting, occasionally shivering from the cold breeze that whistled down the streets of the lifeless city. Once he saw a rat, but a premature whine of hunger had sent it scurrying off into the debris before he could catch it, and so he trotted, his stride a little shorter, his chest hurting a little more, searching for sustenance so that he would live another day to hunt again and eat again and live still another day.

Then suddenly he froze, his mud-caked nostrils testing the wind, the pitiful stump of a tail held rigidly behind him. He remained motionless for almost a minute, except for a spasmodic quivering in one foreleg, then slunk into the shadows and advanced silently down the street.

He emerged at what had once been an intersection, stared at the thing across the street from him, and blinked. His eyesight, none too good even in the days of his youth and health, was insufficient to the task, and so he inched forward, belly to ground, flecks of saliva falling onto his chest.

The Man heard a faint shuffling sound and looked into the shadows, a segment of an old two–by–four in his hand. He, too, was gaunt and dirty, his hair unkempt, four teeth missing and another one half-rotted away. His feet were wrapped in old rags, and the only thing that held his clothes together was the dirt.

"Who's there?" he said in a rasping voice.

The Dog, fangs bared, moved out from between buildings and began advancing, a low growl rumbling in his throat. The Man turned to face him, strengthening his grip on his makeshift warclub. They stopped when they were fifteen feet apart, tense and unmoving. Slowly the Man raised his club to striking position; slowly the Dog gathered his hind legs beneath him.

Then, without warning, a rat raced out of the debris and ran between them. Savage cries escaped the lips of both the

Dog and the Man. The Dog pounced, but the Man's stick was even faster; it flew through the air and landed on the rat's back, pulping it to the ground and killing it instantly.

The Man walked forward to retrieve his weapon and his prey. As he reached down, the Dog emitted a low growl. The Man stared at him for a long moment; then, very slowly, very carefully, he picked up one end of the stick. He sawed with the other end against the smashed body of the rat until it split in half and shoved one pulpy segment toward the Dog. The Dog remained motionless for a few seconds, then lowered his head, grabbed the blood-spattered piece of flesh and tissue, and raced off across the street with it. He stopped at the edge of the shadows, lay down, and began gnawing at his grisly meal. The Man watched him for a moment, then picked up his half of the rat, squatted down like some million-years-gone progenitor, and did the same.

When his meal was done, the Man belched once, walked over to the still-standing wall of a building, sat with his back against it, laid his two-by-four across his thighs, and stared at the Dog. The Dog, licking forepaws that would never again be clean, stared back.

They slept thus, motionless, in the ghost city. When the Man awoke the next morning, he arose, and the Dog did likewise. The Man balanced his stick across his shoulder and began walking, and after a moment the Dog followed him. The Man spent most of the day walking through the city, looking into the soft innards of stores and shops, occasionally cursing as dead store after dead store refused to yield up shoes, or coats, or food. At twilight he built a small fire in the rubble and looked around for the Dog, but could not find it.

The man slept uneasily and awoke some two hours before sunrise. The Dog was sleeping about twenty feet away from him. The Man sat up abruptly, and the Dog, startled, raced off. Ten minutes later he was back, stopping about eighty feet distant, ready to race away again at an instant's warning, but back nonetheless.

The Man looked at the Dog, shrugged, and began walking in a northerly direction. By midday he had reached the outskirts of the city and, finding the ground soft and muddy, he dug a hole with his hands and his stick. He sat down next to it and waited as water slowly seeped into it. Finally he reached his hands down, cupping them together, and drew the precious fluid up to his lips. He did this twice more, then began walking again. Some instinct prompted him to turn back, and he saw the Dog eagerly lapping up what water remained.

He made another kill that night, a medium-sized bird that had flown into the second-floor room of a crumbling hotel and couldn't remember how to fly out before he pulped it. He ate most of it, put the rest into what remained of a pocket, and walked outside. He threw it on the ground and the Dog slunk out of the shadows, still tense but no longer growling. The Man sighed, returned to the hotel, and climbed up to the second floor. There were no rooms with windows intact, but he did find one with half a mattress remaining, and he collapsed upon it.

When he awoke, the Dog was lying in the doorway, sleeping soundly.

They walked, a little closer this time, through the remains of the forest that was north of the city. After they had proceeded about a dozen miles, they found a small stream that was not quite dry and drank from it, the Man first and then the Dog. That night the man lit another fire and the Dog lay down on the opposite side of it. The next day the Dog killed a small, undernourished squirrel. He did not share it with the Man, but neither did he growl or bare his teeth as the Man approached. That night the Man killed an opossum, and they remained in the area for two days, until the last of the marsupial's flesh had been consumed.

They walked north for almost two weeks, making an occasional kill, finding an occasional source of water. Then one night it rained, and there was no fire, and the Man sat, arms hugging himself, beneath a large tree. Soon the Dog approached him, sat about four feet away, and then slowly, ever so slowly, inched forward as the rain struck his flanks. The Man reached out absently and stroked the Dog's neck. It was their first physical contact, and the Dog leaped back, snarling. The Man withdrew his hand and sat motionless, and soon the Dog moved forward again.

After a period of time that might have been ten minutes or perhaps two hours, the Man reached out once more, and this time, although the Dog trembled and tensed, he did not pull away. The Man's long fingers slowly moved up the sore-covered neck, scratched behind the torn ears, gently stroked the scarred head. Finally the Man withdrew his hand and rolled over on his side. The Dog looked at him for a moment, then sighed and laid up against his emaciated body.

The Man awoke the next morning to the feeling of something warm and scaly pressed into his hand. It was not the cool, moist nose of the dogs of literature, because this was not a dog of literature. This was the Last Dog, and he was the Last Man, and if they looked less than heroic, at least there was no one around to see and bemoan how the mighty had fallen.

The Man patted the Dog's head, arose, stretched, and began walking. The Dog trotted at his side, and for the first time in many years the nub of his tail moved rapidly from side to side. They hunted and ate and drank and slept, then repeated the procedure again and again.

And then they came to the Other.

The Other looked like neither Man nor Dog, nor like any-thing else of Earth, as indeed it was not. It had come from beyond Centauri, beyond Arcturus, past Antares. from deep at the core of the galaxy, where the stars pressed so close together that nightfall never came. It had come, and had seen, and had conquered.

"You!" hissed the Man, holding his stick at the ready.

"You are the last," said the Other. "For six years I have scoured and scourged the face of this planet, for six years I have eaten alone and slept alone and lived alone and hunted down the survivors of the war one by one, and you are the last. There is only you to be slain, and then I may go home."

And, so saying, it withdrew a weapon that looked strangely like a pistol, but wasn't.

The Man crouched and prepared to hurl his stick, but, even as he did so, a brick-red, scarred, bristling engine of destruction hurtled past him, leaping through space for the Other. The Other touched what passed for a belt, made a quick gesture in the air, and the Dog bounced back off of something that was invisible, unsensible, but tangible.

Then, very slowly, almost casually, the Other pointed its weapon at the Man. There was no explosion, no flash of light, no whirring of gears, but suddenly the Man grasped his throat and fell to the ground.

The Dog got up and limped painfully over to the Man. He nuzzled his face, whined once, and pawed at his body, trying to turn it over.

"It is no use," said the Other, although its lips no longer moved. "He was the last, and now he is dead."

The Dog whined again, and pushed the Man's lifeless head with his muzzle.

"Come, Animal," said the Other wordlessly. "Come with me and I shall feed you and tend to your wounds."

I will stay with the Man, said the Dog, also wordlessly.

"But he is dead," said the Other. "Soon you will grow hungry and weak."

I was hungry and weak before, said the Dog.

The Other took a step forward, but stopped as the Dog bared his teeth and growled.

"He was not worth your loyalty," said the Other.

He was my— The Dog's brain searched for a word, but the concept it sought was complex far beyond its meager abilities to formulate. *He was my friend.*

"He was my enemy," said the Other. "He was petty and barbarous and unscrupulous and all that is worst in a sentient being. He was Man."

Yes, said the Dog. *He was Man.* With another whimper, he lay down beside the body of the Man and rested his head on its chest.

"There are no more," said the Other. "And soon you will leave him."

The Dog looked up at the Other and snarled again, and then the Other was gone and the Dog was alone with the Man. He licked him and nuzzled him and stood guard over him for two days and two nights, and then, as the Other had said he would, he left to hunt for food and water.

And he came to a valley of fat, lazy rabbits and cool, clear ponds, and he ate and drank and grew strong, and his wounds began to scab over and heal, and his coat grew long and luxuriant.

And because he was only a Dog, it was not too long before he forgot that there had ever been such a thing as a Man, except on those chilly nights when he lay alone beneath a tree in the valley and dreamt of a bond that had been forged by a gentle touch upon the head or a soft word barely audible above the crackling of a small fire.

And, being a Dog, one day he forgot even that, and assumed that the emptiness within him came only from hunger. And when he grew old and feeble and sick, he did not seek out the Man's barren bones and lie down to die beside them, but rather he dug a hole in the damp earth near the pond and lay there, his eyes half-closed, a numbness setting in at his extremities and working its way slowly toward his heart.

And just before the Dog exhaled his last breath, he felt a moment of panic. He tried to jump up, but found that he couldn't. He whimpered once, his eyes clouding over with fear and something else; and then it seemed to him that a bony, gentle hand was caressing his ears, and, with a single wag of his tail, the Last Dog closed his eyes for the last time and prepared to join a God of stubbled beard and torn clothes and feet wrapped in rags.

I am a passionate horse-racing fan. I wrote a weekly column on it for close to fifteen years, and, while I don't bet, I have been known to fly to New York to watch Seattle Slew go up against Affirmed or Dr. Fager take on Damascus. So when Marty Greenberg was putting together the anthology *Horse Fantastic*, nothing was going to keep me out of it. I figured if anyone else wrote about racing, they'd probably write about Secretariat, or perhaps Man o' War, so I chose to write about a rather mediocre horse who actually existed, and even achieved some very brief fame back in the 1930s.

Malish

H is name was Malicious, and you can look it up in the *American Racing Manual*: from ages two to four, he won five of his forty-six starts, had seven different owners, and never changed hands for more than $800.

His method of running was simple and to the point: he was usually last out of the gate, last on the backstretch, last around the far turn, and last at the finish wire.

He didn't have a nickname back then, either. Exterminator may have been Old Bones, and Man o' War was Big Red, and of course Equipoise was the Chocolate Soldier, but Malicious was just plain Malicious.

Turns out he was pretty well-named, after all.

It was at Santa Anita in February of 1935—and *this* you can't look up in the *Racing Manual*, or the *Daily Racing Form Chart Book*, or any of the other usual sources, so you're just going to have to take my word for it—and Malicious was being rubbed down by Chancey McGregor, who had once been a jockey until he got too heavy, and had latched on as a groom because he didn't know anything but the racetrack. Chancey had been trying to supplement his income by betting on the races, but he was no better at picking horses than at riding them—he had a passion for claimers who were moving up in class, which any tout will tell you is a quick way to go broke—and old Chancey, he was getting mighty desperate, and on this particular morning he stopped rubbing Malicious and put him in his stall, and then started trading low whispers with a gnarly little man who had just appeared in the shed row with no visitor's pass or anything, and after a couple of minutes they shook hands and the gnarly little man pricked Chancey's thumb with something sharp and then held it onto a piece of paper.

Well, Chancey started winning big that very afternoon, and the next day he hit a 200-to-1 shot, and the day after that he knocked down a $768.40 daily double. And because he was a good-hearted man, he spread his money around, made a lot of girls happy, at least temporarily, and even started bringing sugar cubes to the barn with him every morning. Old Malicious, he just loved those sugar cubes, and because he was just a horse, he decided that he loved Chancey McGregor too.

Then one hot July day that summer—Malicious had now lost fourteen in a row since he upset a cheap field back in October the previous year—Chancey was rubbing him down at Hollywood Park, adjusting the bandages on his forelegs, and suddenly the gnarly little man appeared inside the stall.

"It's time," he whispered to Chancey.

Chancey dropped his sponge onto the straw that covered the floor of the stall, and just kind of backed away, his eyes so wide they looked like they were going to pop out of his head.

"But it's only July," he said in a real shaky voice.

"A deal's a deal," said the gnarly man.

"But I was supposed to have two years!" whimpered Chancey.

"You've been betting at five tracks with your bookie," said the gnarly man with a grin. "You've had two years worth of winning, and now I've come to claim what's mine."

Chancey backed away from the gnarly man, putting Malicious between them. The little man advanced toward him, and Malicious, who sensed that his source of sugar cubes was in trouble, lashed out with a forefoot and caught the gnarly little man right in the middle of the forehead. It was a blow that would have killed most normal men, but as you've probably guessed by now, this wasn't any normal man in the stall with Malicious and Chancey, and he just sat down hard.

"You can't keep away from me forever, Chancey McGregor," he hissed, pointing a bony finger at the groom. "I'll get you for this." He turned to Malicious. "I'll get you *both* for this, horse, and you can count on it!"

And with that, there was a puff of smoke, and suddenly the gnarly little man was gone.

Well, the gnarly little man, being who he was, didn't have to wait long to catch up with Chancey. He found him cavorting with fast gamblers and loose women two nights later, and off he took him, and that was the end of Chancey McGregor.

But Malicious was another story. Three times the gnarly little man tried to approach Malicious in his stall, and three times Malicious kicked him clear out into the aisle, and finally the gnarly little man decided to change his tactics, and what he did was to wait for Malicious on the far turn with a great big stick in his hand. Being who he was, he made sure that nobody in the grandstand or the clubhouse could see him, but it wouldn't have been a proper vengeance if Malicious couldn't see him, so he made a little adjustment, and just as Malicious hit the far turn, trailing by his usual twenty lengths, up popped the gnarly little man, swinging the paddle for all he was worth.

"I got you now, horse!" he screamed—but Malicious took off like the devil was after him, which was exactly the case, and won the race by seven lengths.

As he was being led to the winner's circle, Malicious looked off to his left, and there was the gnarly little man, glaring at him.

"I'll be waiting for you next time, horse," he promised, and sure enough, he was.

And Malicious won *that* race by nine lengths.

And the gnarly little man kept waiting, and Malicious kept moving into high gear every time he hit the far turn, and before long the crowds fell in love with him, and Joe Hernandez, who called every race in California, became famous for crying, "...and here comes Malish!"

Santa Anita started selling Malish t-shirts thirty years before t-shirts became popular, and Hollywood sold Malish coffee mugs, and every time old Malish won, he made the national news. At the end of his seventh year, he even led the Rose Bowl parade in Pasadena. (Don't take *my* word for it; there was a photo of it in *Time*.)

By the time he turned eight years old, Malish started slowing down, and the only thing that kept him safe was that the gnarly little man was slowing down too, and one day he came to Malish's stall, and this time he looked more tired than angry, and Malish just stared at him without kicking or biting.

"Horse," said the gnarly little man, "you got more gumption than most people I know, and I'm here to declare a truce. What do you say to that?"

Malish whinnied, and the gnarly little man tossed him a couple of sugar cubes, and that was the last Malish ever did see of him.

He lost his next eleven races, and then they retired him, and the California crowd fell in love with Seabiscuit, and that was that.

Except that here and there, now and then, you can still find a couple of railbirds from the old days who will tell you about old Malish, the horse who ran like Satan himself was chasing him down the homestretch.

That's the story. There really was a Malicious, and he used to take off on the far turn like nobody's business, and it's all pretty much the truth, except for the parts that aren't, and they're pretty minor parts at that.

Like I said, you can look it up.

Mike with two of his collie champions, Merlin (left) and Kim (right).
You can read about Kim in the Appendix. From the personal photo
collection of Mike Resnick.

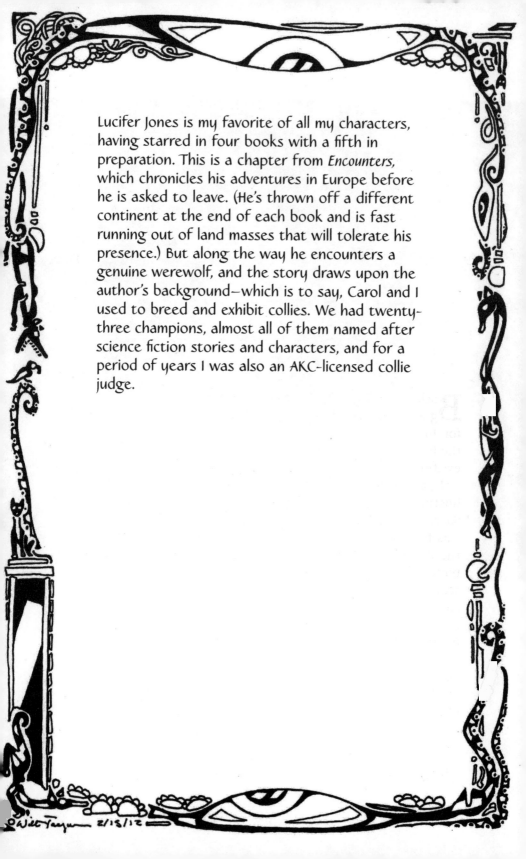

Lucifer Jones is my favorite of all my characters, having starred in four books with a fifth in preparation. This is a chapter from *Encounters*, which chronicles his adventures in Europe before he is asked to leave. (He's thrown off a different continent at the end of each book and is fast running out of land masses that will tolerate his presence.) But along the way he encounters a genuine werewolf, and the story draws upon the author's background—which is to say, Carol and I used to breed and exhibit collies. We had twenty-three champions, almost all of them named after science fiction stories and characters, and for a period of years I was also an AKC-licensed collie judge.

Royal Bloodlines

A Lucifer Jones Story

B ack in 1936, I found myself in Hungary, which ain't never
gonna provide the Riviera with any serious competition
for tourists. Each town I passed through was duller than
the last, until I got to Budapest, which was considerably less
exciting than Boise, Idaho on a Tuesday afternoon.

I passed by an old, run-down arena that did double duty
hosting hockey games on weeknights and dog shows on
Saturdays, then walked by the only nightclub in town, which
was featuring one of the more popular lady tuba soloists in
the country, and finally I came to the Magyar Hotel and
rented me a room. After I'd left my gear there, I set out to
scout out the city and see if there were enough depraved
sinners to warrant building my tabernacle there and setting
up shop in the salvation business. My unerring instincts led
me right to a batch of them, who were holed up in the men's
room of the bus station, playing a game with which I was not
entirely unfamiliar, as it consisted of fifty-two pasteboards
with numbers or pictures on 'em and enough money in the
pot to make it interesting.

"Mind if I join you gents?" I asked, walking over to them.

"Either you put your shirt on backward, or else you're a preacher," said one of 'em in an English accent.

"What's that got to do with anything?" I asked.

"We'd feel guilty taking your money," he said.

"You ain't got a thing to worry about," I said, sitting down with them.

"Well," he said with a shrug, "you've been warned."

"I appreciate that, neighbor," I said, "and just to show my good will, I absolve everyone here of any sins they committed between nine o'clock this morning and noon. Now, who deals?"

The game got going hot and heavy, and I had just about broken even, when the British feller dealt a hand of draw, and I picked up my cards and fanned 'em out and suddenly I was looking at four aces and a king, and two of my opponents had great big grins on their faces, the kind of grin you get when you pick up a flush or a full house, and one of 'em opened, and the other raised, and I raised again, and it was like I'd insulted their manhood, because they raised right back, and pretty soon everyone else had dropped out and the three of us were tossing money into the pot like there wasn't no tomorrow, and just about the time we all ran out of money and energy and were about to show our cards, a little Hungarian kid ran into the room and shouted something in a foreign language—probably Hungarian, now as I come to think on it—and suddenly everyone grabbed their money and got up and started making for the exit.

"Hey, what's going on?" I demanded. "Where do you guys think you're going?"

"Away!" said the British feller.

"But we're in the middle of a hand," I protested.

"Lupo is coming!" said the Brit. "The game's over!"

"Who the hell is Lupo?" I demanded.

"He's more of a what. You'll leave too, if you know what's good for you!"

And suddenly, just like that, I was all alone in the men's room of a Hungarian bus station, holding four totally useless aces and a king, and thinking that maybe Hungarians were more in need of a shrink than a preacher. Then the door opened, and in walked this thin guy with grayish skin and hair everywhere—on his head, his lip, his chin, even the backs of his hands.

"Howdy, Brother," I said, and he nodded at me. "You better not plan on lingering too long," I added. "Someone or something called Lupo is on its way here."

He turned to face me and stared at me intently.

"I am Lupo," he said.

"You are?"

"Count Basil de Chenza Lupo," he continued. "Who are you?"

"The Right Reverend Doctor Lucifer Jones at your service," I said.

"Do you see any reason why you should run at the sight of me?" he continued.

"Except for the fact that you got a predatory look about you and probably ain't on speaking terms with your barber, nary a one," I answered.

"They are fools," he said. "Fools and peasants, nothing more."

"Maybe so," I said, "but you could have timed your call of Nature just a mite better, considering I was holding four bullets and the pot had reached a couple of thousand dollars."

"Bullets?" he said, kind of growling deep in his throat. "What kind?"

"Well, when you got four of 'em, there ain't a lot left except clubs, diamonds, hearts and spades," I said.

"But not silver?" he said.

"Not as I recollect."

"Good," he said, suddenly looking much relieved. "I am sorry I have caused you such distress, Doctor Jones."

"Well, I suppose, when push comes to shove, it ain't really your fault, Brother Basil," I said.

"Nevertheless, I insist that you allow me to take you to dinner to make amends."

"That's right cordial of you," I said. "I'm a stranger in town. You got any particular place in mind?"

"We will dine at The Strangled Elk," he said. "It belongs to some Gypsy friends of mine."

"Whatever suits you," I said agreeably.

We walked out of the station, hit the main drag, and turned left.

"By the way, Brother Basil," I said, "why *were* all them men running away from a nice, friendly gent like you?"

He shrugged. "They are superstitious peasants," he said. "Let us speak no more of them."

"Suits me," I said. "People what entice a man of the cloth into a sinful game like poker and then run off when he's got the high hand ain't headed to no good end anyway."

I noticed as we walked down the street that everyone was giving us a pretty wide berth, and finally we turned down a little alleyway where all the men were dark and swarthy and wearing shirts that could have been took in some at the arms, and the women were sultry and good-looking and wearing colorful skirts and blouses, and Basil told me we were now among his Gypsy friends and no one would bother us, not that anyone had been bothering us before, and after a little while we came to a sign that said we'd reached The Strangled Elk, and we went inside.

It wasn't the cleanest place I'd ever seen, but I'd been a couple of weeks between baths myself, so I can't say that I minded it all that much. There was nobody there except one skinny old waiter, and Basil called him over and said something in Gypsy, and the waiter went away and came back a minute later with a bottle of wine and two glasses.

Well, we filled the glasses and chatted about this and that, and then we drank some more and talked some more, and finally the waiter brought out a couple of steaks.

"Brother Basil," I said, looking down at my plate, "I like my meat as rare as the next man, but I don't believe this has been cooked at all."

"I am sorry, my friend," he said. "That is the way I always eat it, and the cook simply assumed you shared my taste." He signaled to the waiter, said something else in Gypsy, and the waiter took my plate away. "It will be back in a few moments, properly cooked."

"You *always* eat your steak like that?" I asked, pointing to the slab of raw meat in front of him.

"It is the only way," he replied, picking it up with his hands and biting off a goodly chunk of it. He growled and snarled as he chewed it.

"You got a bit of a throat condition?" I asked.

"Something like that," he said. "I apologize if my table manners offend you."

"I've et with worse," I said. In fact, if push came to shove, I couldn't remember having dined with a lot that were much more refined.

Well, my steak came back just then, and after covering it with a pint of ketchup just to bring out the subtle nuances of its flavor, I dug in, and just so Basil wouldn't feel too conspicuous I growled and snarled too, and we spent the next five or ten minutes enjoying the noisiest meal of my experience, after which we polished off a couple of more bottles of wine.

"I have truly enjoyed this evening, my friend," said Basil after we were all done. "So few people will even speak to me, let alone join me in a repast...."

"I can't imagine why," I said. "You'd have to search far and wide to find a more hospitable feller."

"Nonetheless," he said, "it is time for you to leave."

"It's only about nine o'clock," I said. "I think I'll just sit here and digest the repast and maybe smoke a cigar or two, that is if you got any to spare, and then I'll mosey on back to my humble dwelling."

"You really must leave *now*," he said.

"You got a ladyfriend due any minute, right?" I said with a sly smile. "Well, never let it be said that Lucifer Jones ain't the soul of understanding and discretion. Why, I recall one time back in Cairo, or maybe it was Merrakech, that I—"

"*Hurry!*" he shouted. "The moon is rising!"

"Now how could you possibly know that, sitting here in the back of the room?" I asked.

"I *know*!" he said.

I got up and walked over to the doorway and stuck my head out. "Well, son of a gun, the moon *is* out," I said. "I don't see your ladyfriend nowhere, though."

I turned back to face him, but Count Basil de Chenza Lupo wasn't nowhere to be seen. In fact, there wasn't no one in the room except the old waiter and an enormous wolf that must have wandered in through the kitchen door.

"Well, I've heard of restaurants that got roaches," I said, "and restaurants that got rats, but I do believe this is the first eatery I ever been to that was infested by wolves." I turned to the waiter. "What happened to Basil?" I asked. "Did he go off to the necessary?"

The waiter shook his head.

"Then where is he?"

The waiter pointed to the wolf.

"I don't believe I'm making myself clear," I said. "I ain't interested in no four-legged critters with fleas and bad breath. Where is Basil?"

The waiter pointed to the wolf again.

"I don't know why it's so hard to understand," I said. "That there is a wolf. I want to know what became of Basil."

The waiter nodded his head. "Basil," he said, pointing at the wolf again.

"You mean the wolf is named Basil, too?" I asked.

The waiter just threw his hands up and walked out of the room, leaving me alone with the wolf.

Well, I looked at the wolf for a good long while, and he looked right back at me, and as time went by it occurred to me that I hadn't seen no other wolves in all my wanderings through Europe, and that some zoo ought to be happy to pay a healthy price for such a prime specimen, so I walked over kind of gingerly and let him smell the back of my hand, and when I was sure he wasn't viewing me as a potential appetizer, I slipped my belt out of my pants and slid it around his neck and turned it into a leash.

"You come along with me, Basil," I said. "Tonight you can sleep in my hotel room, and tomorrow we'll set about finding a properly generous and appreciative home for you."

I started off toward the door, but he dug his feet in and practically pulled my arm out of the socket.

"Now, Basil," I said, jerking on the leash with both hands, "I ain't one to abuse dumb animals, but one way or the other you're coming with me."

He pulled back and whimpered, and then he snarled, and then he just went limp and laid down, but I was determined to get him out of there, and I started dragging him along the floor, and finally he whined one last time and got to his feet and started trotting alongside of me, and fifteen minutes later we reached the door of the Magyar Hotel. I had a feeling they had some policy or other regarding wild critters in the rooms, so I waited until the desk clerk went off to flirt with one of the maids, and then I opened the door and me and Basil made a beeline for the staircase and reached the second floor without being seen. I walked on down the corridor until I came to my room, unlocked it, and shagged Basil into it. He looked more nervous and bewildered than vicious, and finally he hopped onto the couch and curled up and went to sleep, and I lay back down on the bed and drifted off while I was trying to figure out how many thousands of dollars a real live wolf was worth.

Except that when I woke up, all set to take Basil the wolf off to the zoo, he wasn't there. Instead, laying naked on the couch and snoring up a storm, was Basil the Count, with my belt still around his neck.

I shook him awake, and he sat up, startled, and began blinking his eyes.

"You got something highly personal and just a tad improbable that you want to confide in me, Brother Basil?" I said.

"I *tried* to warn you," he said plaintively. "I told you to leave, to hurry."

"You considered seeing a doctor about this here condition?" I said. "Or maybe a veterinarian?"

He shook his head miserably. "It is a Gypsy curse," he said at last. "There is nothing that can be done about it. I am a werewolf, and that's all there is to it."

"And that's why all them guys were running away from you at the station and looking askance at you on the street?"

He nodded. "I am an outcast, a pariah among my own people."

"Yeah, well, I can see how it probably hampers your social life," I opined.

"It has hampered *all* aspects of my life," he said unhappily. "I have seen so many charlatans and *poseurs* trying to get the curse removed that I am practically destitute. I cannot form a lasting relationship. I dare not be among strangers when the moon comes out. And some of the behavior carries over: you saw me at the dinner table last night."

"Well, it may have been a bit out of the ordinary," I said soothingly, "but as long as you don't lift you leg on the furniture, I don't suppose anyone's gonna object too strenuously. Especially since if they object at the wrong time of day, there's a strong possibility they could wind up getting et."

"You are the most understanding and compassionate man I've ever met, Doctor Jones," he said, "but I am at the end of my tether. I don't know what to do. I have no one to turn to. Only these accursed Gypsies will tolerate my presence, because it amuses them. I think very soon I shall end it all."

At which point the Lord smote me with another of His heavenly revelations.

"Seems to me you're being a mite hasty, Brother Basil," I said.

RESNICK'S MENAGERIE

"What is the use of going on?" he said plaintively. "I will never be able to remove the curse."

"First of all, you got to stop thinking of your condition as a curse," I continued. "What if I was to show you how the werewolf business could be a blessing in disguise?"

"Impossible!"

"You willing to bet five thousand dollars on that?" I asked.

"What are you talking about?" he demanded.

"You see," I said, "the problem is that you ain't never really examined yourself when the moon is out. You ain't simply a werewolf, but you happen to be a damned fine-looking werewolf."

"So what?"

"On my way into town, I passed an arena that holds a dog show every Saturday. The sign said that the prize money was ten thousand dollars."

"You just said five," he pointed out.

"Well, me and the Lord have got to have a little something to live on, too," I said.

"What makes you think a wolf can win a dog show?" he said dubiously.

"Why don't you just concentrate on being a handsome, manly type of critter and let *me* worry about the rest of it?" I said.

Well, we argued it back and forth for the better part of the morning, but finally he admitted that he didn't see no better alternatives, and he could always commit suicide the next week if things didn't work out, and I went off to buy a leash and some grooming equipment at the local pet store, and then stopped by the arena for an entry form. I didn't know if he had an official werewolf name or not, so I just writ down Grand International Champion Basil on the form, and let it go at that.

The biggest problem I had the next two days was finding a vet who was open at night, so I could get Basil his rabies and distemper shots, but finally I convinced one to work late for an extra fifty dollars, which I planned to deduct from Basil's share of the winnings, since the shots didn't do me no good personally, and then it was Saturday, and we just stuck around the hotel until maybe five in the afternoon, Basil getting more and more nervous, and finally we walked on over to the arena.

Basil's class was scheduled to be judged at seven o'clock, but as the hour approached, it began to look like the moon wasn't going to come out in time, and since I didn't want us to forfeit all that money by not showing up on time, I quick ran out into the alley, grabbed the first couple of cats I could find, and set 'em loose in the arena. The newspaper the next morning said that the ruckus was so loud they could hear it all the way over in Szentendre, which was a little town about forty miles up the road, and by the time everything had gone back to normal, Basil was about as far from normal as Hungarian counts are prone to get, and I slipped his leash on him and headed for the ring.

There were three other dogs ahead of us, and after we entered the ring, the judge came over and looked at Basil.

"This is a class for miniature poodles," he said severely. "Just what kind of mongrel is *that*?"

"You know this guy, Basil?" I asked.

Basil nodded.

"He one of the ones who's mean to you when you walk through town?"

Basil growled an ugly growl.

"*Basil*?" said the judge, turning white as a sheet.

Basil gave him a toothy grin.

"Now, to answer your question," I said, "this here happens to be a fully growed miniature poodle what takes umbrage when you insults its ancestry."

The judge stared at Basil for another couple of seconds, then disqualified the other three dogs for not looking like him and handed me a blue ribbon.

Well, to make a long story short, old Basil terrorized the judges in the next three classes he was in and won 'em all, and then the ring steward told me that I had five minutes to prepare for the final class of the day, where they would pick the best dog in the show and award the winner the ten thousand dollars.

Suddenly Basil started whining up a storm. I couldn't see no ticks or fleas on him, and he couldn't tell me what was bothering him, but something sure was, and finally I noticed that he was staring intently at something, and I turned to see what it was, and it turned out to be this lovely-looking lady who was preparing to judge the Best in Show class.

"What's the problem, Basil?" I asked.

He kept whining and staring.

"Is it *her*?"

He nodded.

I racked my mind trying to figure out what it was about her that could upset him so much.

"She's been mean to you before?" I asked.

He shook his head.

"She's got something to do with the Gypsies who cursed you?"

He shook his head again.

"I can't figure out what the problem is," I said. "But what the hell, as long as we let her know who you are, it's in the bag."

He pointed his nose at the ceiling and howled mournfully.

"She's from out of town and doesn't know you're a werewolf?" I asked with a sinking feeling in the pit of my stomach.

He whimpered and curled up in a little ball.

"Will the following dogs please enter the ring?" said the announcer. "Champion Blue Boy, Champion Flaming Spear, Champion Gladiator, Champion Jericho, and Grand International Champion Basil."

Well, we didn't have no choice but to follow these four fluffy little dogs into the ring. The judge just stared at us for a minute with her jaw hanging open, and I figured we were about to get booted out, but then she walked over and knelt down and held Basil by the ears and peered into his face, and then she stood up and stepped back a bit and stared at him some more, and finally she walked over to me and said,

"This is the most handsome, rugged, masculine dog I have ever seen. I have a female I'd love to breed to him. Is he for sale?"

I told her that I was just showing him for a friend, and that she'd have to speak to the Count de Chenza Lupo about it later. She scribbled down her address, and it turned out that she was staying three rooms down the hall from me at the Hotel Magyar.

Finally she examined the other four dogs briefly and with obvious disinterest, and then she announced that Grand International Champion Basil was the best dog in this or any other show and had won the ten thousand dollars.

Well, Basil and me stuck around long enough to have a bunch of photos taken for the papers and then high-tailed it back to the hotel, where we waited until daylight and he became Count Basil again and we divvied up the money. Then he walked down the hall to talk to the judge about selling himself to her, and he came back half an hour later with the silliest grin on his face and announced that he was in love and she didn't mind in the least that he was a werewolf and all was right with the world.

I read in the paper that the other dog owners were so outraged about losing to a wolf that they tore the building down, and, with the dog shows canceled for the foreseeable future, I couldn't see no reason to stick around, so I bid Hungary farewell and decided to try my luck in Paris, where I'd heard tell that the sinners were so thick on the ground you could barely turn around without making the real close acquaintanceship of at least a couple of 'em.

I never saw old Basil again, but a few months later I got a letter from him. He'd married his lady judge and left Budapest for good, and was living on her country estate managing her kennel—and he added a proud little postscript that both his wife and her prize female were expecting.

Not a wolf, but just as fine—if not much better! Mike with his collie champion Gully Foyle (you can read about Gully in the Appendix). From the personal photo collection of Mike Resnick.

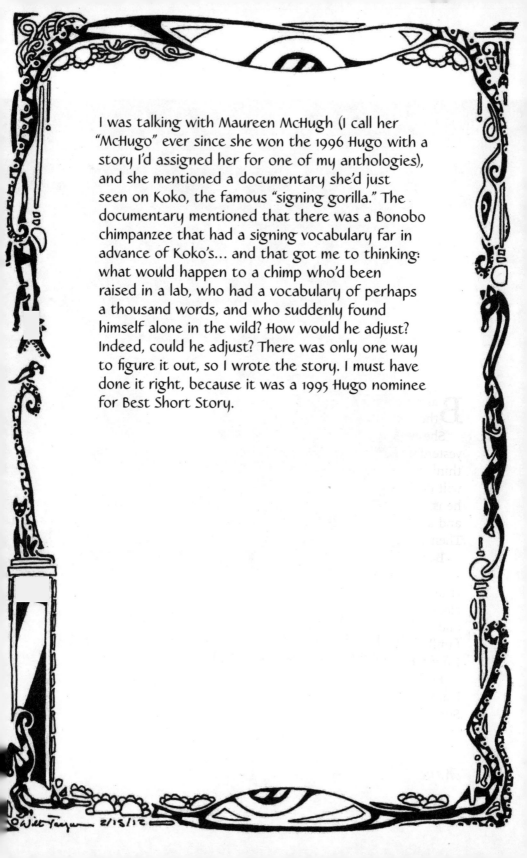

I was talking with Maureen McHugh (I call her "McHugo" ever since she won the 1996 Hugo with a story I'd assigned her for one of my anthologies), and she mentioned a documentary she'd just seen on Koko, the famous "signing gorilla." The documentary mentioned that there was a Bonobo chimpanzee that had a signing vocabulary far in advance of Koko's... and that got me to thinking: what would happen to a chimp who'd been raised in a lab, who had a vocabulary of perhaps a thousand words, and who suddenly found himself alone in the wild? How would he adjust? Indeed, could he adjust? There was only one way to figure it out, so I wrote the story. I must have done it right, because it was a 1995 Hugo nominee for Best Short Story.

Barnaby
in Exile

B arnaby sits in his cage, waiting for Sally to come into the lab.

She will give him the puzzle, the same one he worked on yesterday. But today he will not disappoint her. He has been thinking about the puzzle all night. Thinking is fun. Today he will do it right, and she will laugh and tell him how smart he is. He will lay on his back and she will tickle his stomach, and say, "Oh, what a bright young fellow you are, Barnaby!" Then Barnaby will make a funny face and turn a somersault.

Barnaby is me.

IT GETS LONELY after Sally leaves. Bud comes when it is black and cleans my cage, but he never talks. Sometimes he forgets and leaves the light on. Then I try to talk to Roger and his family, but they are just rabbits and cannot make the signs. I don't think they are very smart, anyway.

Every night when Bud comes in, I sit up and smile at him. I always make the sign for "Hello," but he doesn't answer. Sometimes I think Bud isn't any smarter than Roger. He just pats me on the head. Sometimes he leaves the pictures on after he leaves.

My favorite pictures are Fred and Barney. Everything is so bright and fast. Many times I ask Sally to bring Dino to the lab so that I can play with him, but she never does. I like Barney, because he is not as big or loud as Fred, and I am not big or loud either. Also, my name is Barnaby and that is like Barney. Sometimes, when it is black and I am all alone, I imagine that I am Barney, and that I don't sleep in a cage at all.

THIS DAY IT was white out, and Sally even had white on her when she came to the lab, but it all turned to water.

Today we had a new toy. It looks like the thing on Doctor's desk, with lots of little things that look like flat grapes. Sally told me that she would show me something and then I should touch the grape that had the same picture on it. She showed me a shoe, and a ball, and an egg, and a star, and a square.

I did the egg and the ball wrong, but tomorrow I will do them right. I think more every day. Like Sally says, I am a very bright young fellow.

WE HAVE SPENT many days with the new toy, and now I can speak to Sally with it, just by touching the right grapes.

She will come into the lab and say, "How are you this morning, Barnaby?", and I will touch the grapes that say, "Barnaby is fine" or "Barnaby is hungry."

What I really want to say is "Barnaby is lonely" but there is no grape for "lonely."

TODAY I TOUCH the grapes that say "Barnaby wants out."

"Out of your cage?" she asks.

"Out there," I sign. "Out in the white."

"You would not like it."

"I do not like the black when I am alone," I sign. "I will like the white."

"It is very cold," she says, "and you are not used to it."

"The white is very pretty," I say. "Barnaby wants out."

"The last time I let you out you hurt Roger," she reminds me.

"I just wanted to touch him," I say.

"You do not know your own strength," she says. "Roger is just a rabbit, and you hurt him."

"I will be gentle this time," I say.

"I thought you didn't like Roger," she says.

"I don't like Roger," I say. "I like touching."

She reaches into the cage and tickles my belly and scratches my back and I feel better, but then she stops.

"It is time for your lesson," she says.

"If I do it right, can you bring me something to touch?" I ask.

"What kind of thing?" she says.

I think for a moment. "Another Barnaby," I say.

She looks sad, and doesn't answer.

ONE DAY SALLY brings me a book filled with pictures. I smell it and taste it. Finally I figure out that she wants me to look at it.

There are all kinds of animals in it. I see one that looks like Roger, but it is brown and Roger is white. And there is a kitten, like I see through the window. And a dog, like Doctor sometimes brings to the lab. But there is no Dino.

Then I see a picture of a boy. His hair is shorter than Sally's, and not as gray as Doctor's, or as yellow as Bud's. But he is smiling, and I know he must have many things to touch.

WHEN SALLY COMES back the next morning, I have lots of questions about the pictures. But before I can ask her, she asks me.

"What is this?" she says, holding up a picture.

"Roger," I say.

"No," she says. "Roger is a name. What is this animal called?"

I try to remember. "Rabbit," I say at last.

"Very good, Barnaby," she says. "And what is this?"

"Kitten," I say.

We got through the whole book.

"Where is Barnaby?" I ask.

"Barnaby is an ape," she says. "There is no picture of an ape in the book."

I wonder if there are any other Barnabys in the world, and if they are lonely too.

LATER I ASK, "Do I have a father and a mother?"

"Of course you do," says Sally. "Everything has a father and a mother."

"Where are they?" I ask.

"Your father is dead," says Sally. "Your mother is in a zoo far away from here."

"Barnaby wants to see his mother," I say.

"I'm afraid not, Barnaby."

"Why?"

"She wouldn't know you. She has forgotten you, just as you have forgotten her."

"If I could see her, I would say 'I'm Barnaby,' and then she would know me."

Sally shakes her head. "She wouldn't understand. You are very special; she is not. She can't sign, and she can't use a computer."

"Does she have any other Barnabys?" I ask.

"I don't know," says Sally. "I suppose so."

"How does she speak to them?"

"She doesn't."

I think about this for a long time.

Finally I say, "But she touches them."

"Yes, she touches them," says Sally.

"They must be very happy," I say.

TODAY I WILL find out more about being Barnaby.

"Good morning," says Sally when she comes into the lab. "How are you today, Barnaby?"

"What is a zoo?" I ask.

"A zoo is a place where animals live," says Sally.

62

"Can I see a zoo through the window?"

"No. It is very far away."

I think about my next question for a long time. "Are Barnabys animals?"

"Yes."

"Are Sallys animals?"

"In a way, yes."

"Does Sally's mother live in a zoo?"

Sally laughs. "No," she says.

"Does she live in a cage?"

"No," says Sally.

I think for awhile.

"Sally's mother is dead," I say.

"No, she is alive."

I get very upset, because I do not know how to ask why Sally's mother is different from Barnaby's mother, and the harder I try the worse I do it, and Sally cannot understand me. Finally I start hitting the floor with my fist. Roger and his family all jump, and Doctor opens the door. Sally gives me a little toy that squeeks when I hit it, and very soon I forget to be mad and start playing with the toy. Sally says something to Doctor, and he smiles and leaves.

"Do you want to ask anything else before we begin our lesson?" asks Sally.

"Why?" I ask.

"Why what?"

"Why is Barnaby an ape and Sally a man?"

"Because that is the way God made us," she says.

I start getting very excited, because I think I am very close to learning more about Barnabys.

"Who is God?" I ask.

She tries to answer, but I do not understand again.

WHEN IT GETS black and I am all alone except for Roger and his family, and Bud has already cleaned my cage, I sit and think about God. Thinking can be very interesting.

If he made Sally and he made me, why didn't he make me as smart as Sally? Why can she talk, and do things with her hands that I can't do?

It is very confusing. I decide that I must meet God and ask him why he does these things, and why he forgot that even Barnabys like to be touched.

As soon as Sally comes into the lab, I ask her, "Where does God live?"

"In heaven."

"Is heaven far away?"

"Yes."

"Farther than a zoo?" I ask.

"Much farther."

"Does God ever come to the lab?"

She laughs. "No. Why?"

"I have many questions to ask him."

"Perhaps I can answer some of them," she says.

"Why am I alone?"

"Because you are very special," says Sally.

"If I was not special, would I be with other Barnabys?"

"Yes."

"I have never hurt God," I say. "Why has God made me special?"

The next morning I ask her to tell me about the other Barnabys.

"Barnaby is just a name," explains Sally. "There are other apes, but I don't know if any of them are named Barnaby."

"What is a name?"

"A name is what makes you different from everything else."

"If my name was Fred or Dino, could I be like everyone else?" I ask.

"No," she says. "You are special. You are Barnaby the Bonobo. You are very famous."

"What is famous?"

"Many people know who you are."

"What are People?" I ask.

"Men and women."

"Are there more than you and Doctor and Bud?"

"Yes."

Then it is time for my lessons, but I do them very badly, because I am still thinking about a world that has more People in it than Sally and Doctor and Bud. I am so busy wondering who lets them out of their cages when the dark goes away that I forget all about God and don't think about him any more for many days.

I HEAR SALLY talking to Doctor, but I do not understand what they are saying.

Doctor keeps repeating that we don't have any more fun, and Sally keeps saying that Barnaby is special, and then they both say a lot of things I can't understand.

When they are through, and Doctor leaves, I ask Sally why we can't have fun any more.

"Fun?" she repeats. "What do you mean?"

"Doctor says there will be no more fun."

She stares at me for a long time. "You understood what he said?"

"Why can't we have any fun?" I repeat.

"Fund," she says. "The word was *fund*. It means something different."

"Then Barnaby and Sally can still have fun?" I ask.

"Of course we can."

I lay on my back and sign to her. "Tickle me."

She reaches into the cage and tickles me, but I see water in her eyes. Human People make water in their eyes when they are unhappy. I pretend to bite her hand and then race around my cage like I did when I was a baby, but this time it doesn't make her laugh.

I HEAR VOICES coming from behind the door. It is Sally and Doctor again.

"Well, we can't put him in a zoo," says Doctor. "If he starts signing to the spectators, they'd have a million people demanding his freedom by the end of the month, and then what would happen? What would become of him? Can you picture the poor bastard in a circus?"

"We can't destroy him just because he's too bright," says Sally.

"Who will take him? *You?*" says Doctor. "He's only eight now. What happens when he becomes sexually mature, when he is a surly adult male? It's not that far away. He could rip you apart in seconds."

"He won't—not Barnaby."

"Will your landlord let you keep him? Are you willing to sacrifice the next twenty years of your life caring for him?"

"We might get renewed funding as early as this fall," says Sally.

"Be realistic," says Doctor. "It'll be years, if ever. This program is being duplicated at half a dozen labs around the country, and some of them are much farther along. Barnaby's not the only ape that has learned to use articles and adjectives, you know. There's a twenty-five-year-old gorilla, and three other Bonobo chimps that are well into their teens. There's no reason to believe that anyone will restore our funding."

"But he's *different,*" says Sally. "He asks abstract questions."

"I know, I know... once he asked you who God was. But I studied the tape, and you mentioned God first. If you mention Michael Jordan and he asks who that is, it doesn't mean that he's developed an abiding interest in basketball."

"Can I at least talk to the committee? Show them videotapes of him?"

"They know what a chimpanzee looks like," says Doctor.

"But they don't know what one *thinks* like," says Sally. "Perhaps this will help to convince them...."

"It's not a matter of convincing them," says Doctor. "The funds have dried up. Every program is hurting these days."

"Please...."

66

"All right," says Doctor. "I'll set up a meeting. But it won't do any good."

I hear it all, but I do not understand any of it. Before it got white today I dreamed of a place filled with Barnabys, and I am sitting in a corner, my eyes shut, trying to remember it before it all drifts away.

WE KEEP DOING the lessons each day, but I can tell that Sally is unhappy, and I wonder what I have done to upset her.

THIS MORNING SALLY opens my cage door and just hugs me for a long time.

"I have to talk to you, Barnaby," she says, and I see her eyes are making water again.

I touch the grapes that say, "Barnaby likes to talk."

"This is important," she says. "Tomorrow you will leave the lab."

"Will I go outside?" I ask.

"You will go very far away."

"To a zoo?"

"Farther."

Suddenly I remember God.

"Will I go to heaven?" I ask.

She smiles even as her eyes make more water. "Not quite that far," she says. "You are going to a place where there are no labs and no cages. You will be free, Barnaby."

"Are there other Barnabys there?"

"Yes," she says. "There are other Barnabys there."

"Doctor was wrong," I say. "There will be more fun for Sally and Barnaby."

"I cannot go with you," she says.

"Why?"

"I have to stay here. This is my home."

"If you are good, maybe God will let you out of your cage," I say.

She makes a funny sound and hugs me again.

THEY PUT ME in a smaller cage, one with no light in it. For two days I smell bad things. Most of my water spills, and there are loud noises that hurt my ears. Sometimes People talk, and once a man who is not Bud or Doctor gives me food and more water. He does it through a little hole in the top of the cage.

I touch his hand to show him that I am not angry. He screams and pulls his hand away.

I keep signing, "Barnaby is lonely," but it is dark and there is no one to see.

I do not like my new world.

ON THE THIRD morning they move my crate, and then they move it again. Finally they lift it up and carry it, and when they set it down I can smell many things I have never smelled before.

They open the door, and I step out onto the grass. The sun is very bright, and I squint and look at People who are not Sally or Doctor or Bud.

"You're home, boy," says one of them.

I look around. The world is a much bigger place than the lab, and I am frightened.

"Go on, fella," says another. "Sniff around. Get used to the place."

I sniff around. I do not get used to the place.

I SPEND MANY days in the world. I get to know all the trees and bushes, and the big fence around it. They feed me fruits and leaves and bark. I am not used to them, and for a while I am sick, but then I get better.

I hear many noises from beyond the world—screams and growls and shrieks. I smell many strange animals. But I do not hear or smell any Barnabys.

THEN ONE DAY the People put me back in my crate, and I am alone for a long time, and then they open the crate, and I

68

am no longer in the world, but in a place with so many trees that I almost cannot see the sky.

"Okay, fella," says a Person. "Off into the forest with you now."

He makes a motion with his hands, but it is a sign I do not recognize.

I sign back: "Barnaby is afraid."

The Person pets me on the head. It is the first time anyone has touched me since I left the lab.

"Have a good life," he says, "and make lots of little Barnabys."

Then he climbs into his cage, and it rolls away from me. I try to follow it, but it is much too fast, and soon I can no longer see it.

I look back at the forest and hear strange sounds, and a breeze brings me the sweet smell of fruit.

There is no one around to see me, but I sign "Barnaby is free" anyway.

Barnaby is free.

Barnaby is lonely.

Barnaby is frightened.

I LEARN TO find water, and to climb trees. I see little Barnabys with tails that chatter at me, but they cannot sign, and I see big kittens with spots, and they make terrible noises and I hide from them.

I wish I could hide in my cage, where I was always safe.

TODAY WHEN THE black goes away I wake up and go to the water, and I find another Barnaby.

"Hello," I sign. "I am a Barnaby too."

The other Barnaby growls at me.

"Do you live in a lab?" I ask. "Where is your cage?"

The other Barnaby runs at me and starts biting me. I shriek and roll on the ground.

"What have I done?" I ask.

The other Barnaby runs at me again, and I screech and climb to the top of a tree. He sits at the bottom and stares at me all day until the black returns. It gets very cold, and then wet, and I shiver all night and wish Sally was here.

IN THE MORNING the Barnaby is gone, and I climb down to the ground. I smell where he has been, and I follow his scent, because I do not know what else to do. Finally I come to a place with more Barnabys than I ever imagined there could be. Then I remember that Sally taught me counting, and I count. There are twenty-three of them.

One of them sees me and screams, and before I can make any signs, all of them charge at me and I run away. They chase me for a long time, but finally they stop, and I am alone again.

I AM ALONE for many days. I do not go back to the Barnabys, because they would hurt me if they could. I do not know what I have done to make them mad, so I do not know how to stop doing it.

I have learned to smell the big kittens when they are still far away, and to climb the trees so they cannot catch me, and I have learned to hide from the dogs that laugh like Sally does when I make somersaults, but I am so lonely, and I miss talking, and I am already forgetting some of the signs Sally taught me.

Last night I dreamed about Fred and Wilma and Barney and Dino, and when I woke up, my own eyes were making water.

I HEAR SOUNDS in the morning. Not sounds like the big kittens or the dogs make, but strange, clumsy sounds. I go to see what is making them.

In a little clearing I see four People—two men and two women—and they have brought little brown cages. The cages are not as nice as my old cage, because you cannot see in or out of them.

One of the men has made a fire, and they are sitting on chairs around it. I want to approach them, but I have learned my lesson with the Barnabys, and so I wait until one of the men sees me.

When he doesn't yell or chase me, I sign to him.

"I am Barnaby."

"What has it got in its hands?" asks one of the women.

"Nothing," says a man.

"Barnaby wants to be friends," I sign.

A woman puts something up in front of her face, and suddenly there is a big *pop*! It is so bright that I can't see. I rub my eyes and walk forward.

"Don't let him get too close," says the other man. "No telling what kind of diseases he's carrying."

"Will you play with Barnaby?" I ask.

The first man picks up a rock and throws it at me.

"Shoo!" he yells. "Go away!"

He throws another rock, and I run back into the forest.

WHEN IT IS black out, and they sit around the fire, I sneak as close as I can get, and lay down and listen to the sounds of their voices, and pretend I am back in the lab.

In the morning they throw rocks at me until I go away.

AND THEN ONE day, after they throw the rocks at me and I go for water, I come back and find that they are gone. They were not very good friends, but they were the only ones I had.

What will I do now?

FINALLY, AFTER MANY days, I find a single Barnaby, and it is a female. She has terrible scars on her from other Barnabys, and when she sees me, she bares her teeth and growls. I sit still and hope that she will not go away.

After a long time, she comes closer to me. I am afraid to move, because I do not want to frighten her or make her mad. I ignore her and stare off into the trees.

Finally she reaches out and picks an insect off my shoulder and puts it into her mouth, and soon she is sitting beside me, eating the flowers and leaves that have fallen to the ground.

Finally, when I am sure she will not run away, I sign to her, "I am Barnaby."

She grabs at my hands as if I was playing with a fruit or an insect, then shows her teeth when she sees that I am not holding anything.

She is really not any smarter than Roger, but at least she does not run away from me.

I will call her Sally.

SALLY IS AFRAID of the other Barnabys, so we live at the edge of the forest, where they hardly ever come. She touches me, and that is very nice, but I find that I miss talking and thinking even more.

Every day I try to teach her to sign, but she cannot learn. We have three baby Barnabys, one after each rainy season, but they are no smarter than Sally, and besides I have forgotten most of the signs.

MORE AND MORE People come to the forest in their brown cages. My family is afraid of them, but I love talking and listening and thinking more than anything. I always visit their camps at night, and listen to their voices in the darkness, and try to understand the words. I pretend I am back in the lab, though it is harder and harder to remember what the lab is like.

Each time there are new People, I show myself and say, "I am Barnaby," but none of them ever answers. When one finally does, I will know that he is God.

There were many things I wanted to ask him once, but I cannot remember most of them. I will tell him to be nice to Sally and the other two People at the lab—I forget their names—because what has happened to me is not their fault.

I will not ask him why he hated me so much that he made me special, or why People and Barnabys always chase me away. I will just say, "Please talk to Barnaby," and then I will ask if we can do a lesson.

Once, when I was a very bright fellow, there were many things I wanted to discuss with him. But now that I have left the world, that will be enough.

Nature Magazine, serious, educational, and non-fictional through and through (until the last page), has a delightful habit of closing each issue with a cute 1,000-word science fiction story based on some aspect of nature. My first such piece for them was about communicating with a rude, self-centered flowering plant. This was my second.

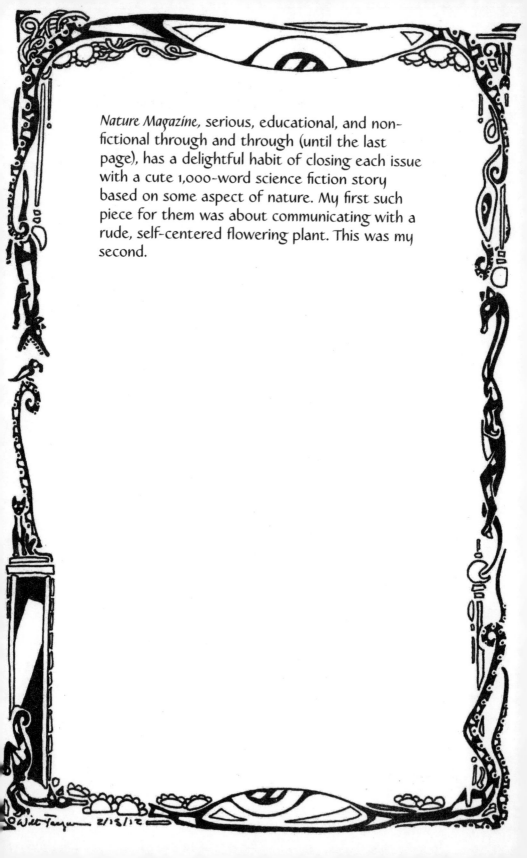

A Better
Mousetrap

M en have always talked about building a better mousetrap,
just the way they talk about a car that runs on water
rather than gasoline, or nuclear fission that doesn't have any
harmful byproducts.

But it wasn't until they re-opened the Heisenberg Space
Station out between Europa and Callisto, two of Jupiter's
moons, that they realized they really *needed* a better mousetrap.

The station had been shut down for almost nine centuries
once Man created the Retarded Tachyon Drive, which allowed
him to circumvent limitations inherent in Einstein's Theory
and let him travel at many multiples of the speed of light. He
spent most of the next millennium exploring the stars and
mapping their planets. It was really only as an afterthought
that some scientific types thought that as long as Heisenberg
was just floating in orbit, it would make a wonderful rent-free
laboratory (and a rent-free boarding house as well).

The first team of scientists—four men and two women—
docked their ship there on the second of November, 3014 A.D.,
at exactly 7:43 PM H.T. (Heisenberg Time). They buttressed

the hatch up against the entrance to the station, sealed it, then opened both doors and stepped into the station, the first humans to do so in more than nine hundred years.

Exactly forty-three seconds later, one of the women, a geneticist, screamed and the other jumped onto a chair that was bolted into the floor. Three of the men started cursing, and the fourth—a wimpy little fellow who specialized in a field so esoteric that most people couldn't pronounce it and he himself had difficulty spelling it—fainted dead away.

It turned out that some of the station's inhabitants were waiting for them. They'd been there nine long centuries and were glad to have some company. Having just eaten the last of the huge stores of preserved food that prior crews had laid in, they were even happier to have a new source of protein.

"What *are* they?" demanded the wimpy scientist when they woke him up.

"Mice," said the nuclear physicist.

"I thought they were extinct," offered the nanotechnologist.

"Well," said the biochemist, "they *could* be rats."

"I don't care what they are!" said the roboticist from atop her chair. "Get them away from me!"

"I suppose we really should get rid of them," said the biochemist. "I'll whip up a fast-acting poison and lay it out for them. They look hungry enough to eat anything."

At which point the wimpy scientist fainted again.

So they mixed up the poison, and left it out for the mice, and went about setting up their work stations, and ate dinner, and went to bed, expecting to find a few hundred dead mice in the morning.

But what they found were some plump mice, happily licking their chops and looking for more poisoned bait.

"They've evolved," said the biochemist. "They've obviously developed an immunity to poison. I suppose it was inevitable, given that they would have laid out various poisons just in case mice or any alien vermin ever found the food storage room. I suppose we'll just have to find some other way to kill them."

"I know just the thing," said the nanotechnologist.

"Oh?"

He nodded. "I'll design a mechanical microbe that will invade their systems and attack them from the inside."

"How will you get it into them?" asked the nuclear physicist.

"I'll just stick my microbes in the food we leave out for them."

And so he did.

The mice came, and they saw, and they ate—and they came back the next morning looking for more.

"I don't understand it," said the nanotechnologist. "Those microbes would kill any one of *us*. Why didn't they kill the mice?"

No one knew, so they captured one of the mice, drew blood samples, stomach samples, gene samples, and still had no answer. The best one came from the biochemist, who suggested that their forced evolution had created an internal environment so hospitable to microbes, even engineered ones, that the microbes ignored their programming and set up shop in the mice's intestines.

The roboticist tried next. She created an army of tiny metal warriors, each six inches in height, and sent them forth to do battle under chairs and beds, inside bulkheads, wherever the mice were hiding.

That was when they found out that the mice had evolved mentally as well as physically, and that their commanders were far superior at warfare to the roboticist, who had programmed her metal army. The robots were outflanked and outmaneuvered, and finally surrendered only seventeen hours into the battle.

The nuclear physicist didn't do much better with his jerry-built disintegrator ray. The mice were impervious to it, and the only harm it did was to two bathrooms and a collection of millennium-old dirty movies that a former crew had brought along to combat the boredom of living on a space station.

"Well, I'm all out of ideas," said the biochemist.

"Me, too," agreed the roboticist.

"The dirty little swine have beaten us at every turn," muttered the nuclear scientist.

"I guess we're either going to have to share the station with the hideous little things or go find another venue," added the nanotechnologist.

"Idiots!" said the wimpy little scientist disgustedly.

"The mice?"

"No," he said. "I was referring to my colleagues."

"You should talk!" snapped the roboticist. "All you ever do is faint."

"I have never denied my limitations," said the scientist, "though it is thoughtless of you to refer to them. Just for that, I've a good mind not to solve your problem."

"So you think you're the one who can build a better mousetrap?" she said sardonically.

"Most certainly."

"Even though they've withstood poison, microbes, military robots, and disintegrator rays?"

"Yes."

"Okay, hot-shot. What will you need?"

"Just a little help from our geneticist."

"And nothing else?"

"Not at the moment," said the scientist.

So they left him and the geneticist alone for a month and tried not to notice all the damage the mice were doing. They would wake up in the morning, put their feet in their slippers, and find a mouse had gotten there first. They would go to the galley to make a sandwich and find a mouse on the counter, waiting for scraps. They would try to use their delicate equipment, only to find that the mice had gnawed through everything that wasn't composed of tightly-bonded titanium molecules.

And then one day the scientist announced that the better mousetrap had been created and was ready to perform its function.

The others all snickered at him.

78

"That's *it?*" asked the nanotechnologist when he displayed it. "That's the better mousetrap that we've been waiting for all month?"

"Maybe no one's told him that this is the 31ˢᵗ Century, and that we've reached the stars," said the roboticist.

"You don't really think something this primitive is going to work, do you?" demanded the biochemist.

"Oh, ye of little faith," muttered the wimpy scientist.

They all laughed. (Well, they laughed at Newton and Einstein too.)

Within a week, every mouse on the station had been eliminated, including three that had somehow migrated onto the docked ship. It had been swift, efficient, and devastating.

"Who'd have believed it?" said the roboticist, as they all gathered around the better mousetrap.

"Too bad mice are extinct now or we could patent this thing," said the nuclear physicist.

"Where did you ever hear about something like this?" asked the nanotechnologist.

"Sometimes you have to read books that aren't exclusive to your field of study," answered the scientist.

"Meow," agreed the better mousetrap.

I'd been to Africa half a dozen times, and had written four Hugo winners and a bunch of nominees about it, but I'd never done a hunting story. Then, when *Asimov's* editor Gardner Dozois found out that I was editing a line of classic African hunting reprints, he waited until we were in the middle of a big crowd and challenged me to write "the ultimate science fiction hunting story." I couldn't back down in front of all those people, so of course I agreed... and then promptly put it out of my mind until he started nagging me for it—and trust me, Gardner can nag with the best of them (and always in public).

I finally came up with the notion of collaborating with Lewis Carroll (the only one of my forty-seven collaborators who never asked for his half of the money), and the story was a Hugo and Nebula nominee for Best Novella in 2000, so I guess I'm glad Gardner is such a good nag.

Hunting
The Snark

B elieve me, the last thing we ever expected to find was a
Snark.

And I'm just as sure we were the last thing he ever expected to meet.

I wish I could tell you we responded to the situation half
as well as he did. But maybe I should start at the beginning.
Trust me: I'll get to the Snark soon enough.

My name's Karamojo Bell. (Well, actually it's Daniel Mathias
Bellman. I've never been within five thousand light years of
the Karamojo district back on Earth. But when I found out
I was a distant descendant of the legendary hunter, I decided
to appropriate his name, since I'm in the same business and I
thought it might impress the clients. Turned out I was wrong;
in my entire career, I met three people who had heard of
him, and none of them went on safari with me. But I kept it
anyway. There are a lot of Daniels walking around; at least
I'm the only Karamojo.)

At that time I worked for Silinger & Mahr, the oldest and
best-known firm in the safari business. True, Silinger died

sixty-three years ago and Mahr followed him six years later and now it's run by a faceless corporation back on Deluros VIII, but they had better luck with their name than I had with mine, so they never changed it.

We were the most expensive company in the business, but we were worth it. Hundreds of worlds have been hunted out over the millennia, but people with money will always pay to have first crack at territory no one else has set foot on or even seen. A couple of years ago the company purchased a ten-planet hunting concession in the newly-opened Albion Cluster, and so many of our clients wanted to be the first to hunt virgin worlds that we actually held drawings to see who'd get the privilege. Silinger & Mahr agreed to supply one professional hunter per world and allow a maximum of four clients per party, and the fee was (get ready for it!) twenty million credits. Or eight million Maria Theresa dollars, if you don't have much faith in the credit—and out here on the Frontier, not a lot of people do.

We pros wanted to hunt new worlds every bit as much as the clients did. They were parceled out by seniority, and as seventh in line, I was assigned Dodgson IV, named after the woman who'd first charted it a dozen years ago. Nine of us had full parties. The tenth had a party of one—an incredibly wealthy man who wasn't into sharing.

Now, understand: I didn't take out the safari on my own. I was in charge, of course, but I had a crew of twelve blue-skinned humanoid Dabihs from Kakkab Kastu IV. Four were gunbearers for the clients. (I didn't have one myself; I never trusted anyone else with my weapons.) To continue: one was the cook, three were skinners (and it takes a lot more skill than you think to skin an alien animal you've never seen before without spoiling the pelt), and three were camp attendants. The twelfth was my regular tracker, whose name—Chajinka—always sounded like a sneeze.

We didn't really need a pilot—after all, the ship's navigational computer could start from half a galaxy away and land on top of a New Kenya shilling—but our clients were paying for luxury, and Silinger & Mahr made sure they got it. So in addition to the Dabihs, we also had our own personal pilot, Captain Kosha Mbele, who'd spent two decades flying one-man fighter ships in the war against the Sett.

The hunting party itself consisted of four business associates, all wealthy beyond my wildest dreams if not their own. There was Willard Marx, a real estate magnate who'd developed the entire Roosevelt planetary system; Jaxon Pollard, who owned a matching chains of cut-rate supermarkets and upscale bakeries that did business on more than a thousand worlds; Philemon Desmond, the CEO of Far London's largest bank—with branches in maybe two hundred systems—and his wife Ramona, a justice on that planet's Supreme Court.

I don't know how the four of them met, but evidently they'd all come from the same home world and had known each other for a long time. They began pooling their money in business ventures early on, and just kept going from one success to the next. Their most recent killing had come on Silverstrike, a distant mining world. Marx was an avid hunter who had brought trophies back from half a dozen worlds, the Desmonds had always wanted to go on safari, and Pollard, who would have preferred a few weeks on Calliope or one of the other pleasure planets, finally agreed to come along so that the four of them could celebrate their latest billion together.

I took an instant dislike to Marx, who was too macho by half. Still, that wasn't a problem; I wasn't being paid to enjoy his company, just to find him a couple of prize trophies that would look good on his wall, and he seemed competent enough.

The Desmonds were an interesting pair. She was a pretty woman who went out of her way to look plain, even severe; a well-read woman who insisted on quoting everything she'd read, which made you wonder which she enjoyed more, reading in private or quoting in public. Philemon, her husband, was a mousy little man who drank too much, drugged too much, smoked too much, seemed in awe of his wife, and actually wore a tiny medal he'd won in a school track meet some thirty years earlier—probably a futile attempt to impress Mrs. Desmond, who remained singularly unimpressed.

Pollard was just a quiet, unassuming guy who'd lucked into money and didn't pretend to be any more sophisticated than he was—which, in my book, made him considerably more sophisticated than his partners. He seemed constantly amazed that they had actually talked him into coming along. He'd packed remedies for sunburn, diarrhea, insect bites, and half a hundred other things that could befall him, and jokingly worried about losing what he called his prison pallor.

We met on Braxton II, our regional headquarters, then took off on the six-day trip to Dodgson IV. All four of them elected to undergo DeepSleep, so Captain Mbele and I put them in their pods as soon as we hit light speeds, and woke them about two hours before we landed.

They were starving—I know the feeling; DeepSleep slows the metabolism to a crawl, but of course it doesn't stop it or you'd be dead, and the first thing you want to do when you wake up is eat—so Mbele shagged the Dabihs out of the galley, where they spent most of their time, and had it prepare a meal geared to human tastes. As soon as they finished eating, they began asking questions about Dodgson IV.

"We've been in orbit for the past hour, while the ship's computer has been compiling a detailed topographical map of the planet," I explained. "We'll land as soon as I find the best location for the base camp."

"So what's this world like?" asked Desmond, who had obviously failed to read all the data we'd sent to him.

"I've never set foot on it," I replied. "No one has." I smiled. "That's why you're paying so much."

"How do we know there's any game to be found there, then?" asked Marx pugnaciously.

"There's game, all right," I assured him. "The Pioneer who charted it claims her sensors pinpointed four species of carnivore and lots of herbivores, including one that goes about four tons."

"But she never landed?" he persisted.

"She had no reason to," I said. "There was no sign of sentient life, and there are millions of worlds out there still to be charted."

"She'd damned well better have been right about the animals," grumbled Marx. "I'm not paying this much to look at a bunch of trees and flowers."

"I've hunted three other oxygen worlds that Karen Dodgson charted," I said, "and they've always delivered what she promised."

"Do people actually hunt on chlorine and ammonia worlds?" asked Pollard.

"A few. It's a highly specialized endeavor. If you want to know more about it after the safari is over, I'll put you in touch with the right person back at headquarters."

"I've hunted a couple of chlorine worlds," interjected Marx.

Sure you have, I thought.

"Great sport," he added.

When you have to live with your client for a few weeks or months, you don't call him a braggart and a liar to his face, but you do file the information away for future reference.

"This Karen Dodgson—she's the one the planet's named for?" asked Ramona Desmond.

"It's a prerogative of the Pioneer Corps," I answered. "The one who charts a world gets to name it anything he or she wants." I paused and smiled. "They're not known for their modesty. Usually they name it after themselves."

"Dodgson," she said again. "Perhaps we'll find a Jabberwock, or a Cheshire Cat, or even a Snark."

"I beg your pardon?" I said.

"That's was Lewis Carroll's real name: Charles Dodgson."

"I've never heard of him," I replied.

"He wrote *Jabberwocky* and *The Hunting of the Snark,* along with the Alice books." She stared at me. "Surely you're read them."

"I'm afraid not."

"No matter," she said with a shrug. "It was just a joke. Not a very funny one."

In retrospect, I wish we'd found a Jabberwock.

"Just the place for a Snark!" the Bellman cried,
As he landed his crew with care;
Supporting each man on the top of the tide
By a finger entwined in his hair.

DODGSON IV WAS lush and green, with huge rolling savannahs, thick forests with trees growing hundreds of feet high, lots of large inland lakes, a trio of freshwater oceans, an atmosphere slightly richer than Galactic Standard, and a gravity that was actually a shade lighter than Standard.

While the Dabihs were setting up camp and erecting the self-contained safari Bubbles near the ship, I sent Chajinka off to collect possible foodstuffs, then took them to the ship's lab for analysis. It was even better than I'd hoped.

"I've got good news," I announced when I clambered back out of the ship. "There are at least seventeen edible plant species. The bark of those trees with the golden blossoms is also edible. The water's not totally safe, but it's close enough, so that if we irradiate it, it'll be just fine."

"I didn't come here to eat fruits and berries or whatever the hell Blue Boy found out there," said Marx gruffly. "Let's go hunting."

"I think it would be better for you and your friends to stay in camp for a day while Chajinka and I scout out the territory and see what's out there. Just unwind from the trip and get used to the atmosphere and the gravity."

"Why?" asked Desmond. "What's the difference if we go out today or tomorrow?"

"Once I see what we're up against, I'll be able to tell you which weapons to take. And while we know there are carnivores, we have no idea whether they're diurnal or nocturnal or both. No sense spending all day looking for a trophy that only comes out at night."

"I hadn't thought of that." Desmond shrugged. "You're the boss."

I took Captain Mbele aside and suggested he do what he could to keep them amused—tell them stories of past safaris, make them drinks, do whatever he could to entertain them while Chajinka and I did a little reconnoitering and learned what we'd be up against.

"It looks pretty normal to me," said Mbele. "A typical primitive world."

"The sensors say there's a huge biomass about two miles west of here," I replied. "With that much meat on the hoof, there should be a lot of predators. I want to see what they can do before I take four novices into the bush."

"Marx brags about all the safaris he's been on," complained Mbele. "Why not take the Great White Hunter with you?"

"Nice try," I said. "But I make the decisions once we're on the ground. You're stuck with him."

"Thanks a lot."

"Maybe he's been on other safaris, but he's a novice on Dodgson IV, and as far as I'm concerned that's all that counts."

"Well, if it comes to that, so are you."

"I'm getting paid to risk my life. He's paying for me to make sure he gets his trophies and doesn't risk *his*." I looked around. "Where the hell did Chajinka sneak off to?"

"I think he's helping the cook."

"He's got his own food," I said irritably. "He doesn't need ours." I turned in the direction of the cooking Bubble and shouted: "Chajinka, get your blue ass over here!"

The Dabih looked up at the sound of my voice, smiled, and pointed to his ears.

"Then get your goddamned t-pack!" I said. "We've got work to do."

He smiled again, wandered off, and returned a moment later with his spear and his t-pack, the translating mechanism that allowed Man and Dabih (actually, Man and just about anything, with the proper programming) to converse with one another in Terran.

"Ugly little creature," remarked Mbele, indicating Chajinka.

"I didn't pick him for his looks."

"Is he really that good?"

"The little bastard could track a billiard ball down a crowded highway," I replied. "And he's got more guts than most Men I know."

"You don't say," said Mbele in tones that indicated he still considered Dabihs one step up—if that—from the animals we had come to hunt.

> *"His form is ungainly—his intellect small—"*
> *(So the Bellman would often remark)—*
> *"But his courage is perfect! And that, after all,*
> *Is the thing that one needs with a Snark."*

I'M NOT MUCH for foot-slogging when transportation is available, but it was going to take the Dabihs at least a day to assemble the safari vehicle and there was no sense hanging around camp waiting for it. So off we went, Chajinka and me, heading due west toward a water hole the computer had mapped. We weren't out to shoot anything, just to see what there was and what kind of weaponry our clients would need when we went out hunting the next morning.

It took us a little more than an hour to reach the water hole, and once there, we hid behind some heavy bush about fifty yards away from it. There was a small herd of brown-and-white herbivores slaking their thirst, and as they left, a pair of huge red animals, four or five tons apiece, came down to drink. Then there were four or five more small herds of various types of grass-eaters. I had just managed to get comfortable when I heard a slight scrabbling noise. I turned and saw Chajinka pick up a slimy five-inch green worm, study its writhing body for a moment, then pop it into his mouth and swallow it. He appeared thoughtful for a moment, as if savoring the taste, then nodded his head in approval, and began looking for more.

Once upon a time that would have disgusted me, but I'd

been with Chajinka for more than a decade and I was used to his eating habits. I kept looking for predators, and finally asked if he'd spotted any.

He waited for the t-pack to translate, then shook his head. "Night eaters, maybe," he whispered back.

"I never saw a world where *all* the carnivores were nocturnal," I answered. "There have to be some diurnal hunters, and this is the spot they should be concentrating on."

"Then where are they?"

"You're the tracker," I said. "You tell me."

He sighed deeply—a frightening sound if you're not used to Dabihs. A few of the animals at the water hole spooked and ran off thirty or forty yards, raising an enormous cloud of reddish dust. When they couldn't spot where the noise had come from, they warily returned to finish drinking.

"You wait here," he whispered. "I will find the predators."

I nodded my agreement. I'd watched Chajinka stalk animals on a hundred worlds, and I knew that I'd just be a hindrance. He could travel as silently as any predator, and he could find cover where I would swear none existed. If he had to freeze, he could stand or squat motionless for up to fifteen minutes. If an insect was crawling across his face, he wouldn't even shut an eye if it was in the insect's path. So maybe he regarded worms and insects as delicacies, and maybe he had only the vaguest notion of personal hygiene, but in his element—and we were in it now—there was no one of any species better suited for the job.

I sat down, adjusted my contact lenses to Telescopic, and scanned the horizon for the better part of ten minutes, going through a couple of smokeless cigarettes in the process. Lots of animals, all herbivores, came by to drink. Almost too many, I decided, because at this rate the water hole would be nothing but a bed of mud in a few days.

I was just about to start on a third cigarette when Chajinka was beside me again, tapping me on the shoulder.

"Come with me," he said.

"You found something?"

He didn't answer, but straightened up and walked out into the open, making no attempt to hide his presence. The animals at the water hole began bleating and bellowing in panic and raced off, some low to the ground, some zig-zagging with every stride, and some with enormous leaps. Soon all of them vanished in the thick cloud of dust they had raised.

I followed him for about half a mile, and then we came to it: a dead catlike animal, obviously a predator. It had a tan pelt, and I estimated its weight at 300 pounds. It had the teeth of a killer, and its front and back claws were clearly made for rending the flesh of its prey. Its broad tail was covered with bony spikes. It was too muscular to be built for sustained speed, but its powerful shoulders and haunches looked deadly efficient for short charges of up to one hundred yards.

"Dead maybe seven hours," said Chajinka. "Maybe eight."

I didn't mind that it was dead. I minded that its skull and body were crushed. And I especially minded that there'd been no attempt to eat it.

"Read the signs," I said. "Tell me what happened."

"Brown cat," said Chajinka, indicating the dead animal, "made a kill this morning. His stomach is still full. He was looking for a place to lie up, out of the sun. Something killed him."

"What killed him?"

He pointed to some oblong tracks, not much larger than a human's. "This one is the killer."

"Where did he go after he killed the brown cat?"

He examined the ground once more, then pointed to the northeast. "That way."

"Can we find him before dark?"

Chajinka shook his head. "He left a long time ago. Four, five, six hours."

"Let's go back to the water hole," I said. "I want you to see if he left any tracks there."

Our presence frightened yet another herd of herbivores away, and Chajinka examined the ground.

Finally he straightened up. "Too many animals have come and gone."

"Make a big circle around the water hole," I said. "Maybe a quarter mile. See if there are any tracks there."

He did as I ordered, and I fell into step behind him. We'd walked perhaps half the circumference when he stopped.

"Interesting," he said.

"What is?"

"There were brown cats here early this morning," he said, pointing to the ground. "Then the killer of the brown cat came along—you see, here, his print overlays that of a cat—and they fled." He paused. "An entire family of brown cats—at least four, perhaps five—fled from a single animal that hunts alone."

"You're sure he's a solitary hunter?"

He studied the ground again. "Yes. He walks alone. Very interesting."

It was more than interesting.

There was a lone animal out there that was higher on the food chain than the 300-pound brown cats. It had frightened away an entire pod of large predators, and—this was the part I didn't like—it didn't kill just for food.

Hunters read signs, and they listen to their trackers, but mostly they tend to trust their instincts. We'd been on Dodgson IV less than five hours, and I was already getting a bad feeling.

"I KIND OF expected you'd be bringing back a little something exotic for dinner," remarked Jaxon Pollard when we returned to camp.

"Or perhaps a trophy," chimed in Ramona Desmond.

"I've got enough trophies, and you'll want to shoot your own."

"You don't sound like a very enthusiastic hunter," she said.

"You're paying to do the hunting," I replied. "My job is to back you up and step in if things get out of hand. As far as I'm concerned, the ideal safari is one on which I don't fire a single shot."

"Sounds good to me," said Marx. "What are we going after tomorrow?"

"I'm not sure."

"You're not sure?" he repeated. "What the hell were you doing all afternoon?"

"Scouting the area."

"This is like pulling teeth," complained Marx. "What did you find?"

"I think we may have found signs of Mrs. Desmond's Snark, for lack of a better name."

Suddenly everyone was interested.

"A Snark?" said Ramona Desmond delightedly. "What did it look like?"

"I don't know," I replied. "It's bipedal, but I've no idea how many limbs it has—probably four. More than that is pretty rare in large animals anywhere in the galaxy. Based on the depth of the tracks, Chajinka thinks it may go anywhere from 250 to 400 pounds."

"That's not so much," said Marx. "I've hunted bigger."

"I'm not through," I said. "In a land filled with game, it seems to have scared the other predators out of the area." I paused. "Well, actually, that could be a misstatement."

"You mean it hasn't scared them off?" asked Ramona, now thoroughly confused.

"No, they're gone. But I called them *other* predators, and I don't know for a fact that our Snark is a predator. He killed a huge, catlike creature, but he didn't eat it."

"What does that imply?" asked Ramona.

I shrugged. "I'm not sure. It could be that he was defending his territory. Or...." I let the sentence hang while I considered its implications.

"Or what?"

"Or he could simply enjoy killing things."

"That makes two of us," said Marx with a smile. "We'll go out and kill ourselves a Snark tomorrow morning."

"Not tomorrow," I said firmly.

"Why the hell not?" he asked pugnaciously.

"I make it a rule never to go after dangerous game until I know more about it than it knows about me," I answered. "Tomorrow we'll go out shooting meat for the pot and see if we can learn a little more about the Snark."

"I'm not paying millions of credits to shoot a bunch of cud-chewing alien cattle!" snapped Marx. "You've found something that practically screams 'Superb Hunting!' I vote that we go after it in the morning."

"I admire your enthusiasm and your courage, Mr. Marx," I said. "But this isn't a democracy. I've got the only vote that counts, and since it's my job to return you all safe and sound at the end of this safari, we're not going after the Snark until we know more about it."

He didn't say another word, but I could tell that at that moment he'd have been just as happy to shoot me as the Snark.

BEFORE WE SET out the next morning, I inspected the party's weapons.

"Nice laser rifle," I said, examining Desmond's brand new pride and joy.

"It ought to be," he said. "It cost fourteen thousand credits. It's got night sights, a vision enhancer, an anti-shake stock...."

"Bring out your projectile rifle and your shotgun, too," I said. "We have to test all the weapons."

"But I'm only going to use *this* rifle," he insisted.

I almost hated to break the news to him.

"In my professional opinion, Dodgson IV has a B3 biosystem," I said. "I already registered my findings via subspace transmission from the ship last night." He looked confused. "For sport hunting purposes, that means you have to use a non-explosive-projectile weapon with a maximum of a .450 grain bullet until the classification is changed."

"But—"

"Look," I interrupted. "We have fusion grenades that can literally blow this planet apart. We have intelligent bullets that will find an animal at a distance of ten miles, respond to evasive maneuvering, and not contact the target until an instant kill is guaranteed. We've got molecular imploders that can turn an enemy brigade into jelly. Given the game we're after, none of them would qualify as sport hunting. I know, we're only talking about a laser rifle in your case, but you don't want to start off the safari by breaking the law, and I'm sure as a sportsman you want to give the animal an even break."

He looked dubious, especially about the even break part, but finally he went back to his Bubble and brought out the rest of his arsenal.

I gathered the four of them around me.

"Your weapons have been packed away for a week," I said. "Their settings may have been affected by the ship's acceleration, and this world's gravity is different, however minimally, from your own. So before we start, I want to give everyone a chance to adjust their sights." *And,* I added to myself, *let's see if any of you can hit a non-threatening target at forty yards, just so I'll know what I'm up against.*

"I'll set up targets in the hollow down by the river," I continued, "and I'll ask you to come down one at a time." *No sense letting the poorer shots get humiliated in front of the better ones—always assuming there* are *any better ones.*

I took a set of the most basic targets out of the cargo hold. Once I reached the hollow, I placed four of them where I wanted them, activated the anti-grav devices, and when they were gently bobbing and weaving about six feet above the ground, I called for Marx, who showed up a moment later.

"Okay, Mr. Marx," I said. "Have you adjusted your sights?"

"I *always* take care of my weapons," he said as if the question had been an insult.

"Then let's see what you can do."

He smiled confidently, raised his rifle, looked along the sights, pulled the trigger, and blew two targets to pieces, then repeated the procedure with his shotgun.

"Nice shooting," I said.

"Thanks," he replied with a look that said: *of course* I'm a crack shot. I told you so, didn't I?

Desmond was next. He raised his rifle to his shoulder, took careful aim, and missed, then missed three more times.

I took the rifle, lined up the sights, and fired. The bullet went high and to the right, burying itself in a tree trunk. I adjusted the sights and took another shot. This time I hit a target dead center.

"Okay, try it now," I said, handing the rifle back to Desmond.

He missed four more times. He missed sitting. He missed prone. He missed using a rest for the barrel. Then he tried the shotgun, and missed twice more before he finally nailed a target. Then, for good measure, he totally misused his laser rifle, trying to pinpoint the beam rather than sweep the area, and missed yet again. We were both relieved when his session ended.

His wife was a little better; she hit the target on her third try with the rifle and her second with the shotgun. She swept the area with her laser rifle, wiping out all the remaining targets.

Pollard should have been next, but he didn't show up, and I went back to camp to get him. He was sitting down with the others, sipping a cup of coffee.

"You're next, Mr. Pollard," I said.

"I'm just going to take holos," he replied, holding up his camera.

"You're sure, Jaxon?" asked Desmond.

"I don't think I'd enjoy killing things," he replied.

"Then what the hell are you doing here?" demanded Marx.

Pollard smiled. "I'm here because you nagged incessantly, Willard. Besides, I've never been on a safari before, and I enjoy taking holographs."

"All right," I said. "But I don't want you wandering more than twenty yards from me at any time."

"No problem," said Pollard. "I don't want *them* killing me any more than I want to kill *them*."

I told his gunbearer to stay behind and help with the camp

and the cooking. You'd have thought I'd slapped him in the face, but he agreed to do as he was ordered.

We clambered into the vehicle and got to the water hole in about half an hour. Within five minutes Marx had coolly and efficiently brought down a pair of spiral-horned tan-and-brown herbivores with one bullet each. Then, exercising his right to name any species that he was the first to shoot, he dubbed them Marx's Gazelles.

"What now?" asked Desmond. "We certainly don't need any more meat for the next few days."

"I'll send the vehicle back to camp for the skinners. They'll bring back the heads and pelts as well as the best cuts of meat, and I'll have them tie the rest of the carcasses to some nearby trees."

"Why?"

"Bait," said Marx.

"Mr. Marx is right. *Something* will come along to feed on them. The smell of blood might bring the catlike predators back. Or, if we're lucky, maybe the Snark will come back and we'll be able to learn a little more about him."

"And what do *we* do in the meantime?" asked Desmond in petulant tones.

"It's up to you," I said. "We can stay here until the vehicle returns, we can march back to camp, or we can footslog to that swamp about four miles to the north and see if there's anything interesting up there."

"Like a Snark?" asked Ramona.

"Five Men and four Dabihs walking across four miles of open savannah aren't about to sneak up and surprise anything. But we're not part of the ecological system. None of the animals will be programmed to recognize us as predators, so there's always a chance—if he's there to begin with—that the Snark will stick around out of curiosity or just plain stupidity."

It was the answer they wanted to hear, so they decided to march to the swamp. Pollard must have taken fifty holos along the way. Desmond complained about the heat, the humidity, the terrain, and the insects. Ramona stuck a chip that read the text of a book into her ear and didn't utter a word until we reached the swamp. Marx just lowered his head and walked.

When we got there, we came upon a small herd of herbivores, very impressive-looking beasts, going about 500 pounds apiece. The males possessed fabulous horns, perhaps sixty inches long, with a triple twist in them. The horns looked like they were made of crystal, and they acted as a prism, separating the sunlight into a series of tiny rainbows.

"My God, look at them!" said Pollard, taking holographs as fast as he could.

"They're magnificent!" whispered Ramona Desmond.

"I'd like one of those," said Marx, studying the herd.

"You took the gazelles," I noted. "Mr. Desmond has first shot."

"I don't want it," said Desmond nervously.

"All right," I said. "Mrs. Desmond, you have first shot."

"I'd never kill anything so beautiful," she replied.

"No," muttered Desmond so softly that she couldn't hear him. "You'd just throw them into jail."

"Then it's Mr. Marx's shot," I said. "I'd suggest you take the fellow on the far right. He doesn't have the longest horns, but he's got the best-matched set. Let's get a little closer." I turned to the others as Marx took his rifle from his gunbearer and loaded it. "You stay here."

I signaled to Chajinka to take a circuitous approach. Marx, displaying the proper crouching walk, followed him, and I brought up the rear. (A hunter learns early on *never* to get between a client and the game. Either that, or he keeps a prosthetic ear company in business.)

When we'd gotten to within thirty yards, I decided we were close enough and nodded to Marx. He slowly raised his rifle and took aim. I could tell he was going for a heart shot rather than take the chance of ruining the head. It was a good strategy, always assuming that the heart was where he thought it was.

Marx took a deep breath, let it out slowly, and began squeezing the trigger.

And just as he did so, a brilliantly-colored avian flew past, shrieking wildly. The horned buck jumped, startled, just as Marx's rifle exploded. The rest of the herd bolted in all directions at the sound of the shot, and before Marx could get off a second shot, the buck bellowed in pain, spun around, and vanished into the nearby bush.

"Come on!" said Marx excitedly, jumping up and running after the buck. "I know I hit him! He won't get far!"

I grabbed him as he hurtled past. "You're not going anywhere, Mr. Marx!"

"What are you talking about?" he demanded.

"There's a large dangerous wounded animal in the bush," I said. "I can't let you go in after it."

"I'm as good a shot as you are!" he snapped. "It was just a fluke that that goddamned bird startled it. You know that!"

"Look," I said. "I'm not thrilled going into heavy bush after a wounded animal that's carrying a pair of five-foot swords on its head, but that's what I get paid to do. I can't look for him and keep an eye on you as well."

"But—"

"You say you've been on safari before," I said. "That means you know the rules."

He muttered and he cursed, but he *did* know the rules, and he rejoined the rest of the party, while Chajinka and I vanished into the bush in search of our wounded prey.

The swamp smelled of rotting vegetation. We followed the blood spoor on leaves and bushes through two hundred yards of mud that sucked at the Dabih's feet and my boots, and then, suddenly, it vanished. I saw a little hillock a few yards off to the right, where the grass was crushed flat, small branches were broken, and flowers were broken off their stems. Chajinka studied the signs for a full minute, then looked up.

"The Snark," he said.

"What are you talking about?"

"He was hiding, watching us," answered Chajinka. He pointed to the ground. "The wounded animal lay down here. You see the blood? The Snark was over there. Those are his tracks. When the animal lay down, the Snark saw it was too weak to get up again, but still dangerous. He circled behind it. See—here is where he went. Then he leaped upon it and killed it."

"How?"

Chajinka shrugged. "I cannot tell. But he lifted it and carried it off."

"*Could* he lift an animal that big?"

"He did."

"He can't be more that a few hundred yards ahead of us," I said. "What do you think? Can we catch up with him?"

"You and I? Yes."

Every now and then, when my blood was up, Chajinka had to remind me that I wasn't hunting for my own pleasure. Yes, was the implication, he and I could catch up with the Snark. Marx might not be a hindrance. But there was no way we could take Pollard and the Desmonds through the swamp, keep an eye out for predators, and hope to make up any ground on the Snark—and of course I couldn't leave them alone while we went after the Snark with Marx.

"All right," I said with a sigh. "Let's get back and tell them what happened."

Marx went ballistic. He ranted and cursed for a good three minutes, and by the end of it I felt he was ready to declare a blood feud against this trophy thief.

When he finally calmed down, I left Chajinka behind to see if he could learn anything more about the Snark while the rest of us began marching back to the water hole, where the vehicle was waiting for us.

"We have sailed many months, we have sailed many weeks,
(Four weeks to the month you may mark),
But never as yet ('tis your Captain who speaks)
Have we caught the least glimpse of a Snark!"

MBELE HAD HIMSELF a good laugh when we got back to camp, hot and tired and hungry.

"You keep talking about the Snark as if it exists!" he said in amusement. "It's an imaginary beast in a children's poem."

"Snark is just a convenient name for it," I said. "We can call it anything you like."

"Call it absent," he said. "No one's seen it."

"Right," I said. "And I suppose when you close your eyes, the whole galaxy vanishes."

"I never thought about it," admitted Mbele. "But it probably does." He paused thoughtfully. "At least, I certainly hope so. It makes me feel necessary."

"Look!" I exploded. "There's a dead 300-pound killer cat out there, and a missing antelope that was even bigger!" I glared at him. "*I* didn't kill one and steal the other. Did *you*?"

He swallowed his next rejoinder and gave me a wide berth for the rest of the day.

CHAJINKA TROTTED INTO camp the next morning and signaled to me. I walked over and joined him.

"Did you learn anything?" I asked.

"It is an interesting animal," he said.

I grimaced, for as everyone knows, the Dabihs are masters of understatement.

> "Come, listen, my men, while I tell you again
> The five unmistakeable marks
> By which you may know, wheresoever you go,
> The warranted genuine Snarks."

I GATHERED THE hunting party around me.

"Well," I announced, "we know a little more about the Snark now than we did yesterday." I paused to watch their reactions. Everyone except Desmond seemed interested; Desmond looked like he wished he were anywhere else.

RESNICK'S MENAGERIE

"Chajinka has been to the tree where we tied the dead meat animals," I continued.

"And?" said Marx.

"The ropes were untied. Not cut or torn apart or bitten through; untied. So we know that the Snark either has fingers, or some damned effective appendages. And some meat was missing from the carcasses."

"All right," said Ramona. "We know he can untie knots. What else?"

"We know he's a carnivore," I said. "We weren't sure about that yesterday."

"So what?" asked Marx. "There are millions of carnivores in the galaxy. Nothing unique about that."

"It means he won't stray far from the game herds. They're his supermarket."

"Maybe he only has to eat once every few months," said Marx, unimpressed.

"No," I said. "That's the third thing we've learned: he's got to eat just about as often as we do."

"How do we know that?" asked Ramona.

"According to Chajinka, he approached the meat very cautiously, but his tracks show that he trotted away once he'd eaten his fill. The trail disappeared after a mile, but we know that he trotted that whole distance."

"Ah!" said Ramona. "I see."

"I sure as hell don't," complained her husband.

"Anything that can sustain that pace, that kind of drain on its energy, has to eat just about every day." I paused. "And we know a fourth thing."

"What is that?" she asked.

"He's not afraid of us," I said. "He had to know we were the ones who killed those meat animals. Our tracks and scent were all over the place, and of course there were the ropes. He knows that we're a party of at least nine—five, if you discount Chajinka and the three gunbearers, and he has no reason to discount them. And yet, hours after learning all that, he hasn't left the area." I paused. "That leads to a fifth conclusion. He's not very bright; he didn't understand that Marx's gun was what wounded the animal he killed yesterday—because if he realized we could kill from a distance, he'd *be* afraid of us."

"You deduce all that just from a few tracks and the signs that Chajinka saw?" asked Desmond skeptically.

"Reading signs and interpreting what they mean is what hunting's all about," I explained. "Shooting is just the final step."

"So do we go after him now?" asked Marx eagerly.

I shook my head. "I've already sent Chajinka back out to see if he can find the creature's lair. If he's like most carnivores, he'll want to lie up after he eats. If we know where to look for him, we'll save a lot of time and effort. It makes more sense to wait for Chajinka to report back, and then go after the Snark in the morning."

"It seems so odd," said Ramona. "We've never seen this creature, and yet we've already reasoned out that he's incredibly formidable."

"Of course he's formidable," I said.

"You say that as if *everything* is formidable," she said with a condescending smile.

"That's the first axiom on safari," I replied. "Everything bites."

"If this thing is as dangerous as you make it seem," said Desmond hesitantly, "are we permitted to use more... well, sophisticated weapons?"

"Show a little guts, Philemon," said Marx contemptuously.

"I'm a banker, not a goddamned Alan Quatermain!" shot back Desmond.

"If you're afraid, stay in camp," said Marx. "Me, I can't wait to get him in my sights."

"You didn't answer my question, Mr. Bell," persisted Desmond.

Mbele pulled out the Statute Book and began reading aloud. "Unless, in the hunter's judgment, the weapons you are using are inadequate for killing the prey, you must use the weapons that have been approved for the world in question."

"So if he presents a serious threat, we can use pulse guns and molecular imploders and the like?"

"Have you ever seen a molecular imploder in action?" I asked. "Aim it at a fifty-story building and you turn the whole thing into pudding in about three seconds."

"What about pulse guns?" he persisted.

"There's not a lot of trophy left when one of those babies hit the target," I said.

"We need *something,* damn it!" whined Desmond.

"We have more than enough firepower to bring down any animal on this planet," I said, getting annoyed with him. "I don't mean to be blunt, but there's a difference between an inadequate hunter and an inadequate weapon."

"You can say that again!" muttered Marx.

"That was *very* blunt, Mr. Bell," said Desmond, getting up and walking to his Bubble. His wife stared at him expressionlessly, then pulled out her book and began reading.

"That's what you get for being honest," said Marx, making no attempt to hide his amusement. "I just hope this Snark is half the creature you make it out to be."

I'll settle for half, I thought uneasily.

CHAJINKA, WHO WAS sitting on the hood of the safari vehicle, raised his spear, which was my signal to stop.

He jumped down, bent over, examined the grasses for a few seconds, then trotted off to his left, eyes glued to the ground.

I climbed out and grabbed my rifle.

"You wait here," I said to the four humans. The Dabih gunbearers, who clung to handles and footholds on the back of the vehicle when it was moving, had released their grips and were now standing just behind it.

"Whose shot is it?" asked Marx.

"Let me think," I said. "You shot that big buck yesterday, and Mrs. Desmond killed the boar-like thing with the big tusks just before that. So Mr. Desmond has the first shot today."

"I'm not getting out of the vehicle," said Desmond.

"It's against regulations to shoot from the safety of the vehicle," I pointed out.

"Fuck your regulations and fuck you!" hollered Desmond. "I don't want the first shot! I don't want *any* shot! I don't even know what the hell I'm doing on this stupid safari!"

"Goddammit, Philemon!" hissed Marx fiercely.

"What is it?" asked Desmond, startled.

"If there was anything there, Mr. Desmond," I explained, trying to control my temper, "you just gave it more than ample reason to run hell for leather in the opposite direction. You *never* yell during a hunt."

I walked away in disgust and joined Chajinka beneath a small tree. He was standing beside a young dead herbivore whose skull had been crushed.

"Snark," he said, pointing to the skull.

"When?" I asked.

He pulled back the dead animal's lips to examine its gums, felt the inside of its ears, examined other parts for a few seconds.

"Five hours," he said. "Maybe six."

"The middle of the night."

"Yes."

> "Its habit of getting up late you'll agree
> That it carries too far, when I say
> That it frequently breakfasts at five-o'clock tea,
> And dines on the following day."

"Can you pick up his trail?" I asked Chajinka.

He looked around, then gave the Dabih equivalent of a frown. "It vanishes," he said at last, pointing to a spot ten feet away.

"You mean some animals obliterated his tracks after he made them?"

He shrugged. "No tracks at all. Not his, not anyone's."

"Why not?"

He had no answer.

RESNICK'S MENAGERIE

I stared at the ground for a long moment. "Okay," I said at last. "Let's get back to the vehicle."

He resumed his customary position on the hood, while I sat behind the control panel and thought.

"Well?" asked Marx. "Did it have something to do with the Snark?"

"Yeah," I said, still puzzled by the absence of any tracks. "He made a kill during the night. His prey was an animal built for what I would call evasive maneuvering. That means he's got excellent nocturnal vision and good motor skills."

"So he's a night hunter?" asked Ramona.

"No, I wouldn't say that," I replied. "He killed the crystal-horned buck at midday, so like most predators he's also an opportunist; when a meal is there for the taking, he grabs it. Anyway, if we can't find his lair, we're probably going to have to build a blind, sit motionless with our guns, hang some fresh bait every evening, and hope it interests him."

"That's not *real* hunting!" scoffed Marx.

"There's no way we can go chasing after him in the dark," I responded.

"I'm not chasing *anything* in the dark!" said Desmond adamantly. "You want to do it, you do it without me."

"Don't be such a coward!" said Marx.

"Fuck you, Willard!" Desmond retorted.

"Bold words," said Marx. "Why don't you take some of that bravery and aim it at the animals?"

"I hate it here!" snapped Desmond. "I think we should go back to camp."

"And do what?" asked Marx sarcastically.

"And consider our options," he replied. "It's a big planet. Maybe we could take off and land on one of the other continents—one without any Snarks on it."

"Nonsense!" said Marx. "We came here to hunt big game. Well, now we've found it."

"I don't know *what* we've found," said Desmond, halfway between anger and panic, "and neither do you."

"That's what makes it such good sport and so exciting," said Marx.

"Exciting is watching sports on the holo," Desmond shot back. *"This is dangerous."*

"Same damned thing," muttered Marx.

WE SPENT THE next two days searching unsuccessfully for any sign of the Snark. For a while I thought he had moved out of the area and considered moving our base camp, but then Chajinka found some relatively fresh tracks, perhaps three hours old. So we didn't move the camp after all—but we also didn't find the creature.

Then, on the third afternoon of the search, as we were taking a break, sitting in the shade of a huge tree with purple and gold flowers, we heard a strange sound off in the distance.

"Thunder?" asked Marx.

"Doesn't seem likely," replied Pollard. "There's not a cloud in the sky."

"Well, it's *something*," continued Marx.

Ramona frowned. "And it's getting closer. Well, louder, anyway."

On a hunch, I set my lenses to Telescopic, and it was a damned lucky thing I did.

"Everybody! Up into the tree—fast!" I shouted.

"But—"

"No arguments! Get going!"

They weren't the most agile tree-climbers I'd ever encountered, but when they were finally able to see what I had seen, they managed to get clear of the ground in one hell of a hurry. A minute later a few thousand Marx's Gazelles thundered past.

I waited for the dust to settle, then lowered myself to the ground and scanned the horizon.

"Okay, it's safe to come down now," I announced.

"Why didn't we climb into the vehicle?" asked Ramona, getting out of the tree and checking her hands for cuts.

"It's an open vehicle, Mrs. Desmond," I pointed out. "You could have wound up with a fractured skull as they jumped over it—or with a gazelle in your lap if one of them was a poor jumper."

"Point taken."

"What the hell would cause something like that?" asked Pollard, staring after the stampeding herd as he brushed himself off.

"I'd say a predator made a sloppy kill, or maybe blew one entirely."

"How do you figure that?"

"Because this is the first time we've seen a stampede… so we can assume that when they're killed quickly and efficiently, the gazelles just move out of the predator's range and then go back to grazing. It's when the predator misses his prey, or wounds it, and then races after it into the middle of the herd that they panic."

"You think it's one of the big cats?" asked Pollard.

"It's possible."

"I'd love to get some holos of those cats on a kill."

"You may get your wish, Mr. Pollard," I said. "We'll back-track to where the stampede started and hope we get lucky."

"That suits me just fine," said Marx, patting his rifle.

WE HEADED SOUTHWEST in the vehicle until the terrain became too rough, then left it behind and started walking as the land-scape changed from hilly and tree-covered to heavily-forested. Chajinka trotted ahead of us, eyes on the ground, spotting things even I couldn't see, and finally he came to a stop.

"What it is?" I asked, catching up with him.

He pointed straight ahead into the dense foliage. "He is there."

"He?"

"The Snark," he said, pointing to a single track.

"How deep is the cover?" I asked. "How do you know he didn't run right through it?"

He pointed to the bushes, which were covered with thorns. "He cannot run through this without pain."

"You've never seen him," said Ramona, joining us. "How do you know?"

"If it did not rip his flesh, he would be a forest creature, created by God to live here," answered Chajinka, as if explaining it to a child. "But we know that he hunts plains game. A forest dweller with thick, heavy skin and bones could not move swiftly enough. So this is not his home—it is his hiding place."

I thought there was a good chance that it was more than his hiding place, that it could very well be his fortress. It was damned near impenetrable, and the forest floor was covered with dry leaves, so no one was going to sneak up on him without giving him plenty of warning.

"What are we waiting for?" asked Marx, approaching with Desmond. He stopped long enough to take his rifle from his gunbearer.

"We're waiting until I can figure out the best way to go about it," I responded.

"We walk in and blow him away," said Marx. "What's so hard about that?"

I shook my head. "This is *his* terrain. He knows every inch of it. You're going to make a lot of noise walking in there, and the way the upper terraces of the trees are intertwined, I've got a feeling that it could be dark as night six hundred yards into the forest."

"So we'll use infrared scopes on our guns," said Marx.

I kept staring at the thick foliage. "I don't like it," I said. "He's got every advantage."

"But *we've* got the weapons," persisted Marx.

"With minimal visibility and maneuverability, they won't do you much good."

"Bullshit!" spat Marx. "We're wasting time. Let's go in after him."

"The four of you are my responsibility," I replied. "I can't risk your safety by letting you go in there. Within a couple of minutes you could be out of touch with me and with each other. You'll be making noise with every step you take, and if I'm right about the light, before long you could be standing right next to him without seeing him. And we haven't explored any Dodgson forests yet—he might not be the only danger. There could be everything from arboreal killer cats to poisonous insects to fifty-foot-long snakes with an attitude."

"So what do you propose?" asked Marx.

"A blind makes the most sense," I said. "But it could take half a day to build one, and who the hell knows where he'll be by then?" I paused. "All right. The three of you with weapons will spread out. Mr. Pollard, stand well behind them. Chajinka and I will go into the bush and try to flush him out."

"I thought you said it was too dangerous," said Ramona.

"Let me amend that," I answered. "It's too dangerous for amateurs."

"If there's a chance that he can harm you, why don't we just forget about it?" she continued.

"I appreciate your concern," I began, "but—"

"I'm not being totally altruistic. What happens to us if he kills you?"

"You'll return to base camp and tell Mbele what happened. He'll radio a subspace message to headquarters, and Silinger & Mahr will decide whether to give you a refund or take you to another planet with a new hunter."

"You make it sound so... so businesslike," she said distastefully.

"It's my business," I replied.

"Why did you ever become a hunter?"

I shrugged. "Why did you become a judge?"

"I have a passion for order," she said.

"So do I," I replied.

"You find order in killing things?"

"I find order in Nature. Death is just a part of it." I paused. "Now, Mr. Marx," I said, turning back to him, "I want you to...."

He wasn't there.

"Where the hell did he go?" I demanded.

No one seemed to know, not even Chajinka. Then his gunbearer approached me.

"Boss Marx went *there*." He pointed to the forest, then ruefully held up the back-up rifle. "He did not wait for me."

"*Shit!*" I muttered. "It's bad enough that I've got to go in after the Snark! Now I stand a hell of a good chance of getting blown away by that macho bastard!"

"Why would he shoot you?" asked Ramona.

"He'll hear me before he sees me," I answered. "He's running on adrenaline. He'll be sure I'm the Snark."

"Then stay out here."

"I wish I could," I said truthfully. "But it's my job to protect him whether he wants me to or not."

That particular argument became academic about five seconds later, when we heard a shot, and then a long, agonized scream.

A *human* scream.

"You two stand about two hundred yards apart," I said to the Desmonds. "Shoot anything that comes out of there that doesn't look like me or a Dabih!" Then, to Chajinka: "Let's go!"

The Dabih led the way into the forest. Then, as it started getting thicker and darker, we lost Marx's trail. "We're more likely to find him if we split up," I whispered. "You go left, I'll go right."

I kept my gun at the ready, wishing I'd inserted my infrared lenses into my eyes that morning. After a minute I couldn't hear Chajinka any more, which meant, when I finally heard footsteps, I was going to have to hold my fire until I could tell whether it was the Dabih or the Snark.

It's no secret that hunters hate going into the bush after a wounded animal. Well, let me tell you something: going into the bush after an *unwounded* animal is even less appealing. Sweat ran down into my eyes, insects crawled inside my shoes and socks and up my shirtsleeves, and my gun seemed to have tripled in weight. I could barely see ten feet in front of me, and if Marx had yelled for help from fifty yards away, I probably would be five minutes locating him.

But Marx was past yelling for help. I was suddenly able to make out the figure of a man lying on the ground. I approached him cautiously, seeing Snarks—whatever they looked like—behind every tree.

Finally I reached him and knelt down to examine him. His throat had been slashed open, and his innards were pouring out of a gaping hole in his belly. He was probably dead before he hit the ground.

"*Chajinka!*" I hollered. There was no response.

I called his name every thirty seconds, and finally, after about five minutes, I heard a body shuffling through the thick bush, its translated, monotone voice saying, "Don't shoot! Don't shoot!"

"Get over here!" I said.

He joined me a moment later. "Snark," he said, looking at Marx's corpse.

"For sure?" I asked.

"For sure."

"All right," I said. "Help me carry his body back out of here."

Then, suddenly, we heard two rifle shots.

"Damn!" I bellowed. "He's broken out!"

"Perhaps he will be dead," said Chajinka, leading the way back out of the forest. "There were two shots."

When we finally got into the open, we found Philemon Desmond sitting on the ground, hyper-ventilating, his whole body shaking. Ramona and Pollard stood a few yards away, staring at him—she with open contempt, he with a certain degree of sympathy.

"What happened?" I demanded.

"He burst out of the woods and came right at me!" said Desmond in a shaky voice.

"We heard two shots. Did you hit him?"

"I don't think so." He began shaking all over. "No, I definitely didn't."

"How the hell could you miss?" I shouted. "He couldn't have been twenty yards away!"

"I've never killed anything before!" Desmond yelled back.

I scanned the hilly countryside. There was no sign of the Snark, and there had to be a good five hundred hiding places just within my field of vision.

"Wonderful!" I muttered. "Just wonderful!"

> The Bellman looked uffish, and wrinkled his brow.
> "If only you'd spoken before!
> It's excessively awkward to mention it now,
> With the Snark, so to speak, at the door!"

WE DRAGGED MARX'S body out of the forest and loaded in into the back of the safari vehicle.

"My God!" whined Desmond. "He's dead! He was the only one of us who knew the first damned thing about hunting, and he's dead! We've got to get out of here!"

"He was also a friend," said Ramona. "You might spare a little of your self-pity for *him*."

"Ramona!" said Pollard harshly.

"I'm sorry," she said with a total lack of sincerity.

Pollard had been staring at Marx's body since we brought it out of the forest. "Jesus, he's a mess!" he said at last. "Did he suffer much?"

"No," I assured him. "Not with wounds like those—he would have gone into shock immediately."

"Well, we can be thankful for that, I suppose," said Pollard. He finally tore his eyes away from the body and turned to me. "What now?"

"Now it's not a matter of sport anymore," I said, morbidly wondering whether the authorities would revoke my license for losing a client or simply suspend it. "He's killed one of us. He's got to die."

"I thought that was the whole purpose of the safari."

"The purpose was a sporting stalk, with the odds all on the game's side. Now the purpose is to kill him as quickly and efficiently as we can."

"That sounds like revenge," noted Ramona.

"Practicality," I corrected her. "Now that he knows how easy it is to kill an armed man, we don't want him to get into the habit."

"How do you stop him?"

"There are ways," I said. "I'll use every trick I know—and I know a lifetime's worth of them—before he has a chance to kill again." I paused. "Now, so I'll know which traps to set, I want you to tell me what he actually looks like."

"Like a huge red ape with big glaring eyes," said Pollard.

"No," said Ramona. "He looked more like a brown bear, but with longer legs."

"He was sleek," offered Pollard.

Ramona disagreed again. "No, he was shaggy."

"Wonderful," I muttered. "I trust you at least took a couple of holos, Mr. Pollard?"

He shook his head. "I was so surprised when he burst out of there that I totally forgot the camera," he admitted shamefacedly.

"Well, that's an enormous help," I said disgustedly. I turned to Desmond. "How about you?"

"I don't know," he whimpered. Suddenly he shuddered. "He looked like Death!"

"You must forgive Philemon," said Ramona, with an expression that said *she* wasn't about to forgive him. "He's really very good at investments and mergers and even hostile takeovers. He's just not very competent at *physical* things." She patted his medal. "Except running."

MARX HAD A wife and three grown children back on Roosevelt III, and his friends felt sure they'd want him shipped home, so we put his body in a vacuum container and stuck it in the cargo hold.

After that was done, Chajinka and I went to work. We set seven traps, then went back to camp and waited.

Early the next morning we went out to see what we'd accomplished.

That was when I learned that the Snark had a sardonic sense of humor.

Each of the traps contained a dead animal. But lest we mistakenly think that *we* had anything to do with it, each one had its head staved in.

The son of a bitch was actually mocking us.

> *"For the Snark's a peculiar creature, that won't*
> *Be caught in a commonplace way.*
> *Do all that you know, and try all that you don't:*
> *Not a chance must be wasted today!"*

I AWOKE THE next morning to the sound of vaguely familiar alien jabbering. It took me a minute to clear my head and identify what I was hearing. Then I raced out of my Bubble and almost bumped into Chajinka, who was running to meet me.

"What's going on?" I demanded.

He responded in his native tongue.

"Where's your t-pack?" I asked.

He jabbered at me. I couldn't understand a word of it.

Finally he pulled me over to the area where the Dabihs ate and slept, and pointed to the shapeless pile of metal and plastic and computer chips. Sometime during the night the Snark had silently entered the camp and destroyed all the t-packs.

I kept wondering: was he just lucky in his choice, or could he possibly have *known* how much we needed them?

Mbele, awakened by the same sounds, quickly emerged from his Bubble.

"What the hell is going on?" he asked.

"See for yourself," I said.

"Jesus!" he said. "Can any of the Dabihs speak Terran?"

I shook my head. "If they could, they wouldn't need t-packs, would they?"

"Was it the Snark?"

I grimaced. "Who else?"

"So what do you do now?"

114

"First, I try to figure out whether it was mischief or malice, and whether he had any idea what havoc it would cause."

"You think he might be a little smarter than your average bear in the woods?"

"I don't know. He lives like an animal, he acts like an animal, and he hunts like an animal. But in a short space of time he's killed Marx, and he's seen to it that the five remaining Men can't communicate with the twelve Dabihs." I forced a wry smile to my mouth. "That's not bad for a dumb animal, is it?"

"You'd better wake the others and let them know what's happened," said Mbele.

"I know," I said. I kicked one of the broken t-packs up against a tree. "Shit!"

I woke the Desmonds and Pollard and told them what had occurred. I thought Philemon Desmond might faint. The others were a little more useful.

"How long ago did this happen?" asked Pollard.

"Chajinka could probably give you a more accurate estimate, but I can't speak to him. My best guess is about two hours."

"So if we go after him, he's two hours ahead of us?"

"That's right."

"We'd better kill him quickly," said Ramona. "He could come back any time, now that he knows where our camp is."

"Give me a laser rifle," added Pollard. "I haven't fired a gun since I was a kid at camp, but how the hell hard can it be to sweep the area with a beam?"

"You look a little under the weather, Mr. Desmond," I said. "Perhaps you'd like to stay in camp."

Actually, he looked incredibly grateful for the out I'd given him. Then his wife ruined it all by adding that he'd just be in the way.

"I'm going," he said.

"It's really not necessary," I said.

"I paid. I'm going."

And that was that.

"There's no sense taking gunbearers," I said as the four of us walked to the safari vehicle. "We can't talk to them, and besides, the rules don't apply in this case. If we see him, we'll take him from the safety of the vehicle, and it'll give you something solid to rest your rifles on while you're sweeping the area." They climbed onto their seats. "Wait here a minute."

I went back, found Mbele, and told him that we were going after the Snark, and that he should use the Dabihs to set up some kind of defensive perimeter. Then I signaled to Chajinka to join me. A moment later he had taken his customary position on the hood of the vehicle, and we were off in pursuit of the Snark.

The trail led due northeast, past the savannah, toward rolling country and a large, lightly-forested valley. Two or three times I thought we'd spot him just over the next hill, but he was a cagy bastard, and by midafternoon we still hadn't sighted him.

As dusk fell, Chajinka couldn't read the signs from the vehicle, so he jumped off and began trotting along, eyes glued to the ground. When we entered the valley, he was following the trail so slowly that Ramona and Pollard got out and walked along with him, while I followed in the vehicle and Desmond stayed huddled in the back of it.

> But the valley grew narrow and narrower still,
> And the evening got darker and colder,
> Till (merely from nervousness, not from good will)
> They marched along shoulder to shoulder.

NIGHT FELL WITH no sign of the Snark. I didn't want to chance damaging the vehicle by driving over that terrain in the dark, so we slept until sunrise, and then drove back to base camp, reaching it just before noon.

Nobody was prepared for the sight that awaited us.

The eleven Dabihs we'd left behind were sprawled dead on

the ground in grotesquely contorted positions, each with his throat shredded or his intestines ripped out. Dismembered arms and legs were everywhere, and the place was swimming in blood. Dead staring eyes greeted us accusingly, as if to say: "Where were you when we needed you?"

The stench was worse than the sight. Ramona gagged and began vomiting. Desmond whimpered and curled up into a fetal ball on the floor of the vehicle so he wouldn't have to look at the carnage. Pollard froze like a statue; then, after a moment, he too began vomiting.

I'd seen a lot of death in my time. So had Chajinka. But neither of us had ever seen anything remotely like this. There hadn't been much of a struggle. It doesn't take a 400-pound predator very long to wipe out a bunch of unarmed 90-pound Dabihs. My guess was that it was over in less than a minute.

"What the hell happened here?" asked Pollard, gesturing weakly toward all the blood-soaked dismembered bodies when he finally was able to speak.

> "The method employed I would gladly explain,
> While I have it so clear in my head.
> If I had but the time and you had but the brain—
> But much yet remains to be said."

"WHERE'S MBELE?" I asked, finally getting past the shock of what I was looking at and realizing that he wasn't among them.

Before anyone could answer, I raced to the hatch and entered the ship, rifle at the ready, half-expecting to be pounced on by the Snark at any moment.

I found what was left of Captain Mbele in the control room. His head had been torn from his body, and his stomach was ripped open. The floor, the bulkheads, even the viewscreen were all drenched with his blood.

"Is he there?" called Ramona from the ground.

"Stay out!" I yelled.

Then I searched every inch of the ship, looking for the Snark. I could feel my heart pounding as I explored each section, but there was no sign of him.

I went back to the control room and began checking it over thoroughly. The Snark didn't know what made the ship work, or even what it was, but he knew it belonged to his enemies, and he did a lot of damage. Some of it—to the pilot's chair and the Deepsleep pods and the auxiliary screens—didn't matter. Some of it—to the fusion ignition and the navigational computer and the subspace radio—mattered a *lot.*

I continued going through the ship, assessing the damage. He'd ripped up a couple of beds in his fury, but the most serious destruction was to the galley. I had a feeling that nothing in it would ever work again.

I went back outside and confronted the party.

"Did you find Captain Mbele?" asked Ramona.

"Yes. He's in the ship." She started walking to the hatch. I grabbed her arm. "Trust me: you don't want to see him."

"That's it!" screamed Desmond. "We were crazy to come here! I want out! Not tomorrow, not later! *Now!*"

"I second the motion," agreed Ramona. "Let's get the hell off this planet before it kills any more of us."

"That's not possible," I said grimly. "The Snark did some serious damage to the ship."

"How long will it take to fix it?" asked Pollard.

"If I was a skilled spacecraft mechanic with a full set of tools and all the replacement parts I needed, maybe a week," I answered. "But I'm a hunter who doesn't know how to fix a broken spaceship. I wouldn't know where to begin."

"You mean we're stranded?" asked Ramona.

"For the time being," I said.

"What do you mean, 'for the time being?'" shrieked Desmond hysterically. "We're here forever! We're dead! We're all dead!"

I grabbed him and shook him, and when he wouldn't stop screaming, I slapped him, hard, on the face.

"That won't help!" I said angrily.

"We'll never get off this goddamned dirtball!" he bleated.

"Yes we will," I said. "Mbele had to check in with Silinger & Mahr every week. When they don't hear from us, they'll send a rescue party. All we have to do is stay alive until they get here."

"They'll never come!" moaned Desmond. "We're all going to die!"

"Stop your whining!" I snapped. *This is just what I needed now,* I thought disgustedly; *we're surrounded by dismembered corpses, the very ground is soaked with blood, the Snark's probably still nearby, and this asshole is losing it.* "We have work to do!" They all looked at me. "I want the three of you to start digging a mass grave for the eleven Dabihs. When that's done, I want us to burn everything—every tree, every bush, everything—to get rid of the smell of blood so it doesn't attract any predators. What we can't burn, we'll bury."

"And what are *you* going to be doing?" demanded Desmond, who had at least regained some shred of composure.

"I'm going to bring what's left of Mbele out of the ship and clean up all the blood," I said bluntly. "Unless you'd rather do it." I thought he was going to faint. "Then, if I can make myself understood to Chajinka, he and I will try to secure the area."

"How?" asked Ramona.

"We got some devices that are sensitive to movement and body heat. Maybe we can rig up some kind of alarm system. Chajinka and I can hide them around the perimeter of the camp. If we finish before you do, we'll pitch in and help with the grave. Now get busy—the sooner we finish, the sooner we can lock ourselves in the ship and decide on our next move."

"*Is* there a next move?" asked Pollard.

"Always," I replied.

It took me almost four hours to clean Mbele's blood and innards from the control room. I put what was left of him into a vacuum pouch, then hefted it to my shoulder and carried it outside.

I found Chajinka helping with the grave. I called him over and showed him, with an elaborate pantomime, what I had in mind, and a few moments later we were planting the sensing devices around the perimeter of our camp. I saw no reason to stay in the Bubbles with such a dangerous enemy on the loose, so I collapsed them and moved them back into the cargo hold. The grave still wasn't done, so Chajinka and I helped finish the job. Desmond wouldn't touch any of the corpses, and Ramona looked like she was going be get sick again, so the Dabih, Pollard and I dragged the corpses and spare body parts to the grave, I added the pouch containing Mbele's remains, and after we four humans and Chajinka filled it in, I read the Bible over it.

"Now what?" asked Ramona, dirty and on the verge of physical collapse.

"Now we burn everything, bury any remaining dried blood, and then we move into the ship," I said.

"And just wait to be rescued?"

I shook my head. "It could be weeks, even a month, before a rescue party arrives. We're going to need meat, and since we've no way to refrigerate it with the galley destroyed, it means we'll probably have to go hunting every day, or at least every other day."

"I see," she said.

"And I'm going to kill the Snark," I said.

"Why don't we just wait for the rescue party and not take any chances?" suggested Ramona fearfully.

"It's killed thirteen beings who were under my protection," I said grimly. "I'm going to kill him if it's the last thing I do."

"Maybe Philemon should give you his laser rifle," Ramona suggested. "He's not very good with it anyway."

Desmond glared at her, but made no reply.

"He may need it," I said. "Besides, I'm happy with my own weapon."

"Where will you hunt for it?" asked Pollard.

"Right in this general area," I answered. "He has no reason to leave it."

"We can't just sit around like bait and wait for him!" whined

Desmond. "In all the time we've been on the planet you've never even seen him—but he's killed Marx and Mbele and our Dabihs. He comes into camp whenever he wants! He sabotages our t-packs and our ship! We'll need an army to kill him!"

"If he comes back, you'll be safe inside the ship," I said.

"Locking himself in the ship didn't help Captain Mbele," noted Ramona.

"He didn't close the hatch. As I read the signs, he saw what was happening and raced into the ship for a gun. The Snark caught him before he found it." I paused. "He knew better than to be out here without a weapon."

"So now it's *his* fault that this monster killed him?" shouted Desmond. "Let's not blame the hunter who fucked up! Let's blame the victim!"

That's when I lost it. "One more word out of you and there'll be another killing!" I shouted back at him.

Pollard stepped between us. "Stop it!" he snapped. "The creature's out there! Don't do his work for him!"

We both calmed down after that, and finally went into the ship. There was no food, but everyone was so physically and emotionally exhausted that it didn't matter. Half an hour later we were all sound asleep.

EACH MORNING CHAJINKA and I walked across the scorched, empty field that had so recently been covered with vegetation. We would climb into the safari vehicle and prepare to go out to bag the day's food—and even though there was no longer any place to hide near the ship, I constantly had the uneasy feeling that *he* was watching us, measuring our strength, biding his time.

We never went more than four miles from camp. I didn't shoot the choicest animals, just the closest. Then we'd cut off the strips of meat we thought we'd need and leave the carcass for the scavengers. We'd return to camp, and after breakfast, we'd set out on foot to look for signs of the Snark.

I knew he was nearby, knew it as surely as I knew my own name, but we couldn't find any physical sign of him. I warned the others not to leave the ship without their weapons, preferably not to leave it at all, and under no circumstance were they to go more than thirty yards away from it unless they were in my company.

By the fifth day after the massacre, everyone was getting tired of red meat, so I decided to take Chajinka down to the river, and see if we could spear a few fish.

"Can I come with you?" asked Ramona, appearing just inside the hatch. "I'm starting to feel distinctly claustrophobic."

I couldn't see any reason why not. Hell, she was safer with Chajinka and me than back at the ship.

"Bring your rifle," I said.

She disappeared inside the ship, then emerged with a laser rifle a moment later.

"I'm ready."

"Let's go," I said.

We marched through heavy bush to the river.

"All the local animals must come down here to drink," noted Ramona. "Wouldn't it be easier to do your hunting right here rather than go out in the safari vehicle each morning?"

"We'd attract too many scavengers," I explained. "And since Chajinka and I come down here twice a day to bring water back to the ship, why cause ourselves any problems?"

"I see." She paused. "Are there any carnivores in the river—the kind that might eat a human?"

"I haven't seen any," I replied. "But I sure as hell wouldn't recommend taking a swim."

When we reached the river, Chajinka grabbed a large branch and beat the water. When he was sure it was safe, he waded out, thigh-deep, and held his spear above his head, poised to strike, while we watched him in total silence. He stayed motionless for almost two full minutes, then suddenly stabbed the water and came away with a large, wriggling fish.

RESNICK'S MENAGERIE

He grinned and said something that I couldn't understand, then clambered onto the bank, picked up a rock, and smashed it down on the fish's head. It stopped moving, and he went back into the water.

"Two more and we'll have our dinner," I remarked.

"He's really something," she said. "Where did you find him?"

"I inherited him."

"I beg your pardon?"

"He was the tracker for the hunter I apprenticed under," I explained. "When he retired, he left me his client list—and Chajinka."

Suddenly there was a yell of triumph from Chajinka. He held up his spear, and there was a huge fish, maybe 25 pounds, squirming at the end of it. The Dabih himself didn't weigh much more than 85 pounds, the current was strong, and the footing was slippery. Suddenly he fell over backward and vanished beneath the surface of the water.

He emerged again a second later, but without the spear and the fish. I saw them floating downstream a good ten yards from him. There was no sense telling him where to look; he couldn't understand a word I said without a t-pack. So I waded into the water and went after the spear myself. It became chest-deep very quickly, and I had to fight the current, but I finally reached the spear and waded back to shore. Chajinka climbed out a moment later with an embarrassed grin on his face. He made another incomprehensible comment, then brained the fish as he had done with the first one.

"See?" I said sardonically. "Even fishing can be exciting when you're on safari."

There was no answer. I spun around. Ramona Desmond was nowhere to be seen.

> So the Snark pronounced sentence, the Judge being quite
> Too nervous to utter a word.
> When it rose to its feet, there was silence like night,
> And the fall of a pin might be heard.

I SQUATTED DOWN next to her corpse. There was no blood; he'd noiselessly broken her neck and left her where she'd fallen.

"He was watching us the whole time," I said furiously. "He waited until she was alone, then grabbed her and pulled her into the bush." A chilling thought occurred to me. "I wonder who's hunting who?"

Chajinka muttered something incomprehensible.

"All right," I said at last. "Let's take her back to camp."

I lifted Ramona's body to my shoulder and signaled him to follow me.

Desmond raced out of the ship when he saw us. He began flagellating himself and pulling tufts of his hair out, screaming nonsense words at the top of his lungs.

"What the hell is happening?" asked Pollard, clambering out through the hatch. Then he saw the body. He had to work to keep his voice under control. "Oh, Jesus! Oh, Jesus!" he kept repeating. When he'd finally calmed down, he said, "It's more than an animal! It's like some vengeful alien god come to life!"

Chajinka went into the cargo hold and emerged with a shovel.

Pollard stared at Desmond, who was still raving. "I'll help with the grave."

"Thanks," I said. "I think I'd better get Desmond to his cabin and give him a sedative."

I walked over and put a hand on his shoulder.

"It was *your* fault!" he screamed. "*You* were supposed to protect her and you let it kill her!"

I couldn't deny it, so I just kept urging him gently toward the ship.

And then, between one second and the next, he snapped. I could see it in his face. His eyes went wide, the muscles in his jaw began twitching, even the tenor of his voice changed.

"That thing is going to learn what it means to kill the wife of the most powerful man on Far London!" He looked off into the bush and hollered: "I'm Philemon Desmond, god-dammit, and I'm through being terrified by some ignorant fucking beast! Do you hear me? It's over! You're dead meat!"

"Come on, Mr. Desmond," I said softly, pushing him toward the ship.

"Who the hell are you?" he demanded, and I could tell that he really didn't recognize me.

I was about to humor him with an answer when everything went black and the ground came up to meet me.

> *And the Banker, inspired with a courage so new*
> *It was a matter for general remark,*
> *Rushed madly ahead and was lost to their view*
> *In his zeal to discover the Snark.*

POLLARD SLOSHED SOME water on my face. I gasped for breath, then sat up and put a hand to my head. It came away covered with blood.

"Are you all right?" he asked, kneeling down next to me, and I saw that Chajinka was behind him.

"What happened?"

"I'm not sure," he said. "We were just starting to dig the grave when I heard Desmond suddenly stop gibbering. Then he whacked you on the head with something, and ran off."

"I never saw it coming," I groaned, blinking my eyes furiously. "Where did he go?"

"I don't know." He pointed to the southwest. "That way, I think."

"*Shit!*" I said. "The Snark is still in the area!"

I tried to get to my feet, but was overwhelmed by pain and dizziness, and sat back down, hard.

"Take it easy," he said. "You've probably got a hell of a concussion. Where's the first aid kit? Maybe I can at least stop the bleeding."

I told him where to find it, then concentrated on trying to focus my eyes.

When Pollard returned and began working on my head, I asked, "Did you see if he at least took his laser rifle with him?"

"If he didn't have it when he hit you, he didn't stop to get it."

"Goddammit!"

"I guess that means he doesn't have it."

"Wonderful," I muttered, wincing as he did something to the back of my head. "So he's unarmed, running through the bush, and screaming at the top of his lungs."

"All done," said Pollard, standing up. "It's not a pretty job, but at least the bleeding's stopped. How do you feel?"

"Groggy," I said. "Help me up."

Once I was on my feet, I looked around. "Where's my rifle?"

"Right here," said Pollard, picking it up and handing it to me. "But you're in no shape to go after Desmond."

"I'm not going after Desmond," I mumbled. "I'm going after *him*!" I signaled Chajinka to join me and set off unsteadily to the southwest. "Lock yourself in the ship."

"I'll finish burying Ramona first."

"*Don't!*"

"But—"

"Unless you're prepared to fend him off with a shovel if he shows up, do what I said."

"I can't leave her body out for the scavengers," Pollard protested.

"Take her with you. Spray her with the preservatives we use for trophies and stash her in the cargo hold. We'll bury her when I get back."

"*If* you get back," he corrected me. "You look like you can barely stand on your feet."

"I'll be back," I promised him. "I'm still a hunter, and he's still just an animal."

"Yeah—he's just an animal. That's why there's just you, me and Chajinka left alive."

DESMOND DIDN'T GET very far—not that I ever expected him to. We found him half a mile away, his skull crushed. I carried him back to camp and buried him next to his wife.

"That bastard's been one step ahead of us from the start," said Pollard bitterly as we sat down next to the ship and slaked our thirst with some lukewarm water. Chajinka sat a few yards away, motionless as a statue, watching and listening for any sign of the Snark.

"He's smarter than I thought," I admitted. "Or luckier."

"Nothing is that lucky," said Pollard. "He must be intelligent."

"Absolutely," I agreed.

Pollard's eyes went wide. "Wait a minute!" he said sharply. "If you *knew* he was intelligent, what the hell were we doing hunting him in the first place?"

"There's a difference between intelligence and sentience," I said. "We know he's intelligent. We don't know that he's sentient."

He looked puzzled. "I thought they were the same thing."

I shook my head. "Back on Earth, chimpanzees were intelligent enough to create crude tools, and to pass that knowledge on from one generation to the next—but no one ever claimed they were sentient. The fact that the Snark can hide his trail, spot my traps and elude us makes him intelligent. It doesn't make him sentient."

"On the other hand, it doesn't prove he's *not* sentient," said Pollard stubbornly.

"No, it doesn't."

"So what do we do?"

"We kill him," I answered.

"Even if he's sentient?"

"What do you do when someone murders fifteen sentient beings?" I said. "If he's a Man, you execute him. If he's an animal, you track him down and kill him. Either way, the result is the same."

"All right," said Pollard dubiously. "We kill him. How?"

"We leave the ship and go after him."

"Why?" he demanded. "We're safe in the ship!"

"Tell that to Mbele and the Desmonds and the Dabihs," I shot back. "As long as we stay here, he knows where we are and we don't know where *he* is. That means he's the hunter and we're the prey. If we leave camp and pick up his trail before he picks up ours, we go back to being the hunters again." I got to my feet. "In fact, the sooner we start, the better."

He wasn't happy about it, but he had no choice but to come along, since the alternative was to remain behind alone. After we loaded the vehicle, I patted the hood, waited for Chajinka to jump onto it, and then we drove to the spot where we'd found Desmond's body.

The Dabih picked up the trail, and we began tracking the Snark. I wanted him so bad I could taste it. It wasn't just revenge for all the Men and Dabihs he'd killed. It wasn't even a matter of professional pride. It was because I knew this was my last hunt, that I'd never get my license back after losing fifteen sentient beings who were under my protection.

The trail led back to the camp, where the Snark had watched us bury Desmond's body. It had kept out of sight until we drove off, and then began moving in a northwesterly direction. We tracked it until late afternoon, when we found ourselves about eight miles from the ship.

"There's no sense going back for the night," I told Pollard. "We might never pick up the trail again."

"Isn't he likely to double back to the camp?"

"Not while we're out here, he isn't," I said with absolute certainty. "This isn't a hunt any longer—it's a war. Neither of us will quit until the other's dead."

He looked at me much the way I'd looked at Desmond earlier in the day. Finally he spoke up: "We can't track him at night."

"I know," I replied. "We'll each keep watch for three hours—you, me, and Chajinka—and we'll start again as soon as it's light enough."

I sat the first watch, and I was so keyed up that I couldn't get to sleep, so I sat through Pollard's watch as well before I woke Chajinka and managed a three-hour nap. As soon as it was light, we started following the trail again.

By noon we were approaching a small canyon. Then, suddenly, I saw a flicker of motion off in the distance. I stopped the vehicle and activated my Telescopic lenses.

He was more than a mile away, and he had his back to us, but I knew I'd finally gotten my first look at the Snark.

> Erect and sublime, for one moment of time,
> In the next, that wild figure they saw
> (As if stung by a spasm) plunge into a chasm,
> While they waited and listened in awe.

I DROVE TO the edge of the canyon. Chajinka hopped off the hood, and Pollard and I joined him a moment later.

"You're sure you saw him?" asked Pollard.

"I'm sure," I said. "Bipedal. Rust-colored. Looks almost like a cross between a bear and a gorilla, at least from this distance."

"Yeah, that's him all right." He peered down into the canyon. "And he climbed down there?"

"That's right," I said.

"I assume we're going after him?"

"There's no reason to believe he'll come out anywhere near here," I said. "If we wait, we'll lose him."

"It looks pretty rocky," he said. "Can we pick up his trail?"

"Chajinka will find it."

Pollard sighed deeply. "What the hell," he said with a shrug. "I'm not going to wait here alone while the two of you go after him. I figure I'll be safer with you—providing I don't break my neck on the terrain."

I motioned for Chajinka to lead the way down, since he was far more sure-footed than any human. He walked along the edge of the precipice for perhaps fifty yards, then came to a crude path we were able to follow for the better part of an hour. Then we were on the canyon floor next to a narrow stream, where we slaked our thirst, hoping the water wouldn't make us too sick, as we'd left the irradiation tablets back at the ship.

We rested briefly, then took up the hunt again. Chajinka was able to find a trail where I would have sworn none existed. By early afternoon, the floor of the canyon was no longer flat, and we had to follow a winding path over and around a series of rock formations. Pollard was game, but he was out of shape. He kept falling behind, actually dropping out of sight a couple of times, which forced us to stop and wait for him to catch up.

When he dropped behind yet again, I wanted to ask him if he needed a break. I didn't dare shout and give away our position to the Snark, so I compromised by signaling Chajinka to slow his pace until Pollard caught up with us.

He didn't—and after a few minutes we went back to see what was the matter.

I couldn't find him. It was like he had vanished off the face of the planet.

> *They hunted till darkness came on, but they found*
> *Not a button, or feather, or mark,*
> *By which they could tell that they stood on the ground*
> *Where the Baker had met with the Snark.*

WE SPENT HALF an hour looking for Pollard. There was no trace of him, and eventually we were forced to admit that somehow the Snark had turned back on his trail and circled around us or hid and waited for us to pass by. Either way, it was obvious that he'd managed to get Pollard.

I knew it was futile to keep looking for him, so I signaled Chajinka to continue searching for the Snark. We hiked over the rocky canyon floor until at last we came to a steep wall.

"We go up, or we go back," I said, looking at the wall. "Which will it be?"

He stared at me expectantly, waiting for me to signal him which way to go.

I looked back the way we'd come, then up in the direction of the path we were following—

—and as I looked up, I saw a large object hurtling down toward me!

I pushed Chajinka out of the way and threw myself to my left, rolling as I hit the ground. The object landed five feet away with a bone-jarring *thud!*—and I saw that it was Pollard's body.

I looked up, and there was the Snark standing on a ledge, glaring down at me. Our eyes met, and then he turned and began racing up the canyon wall.

"Are you all right?" I asked Chajinka, who was just getting to his feet.

He brushed himself off, then made a digging motion and looked questioningly at me.

We didn't have any shovels, and it would take hours to dig even a shallow grave in the rocky ground using our hands. If we left Pollard's body where it was, it would be eaten by scavengers—but if we took the time to bury him, we'd lose the Snark.

> "Leave him here to his fate—it is getting so late!"
> The Bellman exclaimed in a fright.
> "We have lost half the day. Any further delay,
> And we sha'n't catch a Snark before night."

WHEN WE GOT halfway up the wall, I stopped and looked back. Alien raptors were circling high in the sky. Then the first of them landed next to Pollard and began pulling away bits of his flesh. I turned away and concentrated on the Snark.

It took an hour to reach the top, and then Chajinka spent a few minutes picking up the Snark's trail again. We followed it for another hour, and the landscape slowly changed, gradually becoming lush and green.

And then something strange happened. The trail suddenly became easy to follow.

Almost *too* easy.

We tracked him for another half hour. I sensed that he was near, and I was ready to fire at anything that moved.

The humidity made my hands sweat so much that I didn't trust them not to slip on the stock and barrel, so I signaled Chajinka that I wanted to take a brief break.

I took a sip from my canteen. Then, as I leaned against a tree, wiping the moisture from my rifle, I saw a movement half a mile away.

It was *him*!

I pulled my rifle to my shoulder and took aim—but we were too far away. I leaped to my feet and began running after him. He turned, faced me for just an instant, and vanished into the bush.

When we got to where he'd been, we found that his trail led due north, and we began following it. At one point we stopped so I could remove a stinging insect from inside my boot—and suddenly I caught sight of him again. He roared and disappeared again into the heavy foliage as I raced after him.

It was almost as if the son of a bitch was *taunting* us, and I wondered: is he leading us into a trap?

And then I had a sudden flash of insight.

Rather than leading us *into* a trap, was he leading us *away* from something?

It didn't make much sense, but somewhere deep in my gut it felt right.

"Stop!" I ordered Chajinka.

He didn't know the word, but the tone of my voice brought him up short.

I pointed to the south. "This way," I said.

The Dabih frowned and pointed toward the Snark, saying something in his own tongue.

"I know he's there," I said. "But come this way anyway."

I began walking south. I had taken no more than four or five steps when Chajinka was at my side, jabbering again, and pulling my arm, trying to make me follow the Snark.

"No!" I said harshly. It certainly wasn't the word, so it must have been the tone. Whatever the reason, he shrugged, looked at me as if I was crazy, and fell into step behind me. He couldn't very well lead, since there was no trail and he didn't know where we were going. Neither did I, for that matter, but my every instinct said the Snark didn't want me going this direction, and that was reason enough to do it.

We'd walked for about fifteen minutes when I heard a hideous roar off to my left. It was the Snark, much closer this time, appearing from a new direction. He showed himself briefly, then raced off.

"I *knew* it!" I whispered excitedly to Chajinka, who just looked confused when I continued to ignore the Snark.

As we kept moving south, the Snark became bolder and bolder, finally getting within a hundred yards of us, but never showing himself long enough for me to get a shot off.

I could feel Chajinka getting tenser and tenser, and finally, when the Snark roared from thirty yards away, the little Dabih raised his spear above his head and raced after him.

"No!" I cried. "He'll kill you!"

I tried to grab him, but he was much too quick for me. I followed him into the eight-foot-high grasslike vegetation. It was a damned stupid thing to do: I couldn't see Chajinka, I couldn't see the Snark, and I had no room to maneuver or even sidestep if there was a charge. But he was my friend—probably, if I was honest, my *only* friend—and I couldn't let him face the Snark alone.

Suddenly I heard the sounds of a scuffle. There was some growling, Chajinka yelled once, and then all was silent.

I went in the direction I thought the sounds had come from, pushing the heavy grasses aside. Then I was making my way through thornbush, and the thorns ripped at my arms and legs. I paid no attention but kept looking for Chajinka.

I found him in a clearing. He'd put up the fight of his life—his wounds attested to that—but even with his spear he was no match for a 400-pound predator. He recognized me, tried to say something that I wouldn't have understood anyway, and died just as I reached his side.

I knew I couldn't stay in the heavy bush with the Snark still around. This was *his* terrain. So I made my way back to the trail and continued to the south. The Snark roared from cover but didn't show himself.

After another quarter mile, I came to a huge tree with a hollow trunk. I was about to walk around it when I heard a high-pitched whimpering coming from inside it. I approached it carefully, my rifle ready, the safety off—

—and suddenly the Snark broke out of cover no more than fifteen yards away and charged me with an ear-splitting roar.

He was on me so fast that I didn't have time to get off a shot. He swiped at me with a mighty paw. I ducked and turned away, but the blow caught me on the shoulder and sent me flying. I landed on my back, scrambled to my feet, and saw him standing maybe ten feet away. My rifle was on the ground right next to him.

He charged again. This time I was ready. I dove beneath his claws, rolled as I hit the ground, got my hands on my weapon, and got off a single shot as he turned to come at me again.

"Got you, you bastard!" I yelled in triumph.

At first I thought I might have hit him too high in the chest to prove fatal, but he collapsed instantly, blood spurting from the wound—and I noticed that he had a festering wound on his side, doubtless from Marx's shot a week ago. I watched him for a moment, then decided to "pay the insurance," the minimal cost of a second bullet, to make sure he didn't get back up and do any damage before he died. I walked over to stick the muzzle of my rifle in his ear, found that I didn't have a clear shot, and reached out to nudge his head around with my toe.

I felt something like an electric surge within my head, and suddenly, though I'd never experienced anything remotely like it before, I knew I was in telepathic communication with the dying Snark.

Why did you come to my land to kill me? he asked, more puzzled than angry.

I jumped back, shocked—and lost communication with him. Obviously it could only happen when we were in physical contact. I squatted down and took his paw in my hands, and felt his fear and pain.

Then he was dead, and I stood up and stared down at him, my entire universe turned upside down—because during the brief moment that I had shared his thoughts, I learned what had *really* happened.

The Snark's race, sentient but non-technological, was never numerous and had been wiped out by a virulent disease. Through some fluke, he alone survived it. The others had died decades ago, and he had led a life of terrifying loneliness ever since.

He knew our party was on Dodgson IV the very first day we landed. He was more than willing to share his hunting ground with us, and made no attempt to harm us or scare us off.

He had thought the killing of the crystal-horned buck was a gift of friendship; he didn't understand that he was stealing Marx's trophy because the concept of trophies was completely alien to him. He killed Marx only after Marx wounded him.

Even then he was willing to forgive us. Those dead animals we found in my traps were his notion of a peace offering.

He couldn't believe that we really wanted to kill him, so he decided he would visit the camp and try to communicate with us. When he got there, he mistook the Dabihs' t-packs for weapons and destroyed them. Then, certain that this would be seen as an act of aggression even though he hadn't harmed anyone, he left before we woke up.

He came back to try one last time to make peace with us. This time he made no attempt to enter the camp unseen. He marched right in, fully prepared to be questioned and examined by these new races. But what he *wasn't* prepared for was being attacked by the Dabihs. Fighting in self-defense, he made short work of them. Mbele raced into the ship, either to hide or to get a weapon. He knew first-hand what Marx's weapon had done to him at fifty yards, and he didn't dare let

Mbele shoot at him from the safety of the ship, so he raced into it and killed him before he could find a weapon.

After that it was war. He didn't know why we wanted to kill him, but he no longer doubted that we did... and while there was a time when he would have welcomed an end to his unhappy, solitary existence, he now had a reason, indeed a driving urge, to stay alive at all costs...

...because he wasn't a *he* at all; he was an *it*. The Snark was an asexual animal that reproduced by budding. Its final thought was one of enormous regret, not that it would die, for it understood the cycles of life and death, but that now its offspring would die as well.

I stared down at the Snark's body, my momentary feeling of triumph replaced by an overwhelming sense of guilt. What I had thought was my triumph had become nothing less than genocide in the space of a few seconds.

I heard the whimpering again, and I walked back to the hollow tree trunk and looked in. There, trembling and shrinking back from me, was a very small, very helpless version of the Snark.

I reached out to it, and it uttered a tiny, high-pitched growl as it huddled against the back of the trunk.

I spoke gently, moved very slowly, and reached out again. This time it stared at my hand for a long moment, and finally, hesitantly, reached out to touch it. The instant we made contact, I was able to feel its all-encompassing terror.

Do not be afraid, little one, I said silently. *Whatever happens, I will protect you. I owe you that much.*

Its fear vanished, for you cannot lie when you are telepathically linked, and a moment later it emerged from its hiding place.

I looked off into the distance. Men would be coming soon. The rescue party would touch down in the next week or two. They'd find Marx's body in the hold, and they'd exhume the Desmonds and Mbele and the eleven Dabihs. They'd read the Captain's diary and know that all this carnage was caused by an animal called a Snark.

And since they were a hunting company, they'd immediately outfit a safari to kill the Snark quickly and efficiently. No argument could possibly deter them, not after losing an entire party of Men and Dabihs.

But they would be in for a surprise, because *this* Snark not only knew the terrain but knew how Men thought and acted, and was armed with Man's weapons.

The infant reached out to me and uttered a single word. I tried to repeat it, laughed at how badly I mispronounced it, took the tiny creature in my arms, and went off into the bush to learn a little more about being a Father Snark while there was still time.

> *In the midst of the word he was trying to say,*
> *In the midst of his laughter and glee,*
> *He had softly and suddenly vanished away—*
> *For the Snark was a Boojum, you see.*

I had just been reading some of Alexander
Lake's hunting memoirs (wonderful stuff, which
I brought back into print in *Resnick's Library of
African Adventure* a decade ago), and then we went
to a science fiction convention. I guess I must
have seen one sweet, innocent, soft-eyed unicorn
too many in the art show, because when we got
home, I planted my tongue firmly in my cheek
and wrote this article, which incidentally was the
first thing I ever sold to *The Magazine of Fantasy and
Science Fiction*.

Stalking the Unicorn with Gun and Camera

When she got to within 200 yards of the herd of Southern Savannah unicorns she had been tracking for four days, Rheela of the Seven Stars made her obeisance to Quatr Mane, God of the Hunt, then donned the Amulet of Kobassen, tested the breeze to make sure that she was still downwind of the herd, and began approaching them, camera in hand.

But Rheela of the Seven Stars had made one mistake—a mistake of *carelessness*—and thirty seconds later she was dead, brutally impaled upon the horn of a bull unicorn.

HOTACK THE BEASTSLAYER cautiously made his way up the lower slopes of the Mountain of the Nameless One. He was a skilled tracker, a fearless hunter, and a crack shot. He picked out the trophy he wanted, got the beast within his sights, and hurled his killing club. It flew straight and true to its mark.

And yet, less than a minute later, Hotack, his left leg badly gored, was barely able to pull himself to safety in the branches of a nearby Rainbow Tree. He, too, had made a mistake—a mistake of *ignorance*.

Bort the Pure had had a successful safari. He had taken three chimeras, a gorgon, and a beautifully-matched pair of griffons. While his trolls were skinning the gorgon, he spotted a unicorn sporting a near-record horn, and, weapon in hand, he began pursuing it. The terrain gradually changed, and suddenly Bort found himself in shoulder-high kraken grass. Undaunted, he followed the trail into the dense vegetation.

But Bort the Pure, too, had made a mistake—a mistake of *foolishness*. His trolls found what very little remained of him some six hours later.

Carelessness, ignorance, foolishness—together they account for more deaths among unicorn hunters than all other factors combined.

Take our examples, for instance. All three hunters—Rheela, Hotack, and Bort—were experienced safari hands. They were used to extremes of temperature and terrain, they didn't object to finding insects in their ale or banshees in their tents, they knew they were going after deadly game and took all reasonable precautions before setting out.

And yet two of them died, and the third was badly maimed.

Let's examine their mistakes and see what we can learn from them.

Rheela of the Seven Stars assimilated everything her personal wizard could tell her about unicorns, purchased the very finest photographic equipment, hired a native guide who had been on many unicorn hunts, and had a local witch doctor bless her Amulet of Kobassen. And yet, when the charge came, the amulet was of no use to her, for she had failed to properly identify the particular subspecies of unicorn before her—and, as I am continually pointing out during my lecture tours, the Amulet of Kobassen is potent only against the rare and almost-extinct Forest unicorn. Against the Southern Savannah unicorn, the *only* effective charm is the Talisman of Triconis. *Carelessness.*

Hotack the Beastslayer, on the other hand, disdained all forms of supernatural protection. To him, the essence of the hunt was to pit himself in physical combat against his chosen prey. His killing club, a beautifully-wrought and finely-balanced instrument of destruction, had brought down simurghs, humbabas, and even a dreaded wooly hydra. He elected to go for a head shot, and the club flew to within a millimeter of where he had aimed it. But he hadn't counted on the unicorn's phenomenal sense of smell, nor the speed with which these surly brutes can move. Alerted to Hotack's presence, the unicorn turned its head to seek out its preda-tor—and the killing club bounced harmlessly off its horn. Had Hotack spoken to almost any old-time unicorn hunter, he would have realized that head shots are almost impossible, and would have gone for a crippling knee shot. *Ignorance.*

Bort the Pure was aware of the unique advantages accruing to a virgin who hunts the wild unicorn, and so had practiced sexual abstinence since he was old enough to know what the term meant. And yet he naively believed that because his vir-ginity allowed him to approach the unicorn more easily than other hunters, the unicorn would somehow become placid and make no attempt to defend itself—and so he followed a vicious animal which was compelled to let him approach it, and entered a patch of high grass which allowed him no maneuvering room during the inevitable charge. *Foolishness.*

Every year hundreds of hopeful hunters go out in search of the unicorn, and every year all but a handful come back empty-handed—if they come back at all. And yet the uni-corn *can* be safely stalked and successfully hunted, if only the stalkers and hunters will take the time to study their quarry.

When all is said and done, the unicorn is a relatively docile beast (except when enraged). It is a creature of habit, and once those habits have been learned by the hopeful photographer or trophy hunter, bringing home that picture or that horn is really no more dangerous than, say, slaying an Eight-Forked

Dragon—and it's certainly easier than lassoing wild minotaurs, a sport that has become all the rage these days among the smart set on the Platinum Plains.

However, before you can photograph or kill a unicorn, you have to find it—and by far the easiest way to make contact with a unicorn herd is to follow the families of smerps that track the great game migrations. The smerps, of course, have no natural enemies except for the rafsheen and the zumakim, and consequently will allow a human (or preternatural) being to approach them quite closely.

A word of warning about the smerp: with its long ears and cute, fuzzy body, it resembles nothing more than an oversized rabbit—but calling a smerp a rabbit doesn't make it one, and you would be ill-advised to underestimate the strength of these nasty little scavengers. Although they generally hunt in packs of from ten to twenty, I have more than once seen a single smerp, its aura glowing with savage strength, pull down a half-grown unicorn. Smerps are poor eating, their pelts are worthless because of the difficulty of curing and tanning the auras, and they make pretty unimpressive trophies unless you can come up with one possessing a truly magnificent set of ears—in fact, in many areas they're still classified as vermin—but the wise unicorn hunter can save himself a lot of time and effort by simply letting the smerps lead him to his prey.

With the onset of poaching, the legendary unicorn herds numbering upwards of a thousand members no longer exist, and you'll find that the typical herd today consists of from 50 to 75 individuals. The days when a photographer, safe and secure in a blind by a waterhole, could preserve on film an endless stream of the brutes coming down to drink are gone forever—and it is absolutely shocking to contemplate the number of unicorns that have died simply so their horns could be sold on the black market. In fact, I find it appalling that anyone in this enlightened day and age still believes that a powdered unicorn horn can act as an aphrodisiac.

(Indeed, as any magi can tell you, you treat the unicorn horn with essence of gracch and then boil it slowly in a solution of sphinx blood. Now *that's* an aphrodisiac!)

But I digress.

The unicorn, being a non-discriminating browser that is equally content to feed upon grasses, leaves, fruits, and an occasional small fern tree, occurs in a wide variety of habitats, often in the company of grazers such as centaurs and ~~pegasuses~~ ~~pegasim~~ the pegasus.

Once you have spotted the unicorn herd, it must be approached with great care and caution. The unicorn may have poor eyesight, and its sense of hearing may not be much better, but it has an excellent sense of smell and an absolutely awesome sense of *grimsch,* about which so much has been written that there is no point in my belaboring the subject yet again.

If you are on a camera safari, I would strongly advise against trying to get closer than 100 yards to even a solitary beast—that sense of *grimsch* again—and most of the photographers I know swear by an 85–350mm automatic-focus zoom lens, providing, of course, that it has been blessed by a Warlock of the Third Order. If you haven't got the shots you want by sunset, my best advice is to pack it in for the day and return the next morning. Flash photography is possible, of course, but it does tend to attract golem and other even more bothersome nocturnal predators.

One final note to the camera buff: For reasons our alchemists have not yet determined, no unicorn has ever been photographed with normal emulsified film of any speed, so make absolutely sure that you use one of the more popular infrared brands. It would be a shame to spend weeks on safari, paying for your guide, cook, and trolls, only to come away with a series of photos of the forest that you thought was merely the background to your pictures.

As for hunting the brutes, the main thing to remember is that they are as close to you as you are to them. For this reason, while I don't disdain blood sacrifices, amulets, talismans, and blessings, all of which have their proper place, I for one always feel more confident with a .550 Nitro Express in my hands. A little extra stopping power can give a hunter quite a feeling of security.

You'll want a bull unicorn, of course; they tend to have more spectacular horns than the cows—and by the time a bull's horn is long enough to be worth taking, he's probably too old to be in the herd's breeding program anyway.

The head shot, for reasons explained earlier, is never a wise option. And unless your wizard teaches you the Rune of Mamhotet, thus enabling you the approach close enough to pour salt on the beast's tail and thereby pin him to the spot where he's standing, I recommend the heart shot (either heart will do—and if you have a double-barreled gun, you might try to hit both of them, just to be on the safe side).

If you have the bad fortune to merely wound the beast, he'll immediately make off for the trees or the high grass, which puts you at an enormous disadvantage. Some hunters, faced with such a situation, merely stand back and allow the smerps to finish the job for them—after all, smerps rarely devour the horn unless they're completely famished—but this is hardly sporting. The decent, honorable hunter, well aware of the unwritten rules of blood sports, will go after the unicorn himself.

The trick, of course, is to meet him on fairly open terrain. Once the unicorn lowers his head to charge, he's virtually blind, and all you need do is dance nimbly out of his way and take another shot at him—or, if you are not in possession of the Rune of Mamhotet, this would be an ideal time to get out that salt and try to sprinkle some on his tail as he races by.

When the unicorn dictates the rules of the game, you've got a much more serious situation. He'll usually double back and lie in the tall grasses beside his spoor, waiting for you to pass by, and then attempt to gore you from behind.

It is at this time that the hunter must have all his wits about him. Probably the best sign to look for is the presence of Fire-Breathing Dragonflies. These noxious little insects frequently live in symbiosis with the unicorn, cleansing his ears of parasites, and their presence usually means that the unicorn isn't far off. Yet another sign that your prey is nearby will be the flocks of hungry harpies circling overhead, waiting to swoop down and feed upon the remains of your kill; and, of course, the surest sign of all is when you hear a grunt of rage and find yourself staring into the bloodshot, beady little eyes of a wounded bull unicorn from a distance of ten feet or less. It's moments like that that make you feel truly alive, especially when you suddenly realize that it isn't necessarily a permanent condition.

All right. Let us assume that your hunt is successful. What then?

Well, your trolls will skin the beast, of course, and take special care in removing and preserving the horn. If they've been properly trained, they'll also turn the pelt into a rug, the hooves into ashtrays, the teeth into a necklace, the tail into a flyswatter, and the scrotum into a tobacco pouch. My own feeling is that you should settle for nothing less, since it goes a long way toward showing the bleeding-heart preservationists that a unicorn can supply the hunter with a lot more than just a few minutes of pleasurable sport and a horn.

And while I'm on the subject of what the unicorn can supply, let me strongly suggest that you would be missing a truly memorable experience if you were to come home from safari without having eaten unicorn meat at least once. There's nothing quite like unicorn cooked over an open campfire to top off a successful hunt. (And do remember to leave something out for the smerps, or they might well decide that hunter is every bit as tasty as unicorn.)

So get out those amulets and talismans, visit those wizards and warlocks, pack those cameras and weapons—and good hunting to you!

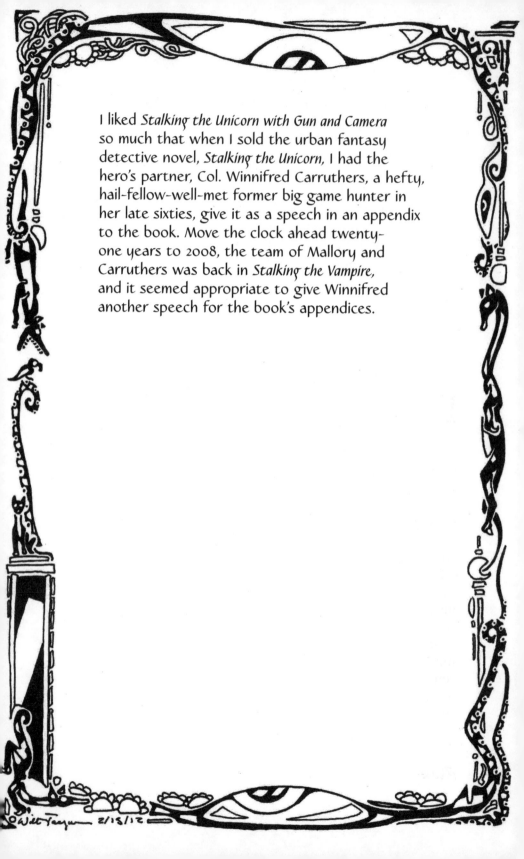

I liked *Stalking the Unicorn with Gun and Camera*
so much that when I sold the urban fantasy
detective novel, *Stalking the Unicorn,* I had the
hero's partner, Col. Winnifred Carruthers, a hefty,
hail-fellow-well-met former big game hunter in
her late sixties, give it as a speech in an appendix
to the book. Move the clock ahead twenty-
one years to 2008, the team of Mallory and
Carruthers was back in *Stalking the Vampire,*
and it seemed appropriate to give Winnifred
another speech for the book's appendices.

Stalking
the Vampire

I have been asked many times: what is the best weapon to use against a vampire?

Are you better off with a wooden stake, or perhaps a wood-shafted arrow shot from a crossbow that has been blessed by a priest? I have even heard of one gentleman who created wooden bullets, which doubtless seemed like a brilliant idea until the first one lost its structural integrity upon firing and caused the pistol to explode in his hand.

The answer, of course, is the very best weapon to use is your brain. Wooden stakes and arrows and other traditional anti-vampiric weapons are all very well and good, but we're not speaking of a dumb herbivore like a gazelle or a unicorn here, an animal that seeks only to escape. No, my friends, the vampire is endowed with a brain every bit as good as your own, and is as anxious to kill you as you are to kill him. Never forget that: he is *not* trying to escape, and while you may trick him from time to time, you are no more likely to outsmart him than he is to outsmart you—perhaps less so, since in all likelihood he has been around longer, and has certainly been hunting men longer than you have been hunting vampires.

I suggest that you study the beasts of the field. The predator never seeks out the strongest member of the herd; he goes after the young, the ancient, and the infirm. It is not a bad principle to apply when hunting the vampire.

No, you won't find any young ones, and the ancient ones are as strong as any of the others. But the principle holds true: you attack the weakest, and since there is no way to differentiate, you attack when your prey is *at* his weakest—in broad daylight, when he's asleep in his coffin.

So just as the predator knows that sooner or later his prey must come to the water hole to slake its thirst, the vampire hunter knows that every day at sunrise the vampire must seek out his coffin, lay down in his native soil, and remain there until sunset.

Which means that just as our hypothetical predator must know the terrain, must know every water hole, every place of concealment, so must the vampire hunter learn *his* terrain, which is to say, he must become intimately acquainted with cemeteries, mausoleums, mortuaries, and any other place where a vampire is likely to store his coffin.

The predator stakes out his territory, usually by leaving signatures of urine or dung on the grass and shrubbery, signals that his rivals can read. It is essential that the vampire hunter stake out *his* territory as well, though by more socially acceptable means, because the mature vampire has heightened senses of perception, and will be more likely to spot three or four of his predators than just one.

Just as the rhino has his tick birds to warn him of approaching danger, just as the gorgon has his smerps, so the vampire has *his* helpers. Usually they are called renfields, though the names vary with the territory. They are the once-bitten and twice-bitten who are in thrall to the vampire, and serve as his lookouts, his informers, and his late-night snacks, or frequently all three. So if you see a renfield walking through the mortuary, keep perfectly still until he has given the all-clear sign to his dark master, and even then you would be wise to wait until the vampire is safely ensconced inside his coffin before showing yourself. Most renfields are cowards at heart, and even those who aren't can usually be bought off with a handful of insects and spiders, which form the staple of their daily diet.

Then, it is simply a matter of waiting until the renfield is gone opening the coffin, and driving home that wooden stake. I prefer hickory, but oak, maple, and even redwood have been used with some success. I would beware of the wood of the African acacia tree, as you never know if a witch doctor has cursed it.

I see some unhappy faces out there. I know, I know—this runs contrary to your sporting instincts, as it doesn't give the vampire a sporting chance to escape. The thing I have to keep emphasizing is that he doesn't *want* to escape. Nor will he meet you on equal footing: when he is awake and on the stalk, even a bullet from a .550 Nitro Express won't slow him down. If you can get close enough to drive in that wooden stake, you'll kill him, of course, but he is as aware of that as you are, and will be on his guard.

How would you approach a vampire?

Again, your greatest weapon is your brain. Let me give you a few examples.

Vampires, as you know, leave no reflection in the mirror. You might stare at him, frown, and offer him a comb. It's a reasonable thing to do, since he has no idea how his hair looks, and as he reaches out to accept the comb, you move in quickly with the stake.

If you are a woman, and this works not only for vampires but any other human-appearing creatures you cannot kill from afar, just stare at his crotch and pretend you are trying very hard to repress a giggle. He will wonder what is wrong, perhaps even ask you. Just blush and say that of course nothing is wrong, then put your hand over your mouth to stifle a laugh. Sooner or later he'll look down to see if his fly is unzipped, and that is the instant you'll move in for the kill.

Or here's one that almost never fails to work. You plan to attend a crowded party, and you know that the vampire has spotted you following him and will try to neutralize you there. You go to the local pet store and buy a small mouse; even a lab rat will do. Then you give it to a confederate who will also be attending the party. When the confederate sees that the vampire has separated you out from the pack, so to speak, and has you cornered, he releases the mouse. Invariably, the first woman to see it will scream (and if not, the confederate can always goose her to elicit a shriek). You will look in her direction with great concern and say words to the effect that a vampire has just attacked a beautiful young woman in front of everyone. The real vampire, whose instinct is to defend his territory, will of course turn to look—and that's when you'll strike.

There are numerous other tried and true methods, but every last one of them requires brainpower, since in all other areas—except the way your pupils adjust to bright sunlight—he is your superior.

There is one method I have to address, simply because it runs against all the finer instincts of blood sports enthusiasts. A number of you have not been members of the Lower South Manhattan Blood Sports Enthusiasts Club as long as I have, so you may not know why Dr. Theodore Van Rhysling was expelled. Dr. Van Rhysling, for those of you who are not aware of the case, specialized in rare blood diseases, and when he found one that was both virulent and incurable, he sent his patient out every night until the vampire that had been terrorizing Dr. Van Rhysling's neighborhood encountered him, took a bite, and died a slow and horrible death. If any of you have had the same idea, be warned that your membership, like Dr. Van Rhysling's, will be revoked. *The true sportsman never uses poisoned bait.*

Let us say that something goes wrong, that the inevitable happens when your prey realizes that he is as close to you are you are to him, and you receive that dreaded first bite. Most people rush to the hospital for an emergency transfusion of blood or plasma, which does absolutely no good, since the bloodstream is already infected and this does nothing to eradicate it. My own suggestion is that you immediately apply leeches to the wound; even ten minutes after being bitten is too late, so carry some leeches with you on the hunt. If sunrise arrives and you still haven't come face-to-face with a vampire, well, the leeches make a hearty breakfast, especially when fried, breaded, and served alongside some scrambled gorgon eggs.

A final warning: numbers mean nothing, so leave your faithful trolls behind. Strength means nothing, so don't take along your pet leopard or lamia. Your only advantage is your brain, and I wouldn't become overconfident, as the last two vampires I killed were a professor of ethics at Harvard and a successful Hollywood agent, truly awesome bloodsuckers both.

So study your prey, learn the territory, sharpen those stakes, gather those leeches, and good hunting to you!

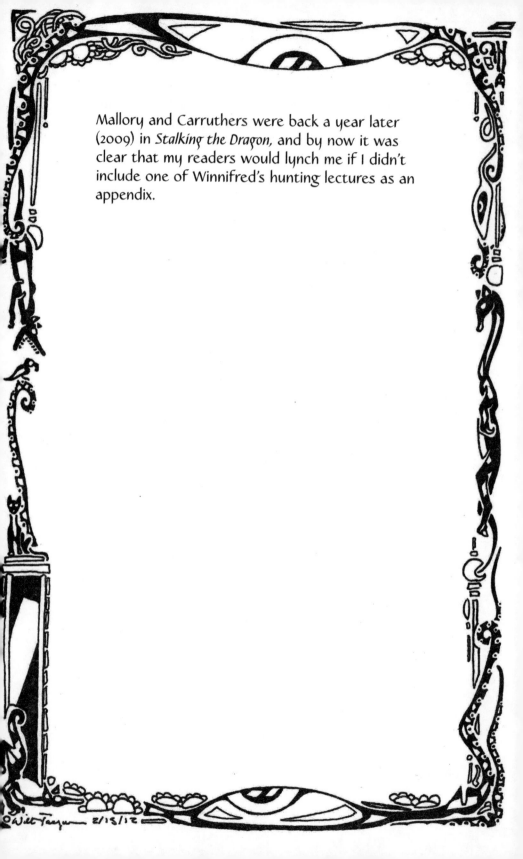

Mallory and Carruthers were back a year later (2009) in *Stalking the Dragon,* and by now it was clear that my readers would lynch me if I didn't include one of Winnifred's hunting lectures as an appendix.

Give Bombing The Suburban Land Dragon

Stalking
the Dragon

Before I begin, I want to make it clear that the true sportsman not only gives his prey a fighting chance to escape, but also gives him a chance to become the predator as well. Hence, my remarks are aimed only at those who hunt the humongous dragons that stand more than eight feet at the shoulder, produce a flame in excess of 300 degrees Fahrenheit, and cruise at an altitude of more than 2,000 feet.

Now what (I hear you ask) is the best weapon to use on a dragon?

If you are a Christian saint, a charmed sword is more than sufficient. If, on the other hand, you are like the rest of us, the first thing you have to do is identify your prey so you will know how best to bait him.

For example, the tree-dwelling dragon of the Ituri Rain Forest lives almost exclusively on a diet of okapis and chimpanzees. The rugged Namibian dragon thrives on young pachyderms, especially the hippopotamus and the black rhinoceros.

Here in New York, the favorite prey of the wild dragon is the drunken sot, followed by the unleashed Great Dane.

Either of these should attract your dragon in a matter of a very few minutes, especially in daylight.

Now, I have always preferred the stopping power of the .550 Nitro Express, especially if you are using soft-nosed bullets. The poisoned arrow usually works, but it simply isn't sporting and we won't mention it here. The Amulet of Kobassen will slow him down enough to deliver the death blow with a blade blessed by a Mage of the Fifth Circle or higher.

If you're going to meet him in close quarters, which where a dragon is concerned constitutes anything his flame can reach, you're going to want protection from the intense heat and fire. My suggestion is that you stop by Alastair Baffle's Emporium of Wonders and pick up a tube of the same ointment magicians, acrobats, and ecdysiasts use to protect their bare flesh from the fire they work with. Failing that, an asbestos body suit and helmet seems to be your best bet.

I've seen would-be daredevils try to douse the dragon's flame with water, totally overlooking the fact that the average six-ton dragon drinks thirty-five gallons of water a day and is not above bathing in it. Actually, the very best way to eradicate a dragon's flame is to toss him something to eat: they're especially fond of suckling pigs, cheese blintzes, and chocolate marshmallow cookies... and it is a little-known fact that dragons do *not* like their food to be well-done, or even medium well. Feed a hungry dragon and you won't have to worry about the flame until he digests his meal.

Once the kill has been made, it's time to enjoy the spoils of conquest. I've never been partial to dragon steaks, but there's a cut of meat along the base of the tail, especially on young dragons, that is almost indistinguishable from veal, and this is the part of the dragon you should reserve for yourself, while doling out the rest to your trolls. Dragon whiskers—on those rare occasions that they haven't been burned away prior to your encounter—are prized religious artifacts, and you should always pluck them out and give them to your gunbearers (or swordbearers) and skinners.

And what if you spend a day tracking your dragon through Central Park, down the wilds of Ninth Avenue, through the caves of the Park Avenue subway, only to find out that he's a mere five feet at the shoulder, or that she is being followed by a brood of infant dragons?

That is why you should always carry a squirt gun filled with indelible and phosphorescent ink. Using the gun, squirt your initials onto the beast's left shoulder. This will tell all other members of the Lower South Manhattan Blood Sports Enthusiasts that you have claimed killing rights to this dragon, and are merely waiting for more sporting circumstances to end its life. Now, the police and the military probably will not honor this claim, especially if the dragon is attacking a lovely, terrified, half-naked woman, which seems to be the kind of human dragons prefer to attack, but under normal circumstances that dragon will be considered untouchable until you once again go a-hunting. (Indeed, an entire religious sect—The Cult of the Untouchable Dragon—has grown up around this practice. In fact, so has the Cult of the Lovely, Terrified, Half-Naked Woman, but that needn't concern us here.)

Once you do slay your dragon, check to see if it is a female, and if so, assiduously seek out her nest, as a clutch of dragon eggs will usually bring a high enough price on the collectors' market to finance your next safari.

So get those weapons ready, assemble your team of trolls, make sure all your mystic protections have been thoroughly upgraded, pack your anti-burn medical kit, and good luck to you!

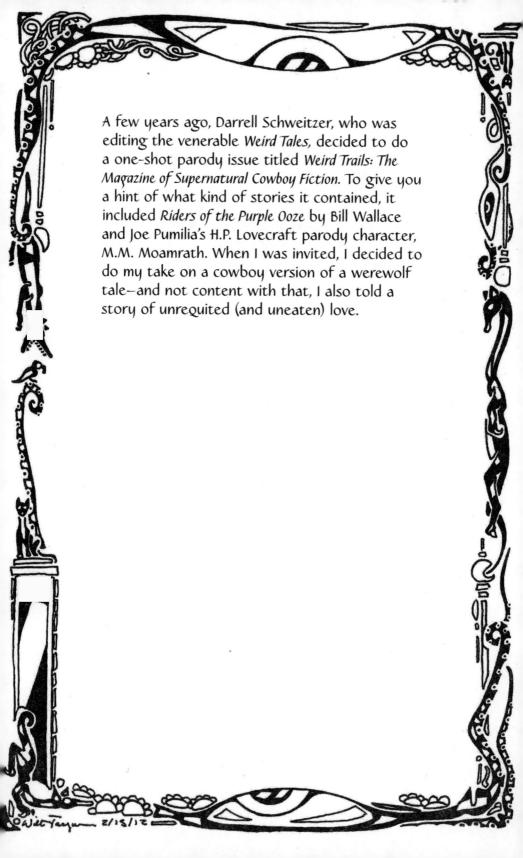

A few years ago, Darrell Schweitzer, who was
editing the venerable *Weird Tales*, decided to do
a one-shot parody issue titled *Weird Trails: The
Magazine of Supernatural Cowboy Fiction*. To give you
a hint of what kind of stories it contained, it
included *Riders of the Purple Ooze* by Bill Wallace
and Joe Pumilia's H.P. Lovecraft parody character,
M.M. Moamrath. When I was invited, I decided to
do my take on a cowboy version of a werewolf
tale—and not content with that, I also told a
story of unrequited (and uneaten) love.

The One That Got Away

W hen cowboys sit around the campfire and tell their mournful stories, they talk of Billy Nightfall, who was shot in the back by the woman he loved, and Texas Slade McBride, who worked seven years breaking the meanest broncs anyone ever saw, and when he'd finally saved up enough money to send for the mail-order bride he'd lost his heart to, got rip-roaring drunk and blew everything he was going to spend on her in a crooked card game. They tell of Westerly Wilson, whose betrothed left him for a fast-talking snake-oil salesman and how his bitterness turned him to a life of crime as a Californy real estate broker.

But the saddest story of all is the story of Howlin' Jack Dawkins.

Nobody knew where he came from. Some say he'd worked alongside Hopalong Cassidy at the Bar-20, others say he'd spent time with Curly Bill Bannerman at the Lazy S. But his tragic tale really begins the day he hired on at the Bar Sinister.

Jack had a way with cattle and sheep. One look from him and they huddled together and did exactly as he wanted. No one could remember ever seeing him fire a shot or crack a whip; when Howlin' Jack glared at an animal, that was all the encouragement it needed.

He didn't have no use for the bunkhouse. Kept everything he owned in his saddle bags, and said he preferred sleeping out under the night sky to layin' in a bed listening to everyone snoring. Besides, he seemed to be one of them guys who didn't need much sleep, because every morning when the others would wake up, there he'd be, squatting by the fire, ready to pour coffee for anyone who came by.

Every now and then, long about midday, he'd fall asleep in his saddle as he was riding along, but everyone just figured he'd been working too hard, and no one mentioned it except to tease him in a good-natured way. They all liked him, and he got along just fine with them, but he couldn't help feeling that there was something lacking in his life, though he didn't know what it was—and then came the fateful day that he rode into town to pick up some supplies, and he saw the stagecoach from Wichita pulling in, and since he'd never seen anyone from a big sophisticated city before, he was kind of curious as to what they looked like and how they dressed, so he stuck around and watched them climb down out of the coach.

And that was when he first saw her. One look was all it took, and he'd lost his heart forever. Her name was Bunny Wigglesworth, and she had golden hair, and she'd been to some finishing school, whatever that is, back East, and she was on her way to Californy to visit an uncle or a cousin or some such who'd made his fortune out there.

Anyway, the second Jack saw her, he felt like baying the moon, which wasn't the first time he'd ever had that urge, but it was the first time it had ever been brung about by a beautiful woman, and Bunny Wigglesworth was as beautiful as they come, especially when you compared her to all the other women who lived in Cougar Claw. He knew he shouldn't approach her in his chaps and buckskin shirt, and dust rising off him with every step he took, and smelling more like a horse than his horse did, but he was just so taken by her that he couldn't help himself. There were a couple of scraggly-looking flowers growing behind a water trough, and he picked 'em up, walked over to her, bowed low like he figured knights of old and maybe Boston gentlemen did, and offered her the flowers. He thought it was kind of strange that she took them and began chewing on 'em after she thanked him, but it was charmingly strange (and probably all the rage back East), and pretty soon Jack, who sometimes went days without saying more then a couple of words, was pouring out his heart to her and begging her not to go out to Californy just yet.

He told her that he loved her with a mad undying passion, and that he just had to see her again. She explained that she was traveling with her maiden aunt, who was a teetotaler and such a stickler for early-to-bed-early-to-rise that her being a maiden was even less surprising than her being an aunt, and that her aunt was dead certain all men were out for just One Thing, or maybe Six Things, which at least showed that what she lacked in experience she made up for in imagination.

But her maiden aunt had been so strict, and her finishing school (whatever that was) so cloistered that, strange as it seems, Howlin' Jack was the very first man she had ever spoken to, except for some exceptionally dull uncles (and one who wasn't dull at all but was currently serving time in Carson City for sins that didn't have no names west of Manhattan, where they were viewed more as a series of popular parlor games than a bunch of crimes against God and Nature). And she allowed that she had plumb lost her heart to him and promised to sneak out of the hotel as soon as her maiden aunt went to bed, and meet Jack on the outskirts of town—not a difficult feat, since town was only one block long—and maybe even steal a forbidden kiss (or perhaps six forbidden kisses, since she wasn't anywhere near as imaginative as her maiden aunt).

So they went their separate ways, each counting the minutes until they met again. (Well, actually, Jack didn't have much schooling, so he could only count the hours. Up to ten, anyway.) Then, after Bunny and her maiden aunt had gone to bed, each in their own rooms, Bunny waited until she heard the gentle snores of the older woman, quickly got out of her nightgown, climbed into her very best outfit, tiptoed out of the room and down the stairs, made her way all eighty-five feet to the edge of town, and a minute later was in Jack's strong, masculine arms.

"I love you, Bunny Wigglesworth," he said, "and I want you to be mine."

"And I love you, Howlin' Jack Dawkins," she said, "and I pledge to be yours forever."

"We will be so happy together, Bunny," he said. And then: "Bunny. That's a curious name. I don't think I've ever met anyone called Bunny. Not that it isn't adorable," he added quickly.

"Well, come to think of it, I've never met anyone called Howlin' Jack before," she replied. "Or even Howlin' Bill, for that matter. Why do they call you that, Jack?"

He had just opened his mouth to answer her when the sun, which had been making its lazy way to the horizon, finally vanished and night fell.

And suddenly he wasn't Howlin' Jack the cowboy any more, but instead was a large red-brown animal with a long muzzle and sharp canines. His answer came out as a howl. Then he cleared his throat and said, "Now you know my deep, dark, shameful secret. I'm a werecoyote."

"Oh my goodness!" said a high-pitched, squeaky, terrified little voice coming from somewhere around Jack's ankle. He looked down and saw a cute, furry blonde rabbit staring at him. "Now you know my secret too."

"You're a wererabbit?" said Jack, trying to sort out his feelings.

"Only at nights," said Bunny. "And please stop drooling on me. I'm getting drenched." She looked up at him. "I hope a little thing like this isn't going to come between us."

"I still love you," said Jack.

"And you don't mind the way I look?" she asked.

"You look... delicious," he said.

"You've changed," said Bunny accusingly.

"Of course I've changed," said Jack. "I'm a coyote. And you're a rabbit. A lovely rabbit. A delicious soft plump blonde juicy rabbit."

"You're drooling again," said Bunny.

She hopped back a step—well, a jump, actually—and he tensed.

"Don't do that!" said Jack.

"Don't do what?" she asked.

"Don't make sudden motions," he said. "I have this urge to chase little things that move fast." He stared at her with a curious expression on his coyote face. "The problem is, I have this urge to eat little things that don't move fast enough."

"Oh, cruel unfeeling Fate!" she cried. "To find you, only to lose you so soon!"

Suddenly Jack howled again. "You ain't losing me, kid!"

"I thought I was a love object, not an appetizer," said Bunny miserably.

"Why limit yourself?" growled Jack, pulling his lips back and exposing his fangs. "You can be both!"

Bunny had time for one little scream, and then she took off like a bat out of hell, or perhaps a rabbit out of finishing school, with Jack in hot pursuit. They ran due West, straight out of Cougar Claw and straight into legend.

Every now and then word comes back about a soft-spoken feller with sad, haunted eyes traveling from town to town looking for a girl with golden tresses named Bunny—and when cowboys sit around the campfire at night telling their sad stories, they always stop when they hear a coyote's mournful wail, because they know it's Howlin' Jack Dawkins, still searching for his lost love.

A year had passed since I wrote and sold *The Last Dog* to *Hunting Dog Magazine*, and the editor contacted me and asked for another. Carol remembered hearing a couple of our favorite folk singers do different versions of the song *Old Dog Blue* and suggested there might be a story there. She was right, as usual.

Blue won me my second consecutive Best Short Fiction Award from the American Dog Writers Association. A few days later, one of their officers asked if I planned to write any more science fictional dog stories. I told them that as long as they gave out the award I'd probably write one a year.

A week later they cancelled the award.

Blue

I had a dog, his name was Blue.
Bet you five dollars he's a good one too.
Come on, Blue!
I'm a-coming too.

They sing that song about him, Burl Ives and Win Stracke and the rest, but they wouldn't have been too happy to be locked in the same room with old Blue. He'd as soon take your hand off as look at you.

He wandered out to my shack one day when he was a pup and just plumped himself down and stayed. I always figured he stuck around because I was the only thing he'd ever seen that was even meaner and uglier than he was.

As for betting five dollars on Blue or anything else, forget it. It's been so long since I've seen five dollars that I don't even remember whose picture is on the bill. Jefferson, I think, or maybe Roosevelt. Money just never mattered much to me, and as long as Blue was warm and dry and had a full belly, nothing much mattered to him.

Each winter we'd shaggy up, me on my face and him just

about everywhere, and each summer we'd naked down. Didn't see a lot of people any time of year. When we did, it'd be a contest to see who could run them off the territory first, me or Blue. He'd win more often than not. He never came back looking for praise, or like he'd done a bright thing; it was more like he'd done a *necessary* thing. Those woods and that river was ours, his and mine, and we didn't see any reason to put up with a batch of intruders, neither city-slickers nor down-home boys either.

It was a pretty good life. Neither of us got fat, but we didn't go hungry very often either. And it was kind of good to sit by a fire together, me smoking and him snorting. I don't think he liked my pipe tobacco, but we had this kind of pact not to bother each other, and he stuck by it a lot better than a couple of women I outlived.

And, Mister, that dog was hell on a cold scent.

> *Blue chased a possum up a cinnamon*
> *tree.*
> *Blue looked at the possum, possum*
> *looked at me.*
> *Come on, Blue.*
> *I'm a-coming too.*

EXCEPT THAT IT wasn't a cinnamon tree at all. I don't ever recollect seeing one. It was just a plain old tree, and I still can't figure out how the possum got up there all in one piece.

It must have been twenty below zero, and neither of us had eaten in a couple of days. Suddenly, Blue put his nose to the ground and started baying just like a bloodhound. Thought he was on the trail of an escaped killer the way he carried on, but it was just an old possum, looking every bit as cold and hungry as we did. The way Blue ran him I thought his heart would burst, but somehow he made it a few feet up the tree trunk. Slashed Blue on the nose a couple of times, just for good measure, but if he thought that would make old

Blue run off with his tail between his legs, he had another think coming. Blue just stood there, kind of smiling up at him, and saying, Possum, let's see you come on down and try that again.

It was a mighty toothy smile.

> *Baked that possum good and brown.*
> *Laid sweet potatoes all around.*
> *Come on, Blue,*
> *You can have some too.*

NEVER DID LIKE possum meat. Even when you bake a possum, it tastes just awful. The sweet potatoes were just to kill the flavor. Folksingers and poets live on steak and praise; let 'em try living on possum for a few days and I bet that verse would come out different.

Anyway, I did offer some to Blue, just like the song says. He looked at it, picked it up, and kind of played with it like a pup dog does when you give him a piece of fruit. At first I thought it was just good taste on Blue's part, but then his nose started to swell where the possum had nailed him. Usually, I'd slap a little mud on a wound like that, but mud's not the easiest thing to come by when it's below zero, so I rubbed some snow on instead.

First time in his life Blue ever snarled at me.

> *When old Blue died, he died so hard,*
> *He jarred the ground in my back yard.*
> *Go on, Blue.*
> *I'll get there too.*

GUESS THE POSSUM had rabies or something, because Blue just got worse and worse. His face swelled up like a balloon, and some of the fire went out of his eyes.

We stayed in the shack, me tending to him, except when I had to go out and shoot us something to eat, and him just getting thinner and thinner. I kept trying to make him rest easier, and I could see him fighting with himself, trying not to bite me when I touched him where it hurt.

Then one day, he started foaming at the mouth and howling something awful. And suddenly he turned toward me and got up on his feet, kind of shaky-like, and I could tell he didn't know who I was anymore. He went for me, but fell over on his side before he got halfway across the floor.

I only had a handful of bullets left to last out the winter, but I figured I'd rather eat fish for a month than let him lie there like that. I walked over to him and put my finger on the trigger, and suddenly he stopped tossing around and held stock-still. Maybe he knew what I was going to do, or more likely it was just that he always held still when I raised my rifle. I don't know the reason, but I know we each made things a little easier for the other in that last couple of seconds before I squeezed the trigger.

> *When I get to Heaven, first thing I'll do*
> *Is grab my horn and call for Blue.*
> *Hello, Blue.*
> *Finally got here too.*

THAT'S THE WAY the song ends. It's a right pretty sentiment, so I suppose they had to sing it that way, but Heaven ain't where I'm bound. Wouldn't like it anyhow; white robes and harp-strumming and minding my manners every second. Besides, winter has always chilled me to the bone; I *like* heat.

But when I get to where I'm going, I'll look up and call for him, and Blue will come running just like he always did. He'll have a long way to go before he finds me, but that never stopped old Blue. He'll just put his nose to the ground, and pretty soon we'll be together again, and he'll know why I did what I did to him.

And we'll sit down before the biggest fire of all, me smoking my pipe and him twitching and snorting like always. And maybe I'll pet him, but probably I won't, and maybe he'll lick me, but probably he won't. We'll just sit there together, and we'll know everything's okay again.

Hello, Blue. I finally got here too.

I wrote an urban fantasy novel, *Stalking the Unicorn*, years before there was a category called "urban fantasy novels." It involved a hardboiled detective named John Justin Mallory, a tongue-in-cheek precursor to Harry Dresden, and the strange Manhattan in which he had to function. When I was through with it, I thought Mallory was permanently retired—there was simply no market for this kind of thing back in 1987, when I was lucky enough to get it published—but over the years, more than half a dozen editors commissioned me to bring Mallory back in short stories and novelettes (of which this was the first, back in 1990). He's not only come back in two more novels, but I now have enough Mallory short fiction that there'll be a collection of it titled *Stalking the Zombie*, coming out in 2012.

Post Time
in Pink

"So who do you like in the sixth?" asked Mallory as he stuck his feet up on the desk and began browsing through the *Racing Form.*

"I haven't the slightest idea," said Winnifred Carruthers, pushing a wisp of gray hair back from her pudgy face and taking a sip of her tea. She was sitting at a table in the kitchen, browsing through the memoirs of a unicorn hunter and trying not to think about what the two donuts she had just eaten would do to her already-ample midriff.

"It's a tough one to call," mused Mallory, staring aimlessly around the magician's apartment that he and Winnifred had converted into their office. Most of the mystic paraphernalia—the magic mirror, the crystal ball, the wands and pentagrams—had been removed. In their place were photos of Joe Dimaggio, Seattle Slew, a pair of Playboy centerspreads (on which Winnifred had meticulously drawn undergarments with a magic marker), and a team picture of the 1966 Green Bay Packers, which Mallery felt gave the place much more the feel of an office and which Winnifred thought was merely in bad taste. "Jumbo hasn't run since he sat on his trainer last fall, and Tantor ran off the course in his last two races to wallow in the infield pond."

"Don't you have anything better to do?" said Winnifred, trying to hide her irritation. "After all, we formed the Mallory & Carruthers Agency two weeks ago, and we're still waiting for our first client."

"It takes time for word to get out," replied Mallory.

"Then shouldn't we be out spreading the word—after you shave and press your suit, of course?"

Mallory smiled at her. "Detective agencies aren't like cars. You can't advertise a sale and wait for customers to come running. Someone has to need us first."

"Then won't you at least stop betting next week's food money on the races?"

"In the absence of a desperate client, this is the only way I know of to raise money."

"But you've had six losing days in a row."

"I'm used to betting on horses in *my* New York," replied Mallory defensively. "Elephants take awhile to dope out. Besides, they're running at Jamaica, and they haven't done that in my New York in thirty-five years; I'm still working out the track bias. But," he added, "I'm starting to get the hang of it. Take Twinkle Toes, for instance. Everything I read in the *Form* led me to believe he could outrun Heavyweight at six furlongs."

"But he didn't," noted Winnifred.

"Outrun Heavyweight? He certainly did."

"I thought he lost."

"By a nose." Mallory grimaced. "Now, how the hell was I supposed to know that his nose was two feet shorter than Heavyweight's?" He paused. "It's just a matter of stockpiling information. Next time I'll take that into consideration."

"What I am trying to say is that we can't afford too many more next times," said Winnifred. "And since you're stranded here, in *this* Manhattan, it would behoove you to start trimming your—*our*—expenses."

RESNICK'S MENAGERIE

"It's my only indulgence."

"No, it's not," said Winnifred.

"It's not?" repeated Mallory, puzzled.

"What do you call *that,* if not an indulgence?" said Winnifred, pointing to the very humanlike but definitely feline creature perched atop the refrigerator.

Mallory shrugged. "The office cat."

"This office can't afford a cat—at least, not *this* one. She's been drinking almost a gallon of milk a day, and the last time I went out shopping, she phoned the local fishmonger and ordered a whale."

"Felina," said Mallory, "is that true?"

The catlike creature shook her head.

"Are you saying you didn't order it?" demanded Winnifred.

"They couldn't fit it through the doorway," answered Felina, leaping lightly to the floor, walking over to Mallory, and rubbing her hip against his shoulder. "So it doesn't count."

"You see?" said Winnifred, shrugging hopelessly. "She's quite beyond redemption."

"This city's got nine million people in it," replied Mallory. "Only two of them didn't desert me when I went up against the Grundy two weeks ago. You're one of them; she's the other. She stays."

Winnifred sighed and went back to sipping her tea, while Felina hopped onto the desk and curled her remarkably humanlike body around Mallory's feet, purring contentedly.

"Do you like the Grundy?" asked Felina after a moment's silence.

"How can one like the most evil demon on the East Coast?" replied Mallory. "Of course," he added thoughtfully, "he makes a lot more sense than most of the people I've met here, but that's a different matter."

"Too bad," purred Felina.

"What's too bad?"

"It's too bad you don't like the Grundy."

"Why?" asked Mallory suspiciously.

"Because he's on his way here."

"How do you know?"

Felina smiled a very catlike smile. "Cat people know things that humans can only guess at."

"I don't suppose you know what he wants?" continued Mallory.

Felina nodded her head. "You."

Mallory was about to reply when a strange being suddenly materialized in the middle of the room. He was tall, a few inches over six feet, with two prominent horns protruding from his hairless head. His eyes were a burning yellow, his nose sharp and aquiline, his teeth white and gleaming, his skin a bright red. His shirt and pants were of crushed velvet, his cloak satin, his collar and cuffs made of the fur of some white polar animal. He wore gleaming black gloves and boots, and he had two mystic rubies suspended from his neck on a golden chain. When he exhaled, small clouds of vapor emanated from his mouth and nostrils.

"We need to talk, John Justin Mallory," said the Grundy, fixing the detective with a baleful glare as Felina arched her back and hissed at him and Winnifred backed away.

"Whatever you're selling, I'm not buying," answered Mallory, not bothering to take his feet off the desk.

"I am selling nothing," said the Grundy. "In fact, I have come as a supplicant."

Mallory frowned. "A supplicant?"

"A client, if you will."

"Why should I accept you as a client?" asked Mallory. "I don't even like you."

"I need a detective," said the Grundy calmly. "It is your function in life to detect."

"I thought it was my function to save people from mad dog killers like you."

"I kill no dogs," said the Grundy, taking him literally. "Only people."

"Well, that makes everything all right, then," said Mallory sardonically.

"Good. Shall we get down to business?"

"You seem to forget that we're mortal enemies, sworn to bring about each other's downfall."

"Oh, *that*," said the Grundy with a disdainful shrug.

"Yes, that."

"The battle is all but over. I will win in the end."

"What makes you think so?" said Mallory.

"Death *always* wins in the end," said the demon. "But I have need of you now."

"Well, I sure as hell don't have any need of you."

"Perhaps not—but you have need of *this*, do you not?" continued the Grundy, reaching into the air and producing a thick wad of bills.

Mallory stared at the money for a moment, then sighed. "All right—what's the deal?"

"John Justin!" said Winnifred furiously.

"You just said that we needed money," Mallory pointed out.

"Not *his* money. It's dirty."

"Between the rent, the phone bill, and the grocery bills, we won't have it long enough for any of the dirt to rub off," said Mallory.

"Well, I won't be a party to this," said Winnifred, turning her back and walking out the front door.

"She'll get over it," Mallory said to the Grundy. "She just has this irrational dislike of Evil Incarnate."

"You both misjudge me," said the Grundy. "I told you once: I am a fulcrum, a natural balance point between this world's best and worst tendancies. Where I find order, I create chaos, and where I find chaos...."

"I believe I've heard this song before," said Mallory. "It didn't impress me then, either. Why don't you just tell me why you're here and let it go at that?"

"You have no fear of me whatsoever, do you?" asked the Grundy.

"Let us say that I have a healthy respect for you," replied Mallory. "I've seen you in action, remember?"

"And yet you meet my gaze, and your voice does not quake."

"Why should my voice quake? I know that you didn't come here to kill me. If you had wanted to do that, you could have done it from your castle... so let's get down to business."

The Grundy glanced at Mallory's desk. "I see that you are a student of the *Racing Form*. That's very good."

"It is?"

The demon nodded. "I have come to you with a serious problem."

"It involves the *Racing Form*?"

"It involves Ahmed of Marsabit."

"Doesn't he run a belly-dance joint over on Ninth Avenue?"

"He is an elephant, John Justin Mallory," said the Grundy sternly. "More to the point, he was *my* elephant until I sold him last week."

"Okay, he was your elephant until you sold him," said Mallory. "So what?"

"I sold him for two thousand dollars."

"That isn't much of a price," noted Mallory.

"He wasn't much of an elephant. He had lost all sixteen of his races while carrying my colors." The Grundy paused. "Three days ago, he broke a track record and won by the entire length of the homestretch."

"Even horses improve from time to time."

"Not *that* much," answered the Grundy harshly, the vapor from his nostrils turning a bright blue. "I own the favorite for the upcoming Quatermaine Cup. I have just found out that Ahmed's new owner has entered him in the race." He paused, and his eyes glowed like hot coals. "Mallory, I tell you that Ahmed is incapable of the kind of performance I saw three days ago. His owner must be running a ringer—a look-alike."

"Don't they have some kind of identification system, like the lip tattoos on race horses?" asked Mallory.

"Each racing elephant is tattooed behind the left ear."

"What's Ahmed's ID number?"

"831," said the Grundy. He paused. "I want you to expose this fraud before the race is run."

"You're the guy with all the magical powers," said Mallory. "Why don't you do it yourself?"

"My magic only works against other magic," explained the Grundy. "For a crime that was committed according to natural law, I need a detective who is forced to conform to natural law."

"Come on," said Mallory. "I've seen you wipe out hundreds of natural-law-abiding citizens who never did you any harm. Were they all practicing magic?"

"No," admitted the Grundy. "But they were under the protection of my Opponent, and *he* operates outside the boundaries of natural law."

"But the guy who bought Ahmed isn't protected by anyone?"

"No."

"Why don't you just kill him and the elephant and be done with it?"

"I may yet do so," said the Grundy. "But first I must know exactly what has happened, or sometime in the future it may happen again."

"All right," said Mallory. "What's the name of the guy who bought Ahmed from you?"

"Khan," said the Grundy.

"Gengis?" guessed Mallory.

"Gengis F.X. Khan, to be exact."

"He must be quite a bastard, if your Opponent doesn't feel compelled to protect him from you."

"Enough talk," said the Grundy impatiently. "John Justin Mallory, will you accept my commission?"

"Probably," said Mallory. He paused. "For anyone else, the firm of Mallory & Carruthers charges two hundred dollars a day. For you, it's a thousand."

"You are pressing your luck, Mallory," said the Grundy ominously.

"And you're pressing yours," shot back Mallory. "I was the only person in this Manhattan that could find your damned unicorn after he was stolen from you, and I'm the only one who can find out what happened to your elephant."

"What makes you so sure of that?"

"The fact that *you're* sure of it," replied Mallory with a confident grin. "We hate each other's guts, remember? You wouldn't have swallowed your pride and come to me unless you'd tried every other means of discovering what really happened first."

The Grundy nodded his approval. "I chose the right man. Sooner or later I shall kill you, slowly and painfully, but for the moment we shall be allies."

"Not a chance," Mallory contradicted him. "For the moment, we're employer and employee... and one of my conditions for remaining your employee is a non-refundable down payment of five thousand dollars." He paused. "Another is your promise not to harass my partner while I'm working." He smiled. "She doesn't know you like I do. You scare the hell out of her."

"Winnifred Carruthers is a fat old woman with a bleak past and a bleaker future. What is she to you?"

"She's my friend."

The demon snorted his contempt.

"I haven't got so many friends that I can let you go around terrifying them," continued Mallory. "Have we got a deal?"

The Grundy stood stock-still for a moment, then nodded. "We have a deal."

"Good. Put the money on my desk before you leave."

But the Grundy had anticipated him, and Mallory found that he was speaking to empty air. He reached across the desk, counted out the bills (which, he noted without surprise, came to exactly five thousand dollars), and placed them in his pocket, while Felina stared at some spot that only she could see and watched the Grundy complete his leave-taking.

MALLORY STOOD BEFORE the grandstand at Jamaica, watching a dozen elephants lumber through their morning workouts and trying to stifle yet another yawn, while all manner of men and vaguely humanoid creatures that had been confined to his nightmares only fifteen days ago went about their morning's chores. The track itself was on the outskirts of the city of Jamaica, which, like this particular Manhattan, was a hodgepodge of skyscrapers, Gothic castles, and odd little stores on winding streets that seemed to have no beginning and no end.

"What the hell am I doing here at five in the morning?" he muttered.

"Watching elephants run in a circle," said Felina helpfully.

"Why is it always animals?" continued Mallory, feeling his mortality as the cold morning air bit through his rumpled suit. "First a unicorn, then an elephant. Why can't it be something that keeps normal hours, like a bank robber?"

"Because the Grundy owns all the banks, and nobody would dare to rob him," answered Felina, avidly watching a small bird that circled overhead as it prepared to land on the rail just in front of the grandstand. Finally, it perched about fifteen feet away, and Felina uttered an inhuman shriek and leaped nimbly toward it. The bird took flight, barely escaping her outstretched claws, but one of the elephants, startled by the sound, turned to pinpoint the source of the commotion, failed to keep a straight course, and broke through the outer rail on the clubhouse turn. His rider went flying through the air, finally landing in the branches of a small tree, while the huge pachyderm continued lumbering through the parking lot, banging into an occasional Tucker or DeLorean.

"Bringing you along may not have been the brightest idea I ever had," said Mallory, futilely attempting to pull her off her perch atop the rail.

"But I like it here," purred Felina, rubbing her shoulder against his own. "There are so many pretty birds here. Fat pretty birds. Fat juicy pretty birds. Fat tasty juicy pretty—"

"Enough," said Mallory.

"You never let me have any fun," pouted Felina.

"Our definitions of 'fun' vary considerably," said Mallory. He shrugged. "Oh, well, I suppose I'd better get to work." He stared at her. "I don't suppose I can leave you here and expect you to stay out of trouble?"

She grinned happily. "Of course you can, John Justin," she replied, her pupils becoming mere vertical slits.

Mallory sighed. "I didn't think so. All right, come on."

She jumped lightly to the ground and fell into step behind him, leaping over any concrete squares that bore the contractor's insignia. They walked around the track and soon reached the backstretch, more than half a mile from where they had started.

Mallory's nose told him where the barns were. The smell of elephants reached him long before he heard the contented gurgling of their stomachs. Finally, he reached the stable area, a stretch of huge concrete barns with tall ceilings and a steady flow of goblins and gnomes scurrying to and fro with hay-filled wheelbarrows.

He approached the first of the barns, walked up to a man who seemed quite human, and tapped him on the shoulder.

"Yes?" said the man, turning to him, and suddenly Mallory became aware of the fact that the man had three eyes.

"Can you tell me where to find Ahmed?"

"You're in the wrong place, pal. I think he's a placekicker for the Chicago Fire."

"He's an elephant."

"He is?" said the man, surprised.

Mallory nodded. "Yes."

"You're absolutely sure of that?"

Mallory nodded again.

The man frowned. "Now why do you suppose the Fire would want an elephant on their team?"

"Beats the hell out of me," conceded Mallory. He decided to try a different approach. "I'm also looking for the barn where Gengis F.X. Khan stables his racing elephants."

"Well, friend, you just found it."

"You work for Khan?"

"Yep."

"Then how come you don't know who Ahmed is?"

"Hey, pal, my job is just to keep 'em cleaned and fed. I let the trainer worry about which is which."

"What's your name?"

"Jake. But everybody calls me Four-Eyes."

"Four-Eyes?" repeated Mallory.

The man nodded. "'Cause I wear glasses."

"Well, I suppose it makes as much sense as anything else in this damned world," Mallory turned and looked down the shed row. "Where can I find Khan?"

"See that big guy standing by the backstretch rail, with the stopwatch in his hand?" said Four-Eyes, gesturing toward an enormous man clad in brilliantly-colored silks and satins and wearing a purple turban. "That's him. He's timing workouts."

"Shouldn't he be standing at the finish line?"

"His watch only goes up to sixty seconds, so he times 'em up to the middle of the backstretch, and then his trainer times 'em the rest of the way home."

"Seems like a lot of wasted effort to me," said Mallory.

"Yeah? Why?"

"Because each time the second hand passes sixty, he just has to add a minute to the final time."

All three of Four-Eyes' eyes opened wide in amazement. "Son of a bitch!" he exclaimed. "I never thought of that!"

"Apparently no one else did, either," said Mallory caustically.

"Look, buddy," said Four-Eyes defensively, "math ain't my specialty. You wanna talk elephant shit, I can talk it with the best of 'em."

"No offense intended," said Mallory. He turned to Felina. "Let's go," he said, leading her toward the backstretch rail. Once there, he waited until Khan had finished timing one of his elephants, and then tapped the huge man on the shoulder.

"Yes?" demanded Khan, turning to him. "What do you want?"

"Excuse me, sir," said Mallory. "But I wonder if you'd mind answering some questions."

"I keep telling you reporters, Jackie Onassis and I are just good friends."

Mallory smiled. "Not that kind of question."

"Oh?" said Khan, frowning. "Well, let me state for the record that all three of them told me they were eighteen, and I don't know where the dead chicken came from. I was just an innocent bystander."

"Can we talk about elephants, sir?"

Khan wrinkled his nose. "Disgusting, foul-smelling animals." He stared distastefully at Felina. "Almost as annoying as cat people." Felina sniffed once and made a production of turning her back to him. "The smartest elephant I ever owned didn't have the intelligence of a potted plant."

"Then why do you own them?"

"My good man, everyone knows that Gengis F.X. Khan is a *sportsman*." The hint of a smile crossed his thick lips. "Besides, if I didn't spend all this money on elephants, I'd just have to give it to the government."

"Makes sense to me," agreed Mallory.

"Is that all you wanted to know?"

"As a matter of fact, it isn't," said Mallory. "I'm not a reporter, sir; I'm a detective—and I'd like to know a little bit about Ahmed of Marsabit."

"Hah!" said Khan. "You're working for the Grundy, aren't you?"

"Yes, I am."

"He finally sells a good one by mistake, and now he's trying to prove that I cheated him out of it!"

"He hasn't made any accusations."

"He doesn't have to. I know the way his mind works." Khan glared at Mallory. "The only thing you have to know about Ahmed is that I'm going to win the Quatermaine Cup with him!"

"I understand that he was a pretty mediocre runner before you bought him."

"Mediocre is an understatement."

"You must have a very good eye for an elephant," suggested Mallory, "to be able to spot his potential."

"To tell you the absolute truth, I wouldn't know one from another," replied Khan. "Though Ahmed does stand out like a sore thumb around the barn."

"If you can't tell one from another, how can he stand out?"

"His color."

"His color?" repeated Mallory, puzzled.

"Didn't you know? One of the restrictions on the Quatermaine Cup is that pink is the only permitted color."

"Ahmed is a pink elephant?"

"Certainly."

Mallory shrugged. "Well, I've heard of white elephants in a somewhat different context... so why not pink?"

"They make the best racers," added Khan.

"Let me ask you a question," said Mallory. "If you don't know one elephant from another, and you don't trust the Grundy to begin with, why did you buy Ahmed?"

"I needed the tax writeoff."

"You mean you purposely bought an elephant you thought couldn't run worth a damn?"

Khan nodded. "And if it wasn't for the fun I'm going to have beating the Grundy's entry in the Cup, I'd be very annoyed with him. If Ahmed wins this weekend, I may actually have to dip into capital to pay my taxes."

"Aren't you afraid the Grundy might be a little upset with you if Ahmed beats his elephant?" asked Mallory.

"I've done nothing wrong," said Khan confidently. "The pure of heart have nothing to fear from demons."

"That's not the way I heard it."

"It's not the way I heard it either," admitted Khan. "But I've also written off a two million dollar donation to my local church, and if *that* doesn't buy me a little holy protection, I'm going to have some very harsh words to say to God's attorneys." He paused. "Perhaps you'd like to take a look at Ahmed now?"

"Very much," responded Mallory. He turned to Felina. "You wait here."

Felina purred and grinned.

"I mean it," said Mallory. "I don't want you to move from this spot. I'll just be a couple of minutes."

"Yes, John Justin," she promised.

"Come along," said Khan, as he began walking back to the barn. When they arrived, Khan whistled, and a number of trunks suddenly protruded from the darkened stalls, each one begging for peanuts or some other tidbit. One of the trunks was pink, and Mallory walked over to it.

"This is Ahmed?" he asked, gesturing toward the huge pink elephant munching contentedly on a mouthful of straw.

"Impressive, isn't he?" said Khan. "As elephants go, that is."

"Do you mind if I pet him?" asked Mallory.

Khan shrugged. "As you wish."

Mallory approached Ahmed gingerly. When the long pink trunk snaked out to identify him, he held it gently in one hand and stroked it with the other, then pulled a handkerchief out of his pocket and rubbed the trunk vigorously. No color came off. Then he checked the tattoo on the back of the animal's left ear: it was Number 831.

Suddenly there was a loud commotion coming from the direction of the track, and a moment later Four-Eyes came running into the barn.

"Hey, buddy," he said, panting heavily, "you'd better do something about your friend!"

"What's she done this time?" asked Mallory.

"Come see for yourself."

Four-Eyes headed back to the track, Mallory and Khan hot on his heels.

The scene that greeted them resembled a riot. Elephants were trumpeting and racing all over the track, while their riders lay sprawled in the dirt. Four of the pachyderms, including a pink one, had broken through the rail and were decimating foreign cars in the parking lot. Track officials were running the length of the homestretch, waving their hands and shouting at Felina, who seemed to be flying a few feet off the ground, just ahead of them.

"What the hell's going on?" demanded Mallory.

"You know how they use a rabbit to make the greyhounds run faster at the dog tracks?" said Four-Eyes. "Well, we use a mouse at the elephant tracks. And instead of the dogs chasing the rabbit, the mouse chases the elephants." He paused for breath. "We don't use it in workouts, but the officials always give it one test run around the track before the afternoon races, just to make sure it's in good working order. Your catgirl pounced on it when it passed by here, and her weight must have fouled up the mechanism, because it's going twice as fast as usual. Panicked every elephant on the track."

Mallory watched as Felina and the mouse hit the clubhouse turn four lengths ahead of the track officials, who soon ran out of breath and slowed down to a walk. The detective stepped under the rail and stood waiting for the catgirl, hands on hips, as she entered the backstretch. As the mouse neared him, Felina gathered herself and sprang high in the air, coming to rest in Mallory's hastily outstretched arms.

"It wasn't real," she pouted.

"I thought I told you to stay where you were," he said severely, setting her down on her feet.

"They cheated," muttered Felina, glaring balefully at the artificial mouse as it continued circling the track.

Mallory looked down the stretch and saw the furious but exhausted officials slowly approaching him. Taking Felina firmly by the hand, he ran to the rail and ducked under it.

"Come on," he said, racing to the barn area. "The last thing I need is to get barred from the grounds because of you."

They zigged and zagged in amongst the buildings, finally ducked into an empty stall, and stood motionless for a few moments until the track officials lost their enthusiasm for the hunt and began slowly returning to the clubhouse.

"Well?" said a voice at his side.

Mallory turned and found himself facing the Grundy.

"Well, what?"

"What have you accomplished for my money thus far, besides causing a small riot?"

"It's early in the day yet," said Mallory defensively.

"You didn't seriously think Khan painted one of his elephants to look like Ahmed, or that I failed to check the tattoo number before hiring you, did you?"

"No—but I felt I ought to check, just to be on the safe side."

"It was a total waste of time."

"Perhaps—but if you don't tell me these things, I have to find them out for myself," replied Mallory. "Is there anything else I should know?"

"Only that I expect results," said the Grundy. "And soon."

"Stop looking over my shoulder and you just might get 'em."

"I have every right to see how my money is being spent."

"That wasn't part of the contract," said Mallory. "I'll let you know when the case is solved. In the meantime, if you pop up again or interfere with me in any way, the deal's off and I'm keeping the retainer. I'm not an actor, and I don't want an audience."

"All right," said the demon after a moment's consideration. "We'll try it your way for the time being."

"I'd thank you, but I don't recall wording that as a request."

"Just remember, Mallory," said the Grundy, "that my patience is not unlimited."

And then he was gone.

"Thanks for warning me that he was about to pay me a visit," said Mallory to Felina.

"They cheated," growled Felina with a single-minded intensity that Mallory had rarely encountered in her before.

"They're not the only ones," said Mallory. He grabbed her hand and began leading her down the shed row. "Let's take a little walk."

He asked a stable girl with scaly green skin and a sullen expression to point out which barn housed the Grundy's stable of elephants, then walked over to it.

RESNICK'S MENAGERIE

Four tweed-clad leprechauns suddenly barred his way.

"No trespassers," said the nearest of them with a malicious smirk.

"I'm working for your boss," replied Mallory.

"And I'm the Sultan of Swat," came the answer.

"I'm telling you the truth," said Mallory. "Check it out."

"Sure," said another one sarcastically. "The worst enemy the Grundy has, and we're supposed to believe you're working for him."

"Believe anything you want, but I'm going into that barn."

"Not a chance, Mallory," said the first leprechaun. "I'll fight to the death to keep you out."

"Fine by me," said Mallory. He turned to Felina, who was eyeing the leprechauns eagerly. "I knew you'd prove useful sooner or later. Felina, fight him to the death."

"Just a minute!" said the leprechaun. "I meant I'd fight you to *his* death." He pointed to one of his companions.

"Okay," said Mallory. "Felina, fight this other one."

"No!" screeched the leprechaun. "I mean, I'd love to fight your cat to the death, really and truly I would, but I strained my back last week and my doctor told me that I couldn't have any more duels to the death 'til a month after Christmas." He pointed to a companion. "How about him? He's a real fighter, old Jules is."

"Right!" chimed in the first leprechaun. "Go get her, Julie! We're behind you one hundred percent."

"What are you talking about?" demanded the second. "I told you: I have a bad back."

"Oh, right," replied the first. "Go get her, Julie! We're behind you almost sixty-seven percent!"

"Uh... count me out, guys," said the fourth leprechaun. "I got a tennis appointment at nine."

"You need a doubles partner?" asked Jules, backing away from the slowly advancing catgirl.

"I thought you were fighting her to the death," said the fourth leprechaun.

"Maybe it'll just be a mild case of death," suggested the first one. "Maybe it won't prove fatal. Go get her, Julie."

The unhappy Jules reached into his pocket and withdrew a wicked-looking knife. Felina merely grinned at him, held out her hand, and displayed four wicked-looking claws, each longer than the knife's blade.

Jules stared at the catgirl's claws for just an instant, then dropped his knife on the ground, yelled "I gotta go to the bathroom!" and lit out for parts unknown at high speed.

"Can we enter the barn now," asked Mallory, "or is someone else interested in a fight to the death?"

"How about if we play checkers instead?" asked the first leprechaun.

"Or we could cut cards," suggested the fourth. "I happen to have a deck right here in my pocket."

Mallory shook his head. "Felina?"

The catgirl began approaching the remaining leprechauns.

"How about a fight to first blood instead?" suggested the nearest leprechaun.

"You and Felina?" asked Mallory.

"Actually, I was thinking more of *you* and Felina," answered the leprechaun.

"Right," chimed in the second one. "If you draw first blood, you get to go into the barn, and if she draws it, she gets to eat you."

"But you're bigger than her, so you gotta tie one hand behind your back," continued the first leprechaun. "After all, fair is fair."

"In fact," added the fourth, "if you could put it off for twenty or thirty minutes, we could sell tickets, and give the winner twenty percent of the take."

"Ten percent!" snapped the first leprechaun. "We've got overhead to consider."

"Split the difference," said the second. "Eleven percent, and let's get this show on the road."

"I'm afraid you guys are missing the point," said Mallory. "If you try to stop us from entering the barn, the only blood that's going to be spilled is leprechaun blood."

"Leprechaun blood?" cried the first one. "That's the most disgusting thought I've ever heard! You have a warped, twisted mind, Mallory!"

"Besides, whoever heard of the combatants attacking the spectators?" demanded the second.

"I'm not a combatant," said Mallory.

"Of course you are," insisted the second leprechaun. "I thought it was all settled: you're fighting *her.*"

"Felina," said Mallory, "I'm walking into the barn now. Do whatever you like to anyone that tries to stop me."

Felina grinned and purred.

The first leprechaun turned to his companions. "Are you gonna let him talk to you like that?"

"What do you mean, *us*?" replied the second one, backing away from Felina. "He was looking at *you* when he said it."

"That's only because I'm so handsome that I just naturally attract the eye. He was definitely addressing you."

"Where's Julie when we need him?" said the fourth. "I'd better go find him." He headed off at a run.

"Wait!" said the second, racing after him. "I'll go with you. Julie wouldn't want to miss the chance to put these interlopers in their place."

"Well?" said Mallory, taking a step toward the one remaining leprechaun.

"The Grundy will kill me if I let anyone in," he said nervously.

"And Felina will kill you if you try to stop me," said Mallory, taking another step. "It's a difficult choice. You'd better consider your options very carefully."

The catgirl licked her lips.

"Well, I don't actually *work* for the Grundy," said the leprechaun hastily. "I mean, he underpays us and we don't even have a union or anything, to say nothing of sick leave and other fringes." He retreated a step. "Who does that Grundy think he is, anyway?" he continued in outraged tones. "How dare he demand that we stop an honest citizen from admiring his elephants. After all, the public supports racing, doesn't it? And you're part of the public, aren't you? These elephants are as much yours as his. The nerve of that Grundy! You go right on in," he concluded, putting even more distance between himself and Felina. "If the Grundy tries to stop you, I'll fight him to the death."

"That's very considerate of you," said Mallory, walking past the trembling leprechaun and entering the barn. "Felina!"

The catgirl reluctantly fell into step behind him.

Mallory walked down the shed row, peering into each stall. When he came to a stall housing a pink elephant, he entered it, checked the tattoo behind its left ear—the ID number was 384—and then left the stall and carefully closed the door behind him. When he finished checking the remainder of the stalls, he walked back outside and then turned to Felina.

"How many pink ones did you see?"

"One," she replied.

"Good. Then I didn't miss any."

Felina searched the sky for birds but saw nothing but airplanes and an occasional harpy.

"It's cloudy," she noted.

"Yes," said Mallory, "but it's getting clearer every minute."

The catgirl shook her head. "It's going to rain."

"I'm not talking about the weather," answered Mallory.

MALLORY DROPPED FELINA off with Winnifred, then paid a visit to Joe the Goniff, his personal bookie.

The Goniff's office was housed in a decrepit apartment building, just far enough from the local police station so that they didn't feel obligated to close him up, and just close enough so that the cops could lay their bets on their lunch breaks.

The Goniff himself looked like something by Lovecraft out of Runyon, a purple-skinned, ill-shapen creature who nonetheless felt compelled to dress the part of his profession, and had somehow, somewhere found a tailor who had managed to create a plaid suit, black shirt, and metallic silver tie that actually fit his grotesque body. He wore a matching plaid visor, and had a pencil tucked behind each of his four ears.

"Hi, John Justin," he hissed in a sibilant voice as Mallory entered the office, which was empty now but would be bustling with activity in another two hours. "Too bad about Twinkle Toes."

"Can't win 'em all," said Mallory with a shrug.

"But you don't seem to win any of 'em," replied Joe the Goniff. "I keep thinking I should give you a discount, like maybe selling you a two-dollar ticket for a buck and a half."

"A big-hearted bookie," said Mallory in bemused tones. "Now I know I'm not in my Manhattan."

The Goniff chuckled, expelling little puffs of green vapor. "So, John Justin, who do you like today?"

"What's the line on the Quatermaine Cup?"

"Leviathan—that's the Grundy's unbeaten elephant—is the favorite at three-to-five. There's been a lot of play on Ahmed of Marsabit since that last race of his, but you can still get four-to-one on him. Hot Lips is eight-to-one, and I'll give you twenty-to-one on any of the others."

"What was Ahmed before his last race?" asked Mallory.

"Eighty-to-one."

"How much money would it take to bring him down to four-to-one?"

"Oh, I don't know," said the Goniff. "Maybe ten grand."

"Can you do me a couple of favors?"

"I love you like a brother, John Justin," said the Goniff. "There is nothing I wouldn't do for you. Just the thought of helping our city's most famous detective is—"

"How much?" interrupted Mallory wearily.

"I would never charge you for a favor, John Justin," replied the Goniff. "However," he added with a grin, "a thousand-dollar bet could buy my kid a new set of braces—if he ever needs them."

"I didn't know you had a kid."

"I don't—but who knows what the future holds?"

"A thousand dollars?"

"Right."

"Okay," said Mallory, pulling out his wallet and counting out ten of the hundred-dollar bills the Grundy had given him. "Put it all on Ahmed of Marsabit in the Cup."

The Goniff shook his massive head sadly. "Ahmed ran a big race the other day, I know—but you're making a mistake, John Justin. Leviathan's unbeaten and unextended. He's got a lock on the race."

"Put it on Ahmed anyway."

"You got inside information?" asked the Goniff, his eyes suddenly narrowing.

"I thought I was buying inside information from *you*," answered Mallory. "Remember?"

"Oh, yeah—right. So what can I do for you?"

"I want to know if anyone made a killing on Ahmed's last race."

"Everyone who bet on him made a killing," replied Joe the Goniff. "He paid better than a hundred-to-one."

"Find out if anyone had more than a hundred dollars on him."

"It may take a day or two," said the Goniff. "I'll have to check with the track and all the O.T.B. offices as well as all the other bookies in town."

"Forget the track and the Off-Track Betting offices," said Mallory. "Whoever made the killing wouldn't want to leave a record of it."

"Then what makes you think the bookies will tell you who it was?"

"They won't—but they'll tell *you*."

"Okay, will do."

"I need to know before they run the Cup."

"Right." The Goniff paused. "You said you needed a couple of favors. What's the other one?"

"If someone plunked down a couple of grand on Ahmed when he was still eighty-to-one for the Cup, would that be the payoff if he won, or would they get the four-to-one you're offering now?"

"If they came to a regular handbook like myself, they'd get the post time odds."

"How could they get eighty-to-one?"

"They'd have to go to a futures book like Crazy Conrad, over on the corner of Hope and Despair."

"What's a futures book?" asked Mallory.

"You get the odds that are on the board that day... but you're stuck with the bet, even if the odds go up, even if he's scratched, even if the damned elephant breaks a leg and they have to shoot him a month before the race. Usually a futures book will close on a race a couple of months before it's run."

"How many futures books are there in town?"

"Three."

"For my second favor, I want you to get in touch with all three, see if any serious money was placed on Ahmed when he was still more than fifty-to-one, and find out who made the bets."

"Can't do it, John Justin."

"Why not?"

"One of those books is run by my brother-in-law, and we haven't spoken to each other since I caught him cheating at Friday night poker. I have my pride, you know."

"How much will it take to soothe your pride?" asked Mallory with a sigh.

"Another five hundred ought to do it."

Mallory withdrew five more bills. "Put four hundred ninety eight on Ahmed, and give me a two-dollar ticket on Leviathan." He paused. "And when you get my information, call Winnifred Carruthers at my office and give it to her."

"You on drugs or something, John Justin?" demanded the Goniff. "I keep telling you Ahmed can't win. You must be snorting nose candy."

"Just do what I said."

"Okay," said the Goniff. "But I got a funny notion that you're a head."

"Not yet," replied Mallory with a sudden burst of confidence. "But I'm catching up."

"WELL?" DEMANDED THE Grundy.

It was Cup day at Jamaica, and the grandstand and clubhouse were filled to overflowing. The sun had finally managed to break through the cover of clouds and smog, and although it had rained the previous night, the maintenance crew had managed to dry out the track, upgrading it from "muddy" in the first race to "good" in the third, and finally to "fast" as post time approached for the Quatermaine Cup.

Mallory was sitting in the Grundy's private box in the clubhouse, sipping an Old Peculiar, and enjoying the awe which the spectators seemed to hold for anyone who was willing to remain in such close proximity to the notorious Grundy.

"I told you," said Mallory. "The case is solved."

"But you haven't told me anything else, and I am fast losing my patience with you."

"I'm just waiting for one piece of information."

"Then the case *isn't* solved, and Khan's elephant might win the cup."

"Relax," said Mallory. "All I'm waiting for is the name of the guilty party. I guarantee you that the real Ahmed will be running in the Cup."

"You're absolutely sure?" demanded the Grundy.

Mallory withdrew his two-dollar win ticket on Leviathan and held it up for the Grundy to see. "I wouldn't be betting on your entry if I wasn't sure."

The Grundy looked out across the track, where eight pink elephants were walking in front of the stands in the post parade.

"It's time for me to lay my bets," he said. "If you have lied to me, John Justin Mallory...."

"As God is my witness, I haven't lied."

"I am considerably more vindictive than God," the Grundy assured him. "You would do well to remember that."

"*You'd* do well to remember that it's only six minutes to post time, and you haven't gotten your bets down yet," responded Mallory.

"Ahmed is definitely on the track right now?" insisted the Grundy.

"For the fifth time, Ahmed is definitely on the track right now."

"You had better be right," said the Grundy, vanishing.

Suddenly, Winnifred Carruthers approached the box.

"I've been wondering what happened to you," said Mallory.

"Your bookie just called the office an hour ago, and traffic was dreadful," she said.

"He gave you a name?"

"Yes," said Winnifred. "I wrote it down." She handed the detective a slip of paper. He looked at it, nodded, and then ripped it into tiny pieces. "By the way," added Winnifred with obvious distaste, "where's your client?"

"Laying his bets," said Mallory.

A sudden murmur ran through the crowd, and Mallory looked up at the tote board. Leviathan had gone down from even money to one-to-five, and the other prices had all shot up. Ahmed of Marsabit was now fifteen-to-one.

"That's it," said Mallory with satisfaction. "All the pieces are in place."

"I hope you know what you're doing, John Justin."

"I hope so too," he said earnestly. He smiled reassuringly at her. "Not to worry. If everything works out the way I have it planned, I'll buy you a new hunting rifle."

"And if it doesn't?"

"We'll worry about that eventuality if and when it comes to pass," said Mallory. He paused. "You'd better be going now. The Grundy is due back any second."

She nodded. "But I'll be standing about thirty rows behind you. If the Grundy tries anything...." She opened her purse, and Mallory could see a revolver glinting inside it.

"Whatever you do, don't shoot him."

"Why not? I'm a crack shot."

"Yeah, but I have a feeling that shooting him would just annoy him," said Mallory. "Besides, you're not going to need the gun. Believe me, everything is under control."

She looked doubtful, but sighed and began walking up the aisle to her chosen vantage point. The Grundy reappeared a few seconds later, just as the elephants were being loaded into the oversized starting gate.

"Well?" demanded the demon.

"What now?"

"I know she talked to you."

"She's my friend and my partner. She's allowed to talk to me."

"Don't be obtuse," said the Grundy coldly. "Did she give you the information you needed?"

"Yes."

"Let me have it."

"As soon as the race is over."

"Now."

"I guarantee the culprit won't get away," said Mallory. "And telling you his name won't affect the outcome of the race."

"You're sure?"

"I may not like you, but I've never lied to you."

The Grundy stared at him. "That is true," he admitted.

"Good. Now sit down and enjoy the race."

Six elephants were already standing in the gate, and the assistant starters soon loaded the last two. Then a bell rang, the doors sprang open, the electric mouse loomed up on the rail, and eight squealing pink elephants pounded down the homestretch.

"And it's Hot Lips taking the early lead," called the track announcer. "Ahmed of Marsabit is laying second, two lengths off the pace, Beer Belly is third, Levithan broke sluggishly and has moved up to fourth, Kenya Express is fifth, Dumbo is sixth, Babar is seventh...."

"He's never broken badly before," muttered the Grundy. "When I get my hands on that jockey...."

"Around the clubhouse turn, and it's still Hot Lips and Ahmed of Marsabit showing the way," said the announcer. "Leviathan is now third, Kenya Express is fourth...."

The order remained unchanged as the pink pachyderms raced down the backstretch, their ears flapping wildly as they tried to listen for signs that the mouse was gaining on them. Then, as they were midway around the far turn, Ahmed's jockey went to the whip—a six-foot wooden club with a spike embedded at the end of it—and Ahmed immediately overtook Hot Lips and opened up a three-length lead by the head of the homestretch.

"Now!" cried the Grundy. "Make your move now!"

But Leviathan began losing ground, his huge sides rising and falling as he labored for breath, and a moment later Ahmed crossed the finish line twelve lengths in front. Leviathan came in dead last, as the lightly-raced Beer Belly caught him in the fifth fifty yards.

"Mallory!" thundered the Grundy, rising to his feet and glaring balefully at the detective. "You lied to me! Your life is forfeit!" He reached into the air and withdrew a huge fireball. "Your bones shall melt within your body, your flesh shall be charred beyond all—"

"I told you the truth!" said Mallory, holding up a hand. "Ahmed lost!"

The Grundy frowned. "What are you talking about?"

"Leviathan won the race."

"I just saw Ahmed win the Cup."

Mallory shook his head. "You just saw *Leviathan* win the Cup."

"Explain yourself," said the Grundy, still holding his fireball at the ready.

"Leviathan's ID number is 384, and Ahmed's is 831. It didn't take much to change them. Then, when Khan came to pick up Ahmed, someone gave him Leviathan instead."

"Then Khan isn't responsible?"

"He's furious. He needed a loser for tax purposes."

"Then who is responsible for this?" demanded the Grundy.

"Someone who had access to both animals, had the time to work on the tattoos, and bet heavily on Leviathan both times he started in Khan's colors."

"Who?" repeated the Grundy.

"A leprechaun named Jules."

"I've never heard of him."

"That's the problem with having your fingers in too many pies, so to speak," said Mallory. "He works for you."

"At the barn?"

"Yes... though he's probably at Creepy Conrad's handbook right now, cashing his ticket."

"I may never have heard of him," said the Grundy, "but he will curse the day he heard of *me*."

"I never doubted it for a minute," replied Mallory.

The Grundy glared at Mallory. "You did not lie, but you purposely deceived me. I will expect my retainer to be returned, and I will not reimburse you for your time. I suspect you made a handsome profit on the race."

"I'll get by okay," answered the detective. "I'll send your money over tomorrow morning."

"See to it that you do," said the Grundy, his fireball finally vanishing. "And now I must take my leave of you, John Justin Mallory. I have urgent business at Creepy Conrad's."

The Grundy vanished, and Mallory walked over to join Winnifred.

"Is it all over?" she asked.

"It will be, as soon as we pick up my winnings from the Goniff. Then I think I'll treat us to dinner and a night on the town."

"Where shall we eat?" asked Winnifred.

"Any place that doesn't serve elephant," replied Mallory. "I've seen quite enough of Ahmed for one day."

"Oh, that poor animal!" said Winnifred. "You don't think the Grundy would—?"

"He hasn't got much use for losers," said Mallory.

"But that's terrible!"

"He's just an elephant."

"We've got to do something, John Justin."

"We've got to collect my money and have dinner."

"We've got to collect your money, yes," said Winnifred. "But forget about dinner. We have more important things to do."

"We have?" asked Mallory resignedly.

"Definitely."

That evening Felina had a new toy. It weighed six tons, and held a very special place in the Guinness Book of World Records for running the slowest mile in the history of Jamaica.

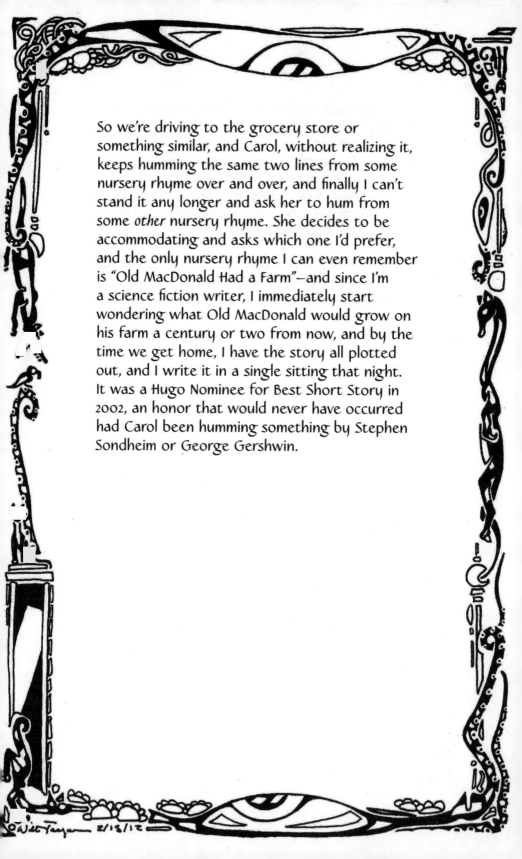

So we're driving to the grocery store or something similar, and Carol, without realizing it, keeps humming the same two lines from some nursery rhyme over and over, and finally I can't stand it any longer and ask her to hum from some *other* nursery rhyme. She decides to be accommodating and asks which one I'd prefer, and the only nursery rhyme I can even remember is "Old MacDonald Had a Farm"—and since I'm a science fiction writer, I immediately start wondering what Old MacDonald would grow on his farm a century or two from now, and by the time we get home, I have the story all plotted out, and I write it in a single sitting that night. It was a Hugo Nominee for Best Short Story in 2002, an honor that would never have occurred had Carol been humming something by Stephen Sondheim or George Gershwin.

Old MacDonald Had a Farm

I came to praise Caesar, not to bury him.

Hell, we all did.

The farm spread out before us, green and rolling, dotted with paddocks and water troughs. It looked like the kind of place you wish your parents had taken you when you were a kid and the world was still full of wonders.

Well, the world may not have been full of wonders any longer, but the farm was. Problem was, they weren't exactly the kind you used to dream of—unless you were coming down from a *really* bad acid trip.

The farm was the brainchild of Caesar Claudius MacDonald. He'd finally knuckled under to public pressure and agreed to show the place off to the press. That's where I came in.

My name's McNair. I used to have a first name, but I dumped it when I decided a one-word byline was more memorable. I work for the *SunTrib*, the biggest newstape in the Chicago area. I'd just broken the story that put Billy Cheever away after the cops had been after him for years. What I wanted for my efforts was my own syndicated column; what I got was a trip to the farm.

For a guy no one knew much about, one who almost never appeared in public, MacDonald had managed to make his name a household word in something less than two years. Even though one of his corporations owned our publishing company, we didn't have much on him in our files, just what all the other news bureaus had: he'd earned a couple of Ph.D.'s, he was a widower who by all accounts had been faithful to his wife, he'd inherited a bundle and then made a lot more on his own.

MacDonald was a Colorado native who emigrated to New Zealand's South Island, bought a 40,000-hectare farm, and hired a lot of technicians over the years. If anyone wondered why a huge South Island farm didn't have any sheep, they probably just figured he had worked out some kind of tax dodge.

Hell, that's what I thought too. I mean, why else would someone with his money bury himself on the underside of the globe for half a lifetime?

Then, a week after his sixty-sixth birthday, MacDonald made The Announcement. That's the year they had food riots in Calcutta and Rio and Manila, when the world was finding out that it was easier to produce eleven billion living human beings than to feed them.

Some people say he created a new life form. Some say he produced a hybrid (though not a single geneticist agrees with that). Some—I used to snicker at them—say that he had delved into mysteries that Man Was Not Meant To Know.

According to the glowing little computer cube they handed out, MacDonald and his crew spent close to three decades manipulating DNA molecules in ways no one had ever thought of before. He did a lot of trial and error work with embryos, until he finally came up with the prototype he sought. Then he spent a few more years making certain that it would breed true. And finally he announced his triumph to the world.

Caesar MacDonald's masterpiece was the Butterball, a meat animal that matured at six months of age and could reproduce at eight months, with a four-week gestation period. It weighed 400 pounds at maturity, and every portion of its body could be consumed by Earth's starving masses, even the bones.

That in itself was a work of scientific brilliance—but to me the true stroke of genius was the astonishing efficiency of the Butterball's digestive system. An elephant, back when elephants still existed, would eat about 600 pounds of vegetation per day, but could only use about forty percent of it and passed the rest as dung. Cattle and pigs, the most common meat animals prior to the Butterballs, were somewhat more efficient, but they, too, wasted a lot of expensive feed.

The Butterballs, on the other hand, utilized one hundred percent of what they were fed. Every pellet of food they ingested went right into building meat that was meticulously bioengineered to please almost every palate. Anyway, that's what the endless series of P.R. releases said.

MacDonald had finally consented to allow a handful of pool reporters to come see for themselves.

We were hoping for a look at MacDonald too, maybe even an interview with the Great Man. But when we got there, we learned that he had been in seclusion for months. Turned out he was suffering from depression, which I would have thought would be the last thing to affect humanity's latest savior, but who knows what depresses a genius? Maybe, like Alexander, he wanted more worlds to conquer, or maybe he was sorry that Butterballs didn't weigh 800 pounds. Hell, maybe he had just worked too hard for too long, or maybe he realized that he was a lot closer to the end of life than the beginning and didn't like it much. Most likely, he just didn't consider us important enough to bother with.

Whatever the reason, we were greeted not by MacDonald himself, but by a flack named Judson Cotter. I figured he had to work in P.R.; his hair was a little too perfect, his suit too up-to-the-minute, his hands too soft for him to have been anything else but a pitchman.

After he apologized for MacDonald's absence, he launched into a worshipful biography of his boss, not deviating one iota from the holobio they'd shown us on the plane trip.

"But I suspect you're here to see the farm," he concluded after paraphrasing the bio for five minutes.

"No," muttered Julie Balch from *NyVid*, "we came all this way to stand in this cold wet breeze and admire your clothes."

A few of us laughed, and Cotter looked just a bit annoyed. I made a mental note to buy her a drink when the tour was done.

"Now let me see a show of hands," said Cotter. "Has anyone here ever seen a live Butterball?"

Where did they find you? I thought. *If we'd seen one, do you really think we'd have flown all the way to hell and gone just to see another?*

I looked around. No one had raised a hand. Which figured. To the best of my knowledge, nobody who didn't work for MacDonald had ever seen a Butterball in the flesh, and only a handful of photos and holos had made it out to the general public. There was even a rumor that all of MacDonald's employees had to sign a secrecy oath.

"There's a reason, of course," continued Cotter smoothly. "Until the international courts verified Mr. MacDonald's patent, there was always a chance that some unscrupulous individual or even a rogue nation would try to duplicate the Butterball. For that reason, while we have shipped and sold its meat all over the world, always with the inspection and approval of the local food and health authorities, we have not allowed anyone to see or examine the animals themselves. But now that the courts have ruled in our favor, we have opened our doors to the press." *Screaming bloody murder every step of the way,* I thought.

"You represent the first group of journalists to tour the farm, but there will be many more, and we will even allow Sir Richard Perigrine to make one of his holographic documentaries here at the farm." He paused. "We plan to open it to public tours in the next two or three years."

Suddenly, a bunch of bullshit alarms began going off inside my head.

"Why not sooner, now that you've won your case?" asked Julie, who looked like she was hearing the same alarms.

"We'd rather that *you* bring the initial stories and holos of the Butterballs to the public," answered Cotter.

"That's very generous of you," she persisted. "But you still haven't told us why."

"We have our reasons," he said. "They will be made apparent to you before the tour is over."

My old friend Jake Monfried of the *SeattleDisk* sidled over to me. "I hope I can stay awake that long," he said sardonically. "It's all rubbish anyway."

"I know," I said. "Their rivals don't even need the damned holos. Any high school kid could take a hunk of Butterball steak and come up with a clone."

"So why haven't they?" asked Julie.

"Because MacDonald's got fifty lawyers on his payroll for every scientist," answered Jake. He paused, his expression troubled. "Still, this guy's lying to us—and it's a stupid lie, and he doesn't look *that* stupid. I wonder what the hell he's hiding?"

We were going to have to wait to find out, because Cotter began leading us across a rolling green plain toward a barn. We circled a couple of ponds, where a few dozen birds were wading and drinking. The whole setting looked like something out of a Norman Rockwell or a Grandma Moses painting, it was so wholesome and innocent—and yet every instinct I had screamed at me that something was wrong here, that nothing could be as peaceful and tranquil as it appeared.

"To appreciate what Mr. MacDonald has done here," said Cotter as we walked toward a large barn on a hillside, "you have to understand the challenge he faced. More than five billion men, women and children have serious protein deficiencies. Three billion of them are quite literally starving to death. And of course the price of meat—*any* meat—had skyrocketed to the point where only the very wealthy could afford it. So what he had to do was not only create an animal as totally, completely nutritious as the Butterball, he had to also create one that could mature and breed fast enough to meet mankind's needs now and in the future."

He stopped until a couple of laggards caught up with the group. "His initial work took the form of computer simulations. Then he hired a bevy of scientists and technicians who, guided by his genius, actually manipulated DNA to the point where the Butterballs existed not just on the screen and in Mr. MacDonald's mind, but in the flesh.

"It took a few generations for them to breed true, but fortunately a Butterball generation is considerably less than a year. Mr. MacDonald then had his staff spend some years mass-producing Butterballs. They were designed to have multiple births, not single offspring, and average ten to twelve per litter—and all of our specimens were bred and bred again so that when we finally introduced the Butterball to the world two years ago, we felt confident that we could keep up with the demand without running out of Butterballs."

"How many Butterballs have you got here?" asked the guy from *Eurocom International*, looking out across the rolling pastures and empty fields.

"We have more than two million at this facility," came the answer. "Mr. MacDonald owns some twenty-seven farms here and in Australia, each as large or larger than this one, and each devoted to the breeding of Butterballs. Every farm has its own processing plant. We're proud to note that while we have supplied food for billions, we've also created jobs for more than eighty thousand men and women." He paused to make sure we had recorded that number or were jotting it down.

"That many?" mused Julie.

"I know it seems like we sneaked up on the world," said Cotter with a smile. "But for legal reasons we were compelled to keep the very existence of the Butterballs secret until we were ready to market them—and once we *did* go public, we were processing, shipping, and selling hundreds of tons from each farm every month right from the start. We had to have all our people in place to do that."

"If they give him the Nobel, he can afford to turn the money down," Jake said wryly.

"I believe Mr. MacDonald is prepared to donate the money to charity should that happy event come to pass," responded Cotter. He turned and began walking toward the barn, then stopped about eighty feet from of it.

"I must prepare you for what you're going to—"

"We've already seen the holos," interrupted the French reporter.

Cotter stared at him for a moment, then began again. "As I was saying, I must prepare you for what you're going to *hear.*"

"Hear?" I repeated, puzzled.

"It was a fluke," he explained, trying to look unconcerned and not quite pulling it off. "An accident. An anomaly. But the fact of the matter is that the Butterballs can articulate a few words, just as a parrot can. We could have eliminated that ability, of course, but that would have taken more experimentation and more time, and the world's hungry masses couldn't wait."

"So what do they say?" asked Julie.

Cotter smiled what I'm sure he thought was a comforting smile. "They simply repeat what they hear. There's no intelligence behind it. None of them has a vocabulary of more than a dozen words. Mostly they articulate their most basic needs."

He turned to the barn and nodded to a man who stood by the door. The man pushed a button, and the door slid back.

The first big surprise was the total silence that greeted us from within the barn. Then, as they heard us approaching—we weren't speaking, but coins jingle and feet scuff the ground—a voice, then a hundred, then a thousand, began calling out:

"Feed me!"

It was a cacophony of sound, not quite human, the words repeated again and again and again: *"Feed me!"*

We entered the barn, and finally got our first glimpse of the Butterballs. Just as in their holos, they were huge and roly-poly, almost laughably cute, looking more like oversized bright pink balloons than anything else. They had four tiny feet, good for balance but barely capable of locomotion. There were no necks to speak of, just a small pink balloon that swiveled atop the larger one. They had large round eyes with wide pupils, ears the size of small coins, two slits for nostrils, and generous mouths without any visible teeth.

"The eyes are the only part of the Butterball that aren't marketable," said Cotter, "and that is really for esthetic reasons. I'm told they are quite edible."

The nearest one walked to the edge of its stall.

"*Pet me!*" it squeaked.

Cotter reached in and rubbed its forehead, and it squealed in delight.

"I'll give you a few minutes to wander around the barn, and then I'll meet you outside, where I'll answer your questions."

He had a point. With a couple of thousand Butterballs screaming "*Feed me!*" more and more frantically, it was almost impossible to think in there. We went up and down the rows of small stalls, captured the place on film and tape and disk and cube, then went back outside.

"That was impressive," I admitted when we'd all gathered around Cotter again. "But I didn't see any two million Butterballs in there. Where are the rest of them?"

"There are more than three hundred barns and other enclosures on the farm," answered Cotter. "Furthermore, close to half a million are outside in pastures."

"I don't see anything but empty fields," remarked Jake, waving a hand toward the pristine enclosures.

"We're a huge farm, and we prefer to keep the Butterballs away from prying eyes. In fact, this barn was built only a month ago, when we finally decided to allow visitors on the premises. It is the only building that's as close as a mile to any of our boundary lines."

"You said that some of them were in pastures," said Julie. "What do they eat?"

"Not grass," answered Cotter. "They're only outside because they're multiplying so fast that we're actually short of barns at the moment." He paused. "If you looked carefully at them, you noticed that grazing is quite beyond their capabilities." He held up a small golden pellet for us to see. "This is what they eat. It is totally artificial, created entirely from chemicals. Mr. MacDonald was adamant that no Butterball should ever eat any product that might nourish a human being. Their digestive systems were engineered to utilize this particular feed, which can provide nourishment to no other species on Earth."

"As long as you tinkered with their digestive systems, why didn't you make them shit-eaters?" asked Jake, only half-jokingly. "They could have served two purposes at once."

"I assume that was meant in jest," said Cotter, "but in point of fact, Mr. MacDonald considered it at one time. After all, some nourishment *does* remain in excrement—but alas, not enough. He wanted an animal that could utilize one hundred percent of what we fed it."

"How smart are they?" asked one of the Brits. "When I was a child, I had a dog that always wanted me to feed it or pet it, but it never told me so."

"Yes it did," said Cotter. "It just didn't use words."

"Point taken," said the Brit. "But I'd still like to know...."

"These are dumb farm animals," said Cotter. "They do not think, they do not dream, they have no hopes or aspirations, they do not wish to become Archbishop. They just happen to be able to articulate a few words, not unlike many birds. Surely you don't think Mr. MacDonald would create a sentient meat animal."

"No, of course not," interjected Julie. "But hearing them speak is still a bit of a shock."

"I know," said Cotter. "And that's the *real* reason we've invited you here, why we're inviting so many other press pools—to prepare the public."

OLD MACDONALD HAD A FARM   207

"That's going to take a lot of preparation," I said dubiously.

"We have to start somewhere," said Cotter. "We have to let the people know about this particular anomaly. Men love to anthropomorphize, and a talking animal makes doing so that much easier. The consumers must be made to understand, beyond any shadow of a doubt, that these are unintelligent meat animals, that they do not know what their words mean, that they have no names and aren't pets, that they do not mourn the loss of their neighbors any more than a cow or a goat does. They are humanity's last chance—note that I did not even say humanity's last *best* chance—and we cannot let the protestors and picketers we know will demonstrate against us go unanswered. No one will believe *our* answers, but they should believe the answers of the unbiased world press."

"Yeah," I said under my breath to Jake. "And if kids didn't want to eat Bambi, or Henry the Turkey, or Penelope Pig, how is anyone going to make them dig into Talky the Butterball, who actually exists?"

"I heard that," said Cotter sharply, "and I must point out that the children who will survive because of the Butterballs will almost certainly never have been exposed to Bambi or Henry or any of the others."

"Maybe not for a year or two," I replied, unimpressed. "But before long you'll be selling Butterburgers on every street corner in the States."

"Not until we've fulfilled our mission among the less fortunate peoples of the world—and by that time the people you refer to should be prepared to accept the Butterballs."

"Well, you can hope," I said.

"If it never comes to that, it doesn't really matter," said Cotter with an elaborate shrug. "Our mission is to feed Earth's undernourished billions."

We both knew it would come to that, and sooner than anyone planned, but if he didn't want to argue it, that was fine with me. I was just here to collect a story.

"Before I show you the processing plant, are there any further questions?" asked Cotter.

"You mean the slaughterhouse, right?" said Jake.

"I mean the processing plant," said Cotter severely. "Certain words are not in our lexicon."

"You're actually going to show us Butterballs being... *processed*?" asked Julie distastefully.

"Certainly not," answered Cotter. "I'm just going to show you the plant. The process is painless and efficient, but I see no value in your being able to report that you watched our animals being prepared for market."

"Good!" said Julie with obvious relief.

Cotter gestured to an open bus that was parked a few hundred meters away, and it soon pulled up. After everybody was seated, he climbed on and stood next to the driver, facing us.

"The plant is about five miles away, at almost the exact center of the farm, insulated from curious eyes and ears."

"*Ears?*" Julie jumped on the word. "Do they scream?"

Cotter smiled. "No, that was just an expression. We are quite humane, far more so than any meat packing plant that existed before us."

The bus hit a couple of bumps that almost sent him flying, but he hung on like a trooper and continued bombarding us with information, about three-quarters of it too technical or too self-serving to be of any use.

"Here we are," he announced as the bus came to a stop in front of the processing plant, which dwarfed the barn we had just left. "Everyone out, please."

We got off the bus. I sniffed the air for the odor of fresh blood, not that I knew what it smelled like, but of course I couldn't detect any. No blood, no rotting flesh, nothing but clean, fresh air. I was almost disappointed.

There were a number of small pens nearby, each holding perhaps a dozen Butterballs.

"You have perhaps noticed that we have no vehicles capable of moving the hundreds and thousands of units we have to process each day?" asked Cotter, though it came out more as a statement than a question.

"I assume they are elsewhere," said the lady from India.

"They were inefficient," replied Cotter. "We got rid of them."

"Then how do you move the Butterballs?"

Cotter smiled. "Why clutter all our roads with vehicles when they aren't necessary?" he said, tapping out a design on his pocket computer. The main door to the processing plant slid open, and I noticed that the Butterballs were literally jumping up and down with excitement.

Cotter walked over to the nearest pen. "Who wants to go to heaven?" he asked.

"*Go to heaven!*" squeaked a Butterball.

"*Go to heaven!*" rasped another.

Soon all twelve were repeating it almost as if it were a chant, and I suddenly felt like I was trapped inside some strange surrealistic play.

Finally Cotter unlocked their pen and they hopped—I hadn't seen any locomote at the other barn—up to the door and into the plant.

"It's as simple as that," said Cotter. "The money we save on vehicles, fuel and maintenance allows us to—"

"There's nothing simple about it!" snapped Julie. "This is somewhere between blasphemy and obscenity! And while we're at it," she added suspiciously, "how can a dumb animal possibly know what heaven is?"

"I repeat, they are not sentient," said Cotter. "Just as you have code words for your pet dog or cat, we have them for the Butterballs. Ask your dog if he wants a treat, and he'll bark or sit up or do whatever you have conditioned him to do. We have conditioned the Butterballs in precisely the same way. They don't know the meaning of the word 'heaven' any more than your pet knows the meaning of the word 'treat,' but we've conditioned them to associate the word with good feelings and with entry into the processing plant. They will happily march miles through a driving rain to 'go to heaven.'"

"But heaven is such a... a *philosophical* concept," persisted the Indian woman. "Even to use it seems—"

"Your dog knows when he's been good," interrupted Cotter, "because you tell him so, and he believes you implicitly. And he knows when he's been bad, because you show him what he's done to displease you and you call him a bad dog. But do you think he understands the abstract philosophical concepts of good and bad?"

"All right," said Julie. "You've made your point. But if you don't mind, I'd rather not see the inside of the slaughterhouse."

"The processing plant," he corrected her. "And of course, you don't have to enter it if it will make you uncomfortable."

"I'll stay out here too," I said. "I've seen enough killing down in Paraguay and Uruguay."

"We're not killing anything," explained Cotter irritably. "I am simply showing you—"

"I'll stay here anyway," I cut him off.

He shrugged. "As you wish."

"If you have no vehicles to bring them to the plant," asked the Brit, approaching the entrance, "how do you move the... uh, the finished product out?"

"Through a very efficient system of underground conveyers," said Cotter. "The meat is stored in subterranean freezers near the perimeter of the property until it is shipped. And now...." He opened a second pen, offered them heaven, and got pretty much the same response.

Poor bastards, I thought as I watched them hop and waddle to the door of the plant. *In times gone by, sheep would be enticed into the slaughterhouse by a trained ram that they blindly followed. But leave it to us to come up with an even better reward for happily walking up to the butcher block: heaven itself.*

The Butterballs followed the first dozen into the belly of the building, and the rest of the pool followed Cotter in much the same way. There was a parallel to be drawn there, but I wasn't interested enough to draw it.

I saw Julie walking toward one of the pens. She looked like

she didn't want any company, so I headed off for a pen in the opposite direction. When I got there, four or five of the Butterballs pressed up against the fence next to me.

"*Feed me!*"

"*Feed me!*"

"*Pet me!*"

"*Feed me!*"

Since I didn't have any food, I settled for petting the one who was more interested in being petted than being fed.

"Feel good?" I asked idly.

"*Feel good!*" it said.

I almost did a double-take at that.

"You're a hell of a mimic, you know that?" I said.

No reply.

"Can you say what I say?" I asked.

Silence.

"Then how the hell did you learn to say it feels good, if you didn't learn it just now from me?"

"*Pet me!*"

"Okay, okay," I said, scratching it behind a tiny ear.

"*Very good!*"

I pulled my hand back as if I'd had an electric shock. "I never said the word 'very.' Where did you learn it?" *And more to the point, how did you learn to partner it with 'good?'*

Silence.

For the next ten minutes, I tried to get it to say something different. I wasn't sure what I was reaching for, but the best I got was a "*Pet me!*" and a pair of "*Good!*"

"All right," I said at last. "I give up. Go play with your friends, and don't go to heaven too soon."

"*Go to heaven!*" it said, hopping up and down. "*Go to heaven!*"

"Don't get so excited," I said. "It's not what it's cracked up to be."

"*See Mama!*" it squealed.

"What?"

"*See God! See Mama!*"

Suddenly I knew why MacDonald was being treated for depression. I didn't blame him at all.

I hurried back to the slaughterhouse, and when Cotter emerged alone a moment later, I walked up to him.

"We have to talk," I said, grabbing him by the arm.

"Your colleagues are all inside inspecting the premises," he said, trying to pull himself loose from my grip. "Are you sure you wouldn't care to join them?"

"Shut up and listen to me!" I said. "I just had a talk with one of your Butterballs."

"He told you to feed him?"

"He told me that he would see God when he went to heaven."

Cotter swallowed hard. "Oh, shit—another one!"

"Another one of *what*?" I demanded. "Another sentient one?"

"No, of course not," said Cotter. "But as often as we impress the need for absolute silence among our staff, they continue to speak to each other in front of the Butterballs, or even to the Butterballs themselves. Obviously this one heard someone saying that God lives in heaven. It has no concept of God, of course; it probably thinks God is something good to eat."

"He thinks he's going to see his mother, too," I said.

"He's a *mimic*!" said Cotter severely. "Surely you don't think he can have any memory of his mother? For Christ's sake, he was weaned at five weeks!"

"I'm just telling you what he said," I replied. "Like it or not, you've got a hell of a P.R. problem: Just how many people do you want him saying it to?"

"Point him out to me," said Cotter, looking panicky. "We'll process him at once."

"You think he's the only one with a vocabulary?" I asked.

"One of the very few, I'm sure," said Cotter.

"Don't be *that* sure," said Julie, who had joined us while I was talking to Cotter. She had an odd expression on her face, like someone who's just undergone a religious experience and wishes she hadn't. "Mine looked at me with those soft brown eyes and asked me, very gently and very shyly, not to eat it."

I thought Cotter would shit in his expensive suit. "That's impossible!"

"The hell it is," she shot back.

"They are *not* sentient," he said stubbornly. "They are *mimics*. They do not think. They do not know what they are saying." He stared at her. "Are you sure he didn't say '*feed*?' It sounds a lot like '*eat*.' You've got to be mistaken."

It made sense. I hoped he was right.

"'Don't feed me?'" repeated Julie. "The only un-hungry Butterball on the farm?"

"Some of them speak better than others. He could have been clearing his throat, or trying to say something that came out wrong. I've even come across one that stutters." It occurred to me that Cotter was trying as hard to convince himself as he was to convince her. "We've tested them a hundred different ways. They're not sentient. They're *not*!"

"But—"

"Consider the facts," said Cotter. "I've explained that the words sound alike. I've explained that the Butterballs are not all equally skilled at articulation. I've explained that after endless lab experiments, the top animal behavioral scientists in the world have concluded that they are not sentient. All that is on one side. On the other is that you *think* you may have heard something that is so impossible that any other explanation makes more sense."

"I don't know," she hedged. "It sounded exactly like...."

"I'm sure it did," said Cotter soothingly. "You were simply mistaken."

"No one else has ever heard anything like that?" she asked.

"No one. But if you'd like to point out which of them said it...."

She turned toward the pen. "They all look alike."

I tagged along as the two of them walked over to the Butterballs. We spent about five minutes there, but none of them said anything but "*Feed me!*" and "*Pet me!*"; and finally Julie sighed in resignation.

"All right," she said wearily. "Maybe I was wrong."

"What do you think, Mr. McNair?" asked Cotter.

My first thought was: what the hell are you asking *me* for? Then I looked into his eyes, which were almost laying out the terms of our agreement, and I knew.

"Now that I've had a few minutes to think about it, I guess we were mistaken," I said. "Your scientists know a lot more about it than we do."

I turned to see Julie's reaction.

"Yeah," she said at last. "I suppose so." She looked at the Butterballs. "Besides, MacDonald may be a zillionaire and a recluse, but I don't think he's a monster, and only a monster could do something like... well... yes, I must have been mistaken."

And that's the story. We were not only the first pool of journalists to visit the farm. We were also the last.

The others didn't know what had happened, and of course Cotter wasn't about to tell them. They reported what they saw, told the world that its prayers were answered, and only three of them even mentioned the Butterballs' special talent.

I thought about the Butterballs all during the long flight home. Every expert said they weren't sentient, that they were just mimics. And I suppose my Butterball could very well have heard someone say that God lived in heaven, just as he could have heard someone use the word "very." It was a stretch, but I could buy it if I had to.

But where did Julie Balch's Butterball ever hear a man begging not to be eaten? I've been trying to come up with an answer to that since I left the farm. I haven't got one yet—but I *do* have a syndicated column, courtesy of the conglomerate that owns the publishing company.

So am I going to use it to tell the world?

That's my other problem: Tell it what? That three billion kids can go back to starving to death? Because whether Cotter was telling the truth or lying through his teeth, if it comes down to a choice between Butterballs and humans, I know which side I have to come down on.

OLD MACDONALD HAD A FARM

There are things I can control and things I can't, things I know and things I am trying my damnedest not to know. I'm just one man, and I'm not responsible for saving the world.

But I am responsible for me—and from the day I left the farm, I've been a vegetarian. It's a small step, but you've got to start somewhere.

Mike with a black rhino on the slopes of Kirinyaga in Kenya. From the personal photo collection of Mike Resnick.

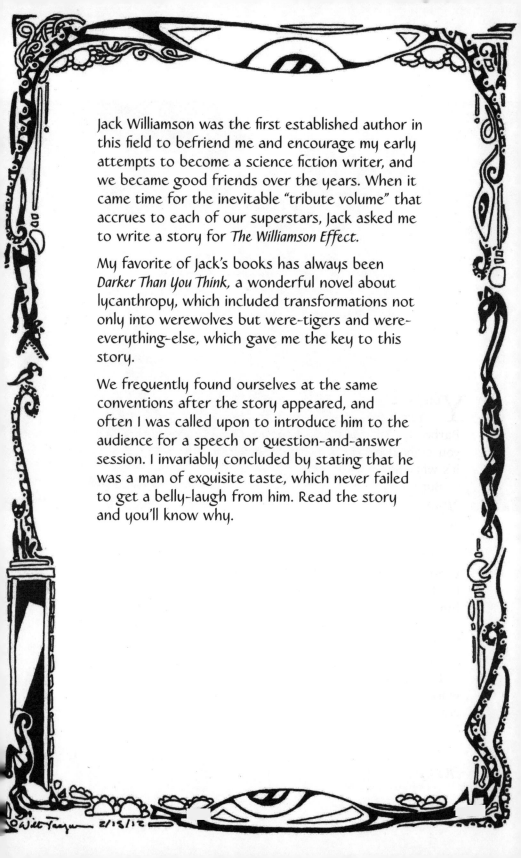

Jack Williamson was the first established author in this field to befriend me and encourage my early attempts to become a science fiction writer, and we became good friends over the years. When it came time for the inevitable "tribute volume" that accrues to each of our superstars, Jack asked me to write a story for *The Williamson Effect*.

My favorite of Jack's books has always been *Darker Than You Think*, a wonderful novel about lycanthropy, which included transformations not only into werewolves but were-tigers and were-everything-else, which gave me the key to this story.

We frequently found ourselves at the same conventions after the story appeared, and often I was called upon to introduce him to the audience for a speech or question-and-answer session. I invariably concluded by stating that he was a man of exquisite taste, which never failed to get a belly-laugh from him. Read the story and you'll know why.

Darker Than You Wrote

You lied, Jack.

Yeah, I know, you had to change his name to Will Barbee for legal reasons. I have no problem with that. And you embellished a little here and a little there. That's okay; it's what novelists do.

But you know what they say about Karen Blixen's *Out of Africa*—that every single sentence is true, but the book, taken as a whole, is a lie?

Same thing with *Darker Than You Think*.

You took Jacob Bratzinger—I'm sorry: Will Barbee; whoever heard of a protagonist called Bratzinger?—and romanticized the hell out of him. Made him some kind of hero. Even gave him a happy ending. You did all that just to make a sale.

Well, let me state just for the record that he wasn't romantic, and he was no hero, and, above all, he didn't end happily.

I know. I was there.

I'm sure shrinks hear a lot of strange stories during their working hours. So do fantasy editors and Hollywood producers, and any tourist who ever tries to walk past a beggar in a Third World city. But let me tell you, *nobody* hears as much out-and-out unbelievable bullshit as your friendly neighborhood bartender.

That's me.

I remember that Jake used to come around in the afternoons. A lonely drinker. Never had anyone with him, never tried to make friends with anyone once he got here. Stayed down at the far end of the bar and minded his own business. Always had an expression on his face that made you hope he was drinking to forget and that he'd succeed, because it looked like what he was remembering was pretty grim stuff.

He always left before sundown. Made no difference to me: I figured he worked a night shift. But then he started coming in all torn up, like he spent his nights prizefighting. Except that he wasn't black-and-blue, the way you'd expect him to be after a fight. No, sir, he was all ripped up, just like I said. He healed pretty fast, didn't bother going to the doctor except for some of the more serious wounds, never complained about the pain.

Since he usually showed up around two or maybe two-thirty, and he left before six, he and I spent a lot of time together with nobody else around, and finally, after maybe half a year, he loosened up and started telling me his story. I didn't believe it at first, but what the hell, it helped pass the time, so I dummied up and listened to him.

I gather that he was telling it to you at pretty much the same time, maybe in the mornings, and he kept waiting for your book to come out. He was sure some scientist would read about him and do something to cure him, though in retrospect I don't know what they could have done.

But then you crossed him up, Jack. You changed his name and gave him a girlfriend and passed it off as science fiction. You'll never know how close he came to killing you when *Darker Than You Think* came out.

Only one thing stopped him, and that was that he was sick of killing. You know, if he'd been a werewolf, if lycanthropy was all there was to it, if the old legends were right, I think he could have adjusted, I really do.

But you know that wasn't true, and you even told your readers. Jake didn't turn into a wolf. Not him. He was a tiger one day, and a roc—you called him a pterosaur—the next. He knew a girl—he wasn't involved with her, he just happened to share a hunting ground—named June (you called her April, remember?) who became a she-wolf at nights. And then there was Ben Sacks—you wrote him out of the book completely—who was a puma.

And even knowing all that, knowing that the flesh-eaters weren't confined to one kind of body, that they weren't all wolves or vampire bats or any of the other creatures out of legend, you still didn't see it, you never drew the connection.

But Jake learned it early on, and so did all of the others. He didn't shrivel in the sunlight like some bad Dracula movie, you know. He didn't instantly turn back into a man, either. It was a slow process, a gradual transformation, that took maybe ten or twelve minutes.

And during that time, he learned the awful, hideous truth, not about himself but about his world. *Our* world. For just as followers outnumber leaders and prey outnumber predators, so did those humans who turned into sheep and goats and cattle far outnumber Jake and his kind. It was presumptuous of him—and you—to think that only a handful of men and women underwent the Change at nights, or that those who changed all became nocturnal hunters.

Jake would make his kills, clean and swift, in the dead of night. He'd drag the carcasses to places of safety, where competing carnivores couldn't see or scent them. And then he'd dine on them, as he was meant to dine: tearing at their flesh, lapping up their blood, swallowing huge mouthfuls of meat. It was perfectly natural.

Until morning came, and the Change began, and it afflicted both predator and prey, and he'd find himself crouching over a half-eaten child, or a partially-consumed woman, and he realized how true was the old saying that you are what you eat, and he was once again a man.

He hated himself for it. His only hope was your book, and then you turned it into a novel, and after that he didn't have any hope at all. He started drinking more heavily, and the haunted look in his eyes grew worse and worse.

It only took another two weeks before he put a gun to his head, right there in the bar, and blew his brains out. Yeah, I know you hadn't heard, Jack; he asked me not to tell you.

That was, let me see, damned near half a century ago. Of course, I don't age the way normal men do. No reason why I should; I'm no more normal than Jake was. The Change just hit me a little later, that's all.

His very last wish was that I avenge him. It took me a long time to figure out what he meant. I mean, hell, he killed himself, so I could hardly take my vengeance out on him. And while it's true that the world made him what he was, I wouldn't begin to know how to destroy the world. So I thought about it, and thought about it, and finally I decided that he meant I should pay you a visit, Jack. He counted on that book of yours, and you let him down. I finally sold my business and retired last month, so now I'm ready to do what has to be done.

They tell me you're a pretty smart fellow, and that you're still working well into your eighties. That's good; I admire brains and industry. I figure you're probably a raccoon, or maybe a badger.

Me, I'm a wolverine. And unlike Jake Bratzinger, I don't have a problem with guilt at all. I *like* meat.

See you soon, Jack.

A cute lil' kitty cat on the Serengeti Plains, Tanzania. From the personal photo collection of Mike Resnick.

Tamora Pierce and Josepha Sherman invited me to write a fantasy story for their anthology, *Young Warriors*. I figured that everyone else would do teenagers with swords, but since no one had actually defined "young," I'd do something a little different. And since it was a fantasy, why not go all the way and examine the problems not only of an unpopular under-age dragon slayer but an unpopular under-age dragon as well?

The Boy Who Cried "Dragon!"

You've all heard the story about the boy who cried "Wolf!" Teachers and parents have been using it to teach children a lesson for centuries now. It's become a part of our culture. *Everybody* knows about the boy who cried "Wolf," just as they know about the three blind mice and the little Dutch boy who put his finger in the dike and the day Michael Jordan scored 63 points in a playoff game.

But would you like to know the *real* story?

It began a long, long time ago, in a mythical land to the north and west which, for a lack of a better term, we shall call The Mythical Land To The North And West.

Now, this Land was the home of exceptionally brave warriors and beautiful damsels (and occasionally they were the same person, since beautiful damsels were pretty assertive back then). Each young boy and girl was taught all the arts of warfare and was soon adept with sword, mace, lance, bow and arrow, dagger, and the off-putting snide remark. They were schooled in horsemanship, camouflage, and military strategy. They learned eye-gouging, ear-biting, kidney-punching, and—since they were destined to become knights and ladies—gentility.

So successful was their training that before long enemy armies were afraid to attack them. Within the borders of the Land justice was so swift that there was not a single criminal left. It would have been a very peaceful and idyllic kingdom indeed—except for the dragons.

You see, the Land was surrounded by hundreds of huge, red-eyed, razor-toothed, fire-breathing dragons, covered with thick scaly skin and armed with vicious-looking claws, and just as fifty years ago a Maasai warrior became a man by slaying a lion with his spear, and today you are hailed as an adult when you can break through Microsoft's firewall, back in the days we are talking about, a boy or girl would be recognized as a young man or woman only after slaying a dragon.

Okay, you've got enough background now, so it's time to introduce Sir Meldrake of the Shining Armor. Well, that's the way he envisioned himself, and that's the name he planned to take once he had slain a dragon and found someone who could actually make a suit of shining armor, but for the moment he was just plain Melvin, tall, gangly, a little underweight, shy around damsels, more worried about pimples than mortal wounds received in glorious battle. His number had come up in the draft, and it was his turn to sally forth and slay a dragon.

He climbed into his older brother's hand-me-down armor, took out the garbage, kissed his mother good-bye (but only after he made sure none of his friends were watching and snickering), climbed aboard the family horse, and armed with lance, sword, mace, and a desire to show Mary Lu Penworthy that he was everything she said he wasn't, he set off to slay a dragon, bring back both ears and the tail (or whatever it was one brought back to prove he had been victorious), and become a knight rather than a skinny teen-aged boy who couldn't get a date for the prom.

Soon the city was far behind him, and before long he had crossed the border of the Land itself and was now in unknown territory. He hummed a little song of battle to keep his spirits up, but he was tone-deaf and his humming annoyed his horse, so finally he fell silent, scanning the harsh, rocky landscape for dragons. He found himself wishing he had paid a little more attention in biology class, so he would know what dragons ate when they weren't eating people, and where they slept (if indeed they slept at all), and especially what kind of terrain they liked to hide in when preparing to ambush young men who suddenly wished they were back home in bed looking at naughty illuminated manuscripts beneath the covers.

At night, he found a cozy cave and, lighting a fire to keep warm and ward off anything that might want to annoy him—like, for example, a pride of dragons (or did they come in flocks, or perhaps gaggles?)—he sang himself to sleep, which kept his spirits up but almost drove his horse to distraction.

When morning came, he peeked out of the cave, just to be certain that nothing lay in wait for him. Then he peeked again, to be doubly certain. Then he thought about Mary Lu Penworthy and decided the mole on her chin that had seemed charming only two days ago was really rather ugly in the cold light of day and hardly worth slaying a dragon for. The same could be said for her eyes (not blue enough), her lips (not rosy red enough), and her nose (which seemed to exist solely to keep her eyes from bumping into each other).

One by one he considered every young lady of his acquaintance. This one was too tall, that one too short, this one too loud, that one too quiet, and to his surprise, he decided that none of them were really worth risking his life in mortal combat with a dragon. In fact, the more he thought about it, the more he couldn't come up with a single reason to seek out a dragon. It was a silly custom, and when he returned to the Land, which he planned to do the moment his horse calmed down and stopped looking at him as if he might burst into song again, he would seek out the Council of Elders and suggest that in the future the rite of passage to adulthood should consist of slaying a chipmunk. They were certainly more numerous, and what purpose was served by slaying a dragon anyway?

His mind made up, Melvin climbed atop his steed and turned him for home—and found his way barred by a huge dragon, twenty feet high at the shoulder, with little beady eyes, thin streams of smoke flowing out of his nostrils, claws the size of butcher knives, and a serious case of halitosis.

"Why have you come to my kingdom?" demanded the dragon.

"I didn't know dragons could talk," said Melvin, surprised.

"I don't mean to be impertinent," said the dragon, "but I could probably fill a very thick book with what you don't know about dragons."

"Yes, I suppose you could," admitted Melvin. He didn't quite know what to say next, so he finally blurted: "By the way, my name is Sir Meldrake of the Shining Armor."

"Are you quite sure?" asked the dragon. "No offense, but you look rather rusty to me."

"My own armor's in the shop getting dry-cleaned," said Melvin, starting to feel rather silly.

"Oh. Well, that explains it," said the dragon charitably. "And since we're doing introductions, my name is Horace. Spelled H-O-R-A-C-E, and not to be mistaken for Horus the Egyptian god."

"That's a strange name for a dragon," said Melvin.

"Just how many dragons do you know on a first-name basis?" asked Horace.

"Counting you, one," admitted Melvin. "Just out of curiosity, how many men have you encountered?"

"The downstate returns aren't all in yet, but so far, rounded off, it comes to one." Horace paused uneasily. "What do we do now?"

"I don't know," said Melvin. "I suppose we battle to the death."

"We do?" said the dragon, surprised. "Why?"

"Those are the ground rules. You meet a dragon, you slay him."

"That's the silliest thing I ever heard!" protested Horace. "I meet dragons all the time, and I've never slain one. In fact, I plan to marry one when I'm an adult, and sire twenty or thirty thousand little hatchlings."

"Had you someone in mind?" asked Melvin, interested in spite of himself.

"Nancy Jo Billingsworth," said the dragon with a sigh. "The most beautiful seventeen tons of wings and scales I've ever seen." He looked at Melvin. "How about you? Have you picked out your lady yet—always assuming you survive our battle to the death?"

"I'm playing the field at the moment," said Melvin.

"So you can't get a date either," said Horace knowingly.

"It's these darned zits," said Melvin, trying not to whine.

"Take off your helmet and let me get a good look at you," said Horace.

"You'll be disgusted," said Melvin. "Everyone is."

"Try me," said the dragon.

Melvin removed his helmet.

"God, I would *kill* for zits like those!" said Horace fervently.

"You would?" said Melvin. "Why?"

"Look at this hideous smooth skin on my face," said Horace, holding back a little whimper of self-loathing. "Let's be honest. Nancy Jo Billingsworth winces every time she looks at me. She'd die before she'd go out with me."

"I know exactly how you feel," said Melvin sympathetically.

"It's not just my face," said Horace, a tear rolling down his smooth green cheek. "It's *me*. Whenever we choose up sides for basketball, I'm always the last one picked. When it's Girls' Choice at the dance, I'm the only one who's never asked."

"They won't even let me in the locker room," Melvin chimed in. "They say I'm just wasting space. And the girls draw straws in the cafeteria, and the loser has to sit next to me."

Before long the young man and the young dragon were pouring out their hearts to each other, and because no one had ever listened before, they continued until twilight.

"Well, we might as well get on with it," said Horace when they had finished their litany of misery.

"Yeah, I suppose so," said Melvin unenthusiastically.

"I want you to know that if you win, I won't hold it against you," said the dragon. "No one will miss me anyway. I haven't got a friend in the world."

"That's not true," protested Melvin. "*I* like you."

Horace's homely green face lit up. "You do?"

Melvin nodded. "Yes, I do." He paused thoughtfully. "You know, I've never had a real friend before. It seems a shame that one of us has to kill the other."

"I know," said the dragon. "Still, rules are rules."

Suddenly Melvin stood up decisively. "Who says so?"

Horace looked around, confused. "I think I just did."

"Well, I'm going to break the rules. You're my only friend, and I'm not going to kill you."

"You're *my* only friend, and I'm not going to kill you either." Horace paused, as if considering what to do next. "Let's kill the horse. At least we'll have something to eat."

Melvin shook his head. "I need him to get home."

"I kind of thought we'd stay out here and be friends forever," said Horace in hurt tones.

"Oh, we'll be friends forever," promised Melvin. "And as my first act of friendship, I'm going to save your life."

"That's very thoughtful of you," said Horace. "But don't be so sure I wouldn't have killed you instead."

"I'm not talking about me," said Melvin. "But every week a new candidate is chosen to go forth and slay a dragon, and next week it's Spike Armstrong's turn."

"Who is Spike Armstrong?" asked Horace.

"He's everything I'm not," said Melvin bitterly. "He's the captain of every sports team, he's the most handsome boy in the Land, and even though he has the brains of a newt, all the cheerleaders fight to sit near him in the cafeteria."

"I dislike him already," said Horace.

"Anyway, if he finds you, he'll kill you," concluded Melvin.

"So you're going to fight him in my place?" asked Horace. "I call that exceptionally decent of you, Melvin. I'll always honor your memory and put flowers on your grave."

"No, I'm not going to fight him," replied Melvin. "I wouldn't fare any better against him than you would. But any time I know he's sallying forth in your direction, I'll go to the far side of the city and tell everybody that a dragon is approaching, and Spike will immediately head off in that direction and you'll be safe."

"That's a splendid idea!" enthused Horace. "And whenever Thunderfire goes out hunting for a man to eat, I'll do the same thing to him."

"Thunderfire?" repeated Melvin.

Horace grimaced. "Females swoon over him. He's got lumps the size of baseballs all over his face, and his flame shoots out ten feet, and he just struts around like he owns the place. But I'll see to it that he never finds you."

"You know," said Melvin, "I *like* having a friend."

"Me too," said Horace. "My mother says one should always seek out new experiences."

Their ruses worked. Spike Armstrong never did slay Horace, and Thunderfire never did eat Melvin. As for Melvin and Horace, they continued to sneak away and meet every Saturday afternoon except when it was raining, and although neither of them ever did become king or marry the damsel of their dreams, they each had a friend they could trust and confide in, which in many ways is better than being a king or marrying a dream.

And that is the story of the boy who cried "Dragon!"

Of course, when dragons sit around the campfire at night, or tuck their children into bed, they tell the story of the dragon who cried "Boy!"

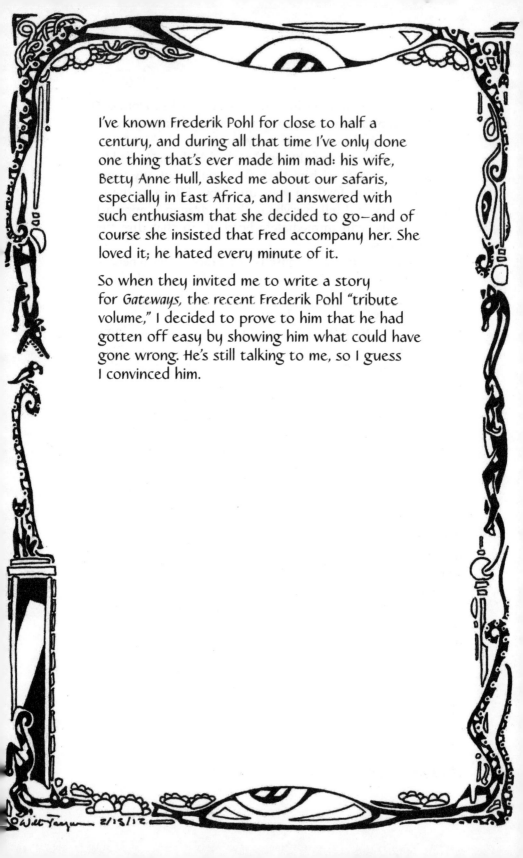

I've known Frederik Pohl for close to half a century, and during all that time I've only done one thing that's ever made him mad: his wife, Betty Anne Hull, asked me about our safaris, especially in East Africa, and I answered with such enthusiasm that she decided to go—and of course she insisted that Fred accompany her. She loved it; he hated every minute of it.

So when they invited me to write a story for *Gateways*, the recent Frederik Pohl "tribute volume," I decided to prove to him that he had gotten off easy by showing him what could have gone wrong. He's still talking to me, so I guess I convinced him.

On Safari

It was a sunny summer day on Selous, as it always was. The sky was a perfect blue, the grass was green, and you could smell excitement in the air.

"Just think," said Anthony Tarica, as he and his companion stepped through the hatch of the ship and began walking down the ramp to the ground. "We might have won a negatronic washer and dryer instead."

"Poor Roberts," agreed Linwood Donahue, following him down the ramp. "If he'd sold just three more units, he'd have replaced one of us here." He snickered. "I hope the poor sonuvabitch has a lot of laundry."

"I can't believe we're really here!" enthused Tarica. "All my life I've wanted to go on a real safari."

"I wonder how they could afford it," said Donahue. "I mean, a safari has to cost a lot more than a washer and dryer."

"Why worry about it?" said Tarica, taking a deep breath and scenting adventure. "We're here for the next five days, and that's all that matters."

They cleared Customs and walked out of the tiny spaceport. They looked around, but there were no people in sight, just a few parked vehicles.

"That's funny," said Tarica. "I'd have thought there'd be someone from the safari company here to meet us."

"Yeah," said Donahue. "What do we do now?"

"If you gentlemen will step this way," said a cultured masculine voice, "I will attend to all your needs."

Tarica looked around. "Who said that?"

"I did."

Tarica and Donahue exchanged looks. "Am I going crazy, or did that safari vehicle just speak to us?" asked Donahue.

"I most certainly did," said the vehicle.

"I never saw a talking car before," said Tarica. "Oh, back home mine reminds me to fasten my seat belt and take the keys out of the ignition and not to try to beat the yellow light, and it castigates me when I go over the speed limit, but I've never actually had a conversation with one."

"I am Quatermain, your fully-equipped safari car and guide, trained in every aspect of safaris and safari life. I have an encyclopedic knowledge of the flora and fauna of Selous, I know every watering hole, every secret trail, every hidden hazard. I come equipped with a mini-kitchen in my trunk, an auxiliary trunk for your luggage, and a supply of water that will last for the duration of your safari. Furthermore, I am capable of erecting your rustic tent at day's end, and of protecting your safety at all times. I run on a small plutonium chip, and will not run out of energy for another 27.348 Earth years." One of the trunks popped open. "If you gentlemen will please deposit your luggage in here, we can begin our exotic adventure."

"Right now?" asked Tarica, surprised.

"Have you a problem with that?" responded Quatermain.

"No," said Tarica hastily. "I just expected that we'd spend a day unwinding in some luxury lodge before we set out on the actual safari."

"Luxury lodges are incompatible with safari experience," replied Quatermain. "If you gentlemen will climb into my back seat, we can be off on the adventure of a lifetime."

"Do you do this every day?" asked Donahue, as he joined Tarica on the back seat and the door automatically shut and locked.

"Yes, sir," responded the car. "This is old hat to me, but each excursion is still thrilling, because each is unique."

"Have you ever lost a client?"

"No, sir," said Quatermain. "I always know right where they are."

Tarica pulled out a cigar. "Well, I can't tell you how much I'm looking forward to this."

"I'd prefer that you didn't smoke, sir."

"But you've got an ashtray built into the arm rest here, and I assure you my friend here doesn't object."

"It's bad for your health, sir."

"I've been smoking for thirty-five years," said Tarica, "and I'm in perfect health."

There was a brief humming sound.

"I have just given you a Level 3 scan, sir," said Quatermain, "and you have incipient emphysema, an eight percent blockage of the arteries leading to your heart, adult onset diabetes, and an undefined gum disease. You really must take better care of yourself, sir."

"I feel fine," said Tarica.

"I could give you a print-out of the scan, sir."

"All right, I'll take better care of myself."

"You could begin by not lighting that cigar, sir," said Quatermain. "I notice you're still holding it."

"Aren't you supposed to be looking for animals?" complained Tarica.

"I can see in every direction at once, sir."

Tarica sighed and put the cigar back in his pocket.

"I'm sure you'll be much happier for doing that, sir."

"You have two more guesses," growled Tarica.

They rode in silence for a few minutes. Then Donahue asked Quatermain how to open the windows.

"Why bother, sir?" replied the car. "I am equipped with the most modern climate control system. You name the conditions and I will accommodate you."

"But I'd like to feel the wind in my face," said Donahue.

Suddenly a blast of cold air hit his face.

"Simulated wind at 32 miles per hour, 82 degrees Fahrenheit, 7% humidity," announced Quatermain. "Would you like any adjustment, sir?"

"I'd just like some fresh air," complained Donahue.

"All right," said Quatermain. "Just let me slow down first."

"Why?"

"Even a small insect could damage your eye at the speed I was going," answered Quatermain. "It will take us an extra hour to reach the closest of the great herds, but your comfort is more important than an extra hour of daylight."

"All right, forget it," said Donahue. "Close the windows and get back up to speed."

"You're sure?" asked the car.

"I'm sure."

"You're not just doing it to make me feel better?"

"Just speed up, goddamit!"

They drove for twenty minutes in absolute silence. Then Quatermain slowed down to a crawl. "Bluebucks at nine o'clock," it announced.

"It's three-thirty," said Tarica. "Do you expect to wait five and a half hours for them to show up?"

"Nine o'clock means to your left, sir," explained Quatermain. "Three o'clock is to your right, twelve o'clock is straight ahead, and six o'clock is straight behind us."

"And I suppose twenty o'clock is some bird that's directly overhead?" asked Donahue with a smug smile.

"I don't call that by an o'clock, sir."

"Oh? What *do* you call it?"

"Up, sir." A brief pause. "Daggerhorns at two o'clock."

"There must be a thousand of 'em!" said Tarica enthusiastically.

"1,276 by my count, sir," said the car.

"Drive a little closer. I'd like to get a good look at them."

"I think this is as close as we should go, sir."

"But we're still half a mile away from them!" complained Tarica.

"783 yards from the nearest, to be exact, sir—or 722.77 meters, if you prefer."

"Well, then?"

"Well what, sir?"

"Drive closer."

"My job is to protect you from danger, sir."

"They're grass-eaters, for God's sake!"

"There are two cases on record of tourists being killed by daggerhorns," said Quatermain.

"Out of how many?" demanded Tarica.

"There have been 21,843 safaris on Selous, comprised of 36,218 tourists, sir."

"So the odds are eighteen thousand to one against our being killed," said Tarica.

"Actually, the odds are 18,109 to 1, sir."

"Big difference," snorted Tarica. "Drive closer."

"I really advise against it, sir."

"Then take us back to the spaceport and we'll get a vehicle that caters to our needs."

"You don't *need* to see a daggerhorn close up, sir," noted Quatermain reasonably. "You merely *want* to."

"The spaceport or the daggerhorns," insisted Tarica. "Make your decision before they all move away."

"You are adamant?"

"I am."

"Very well," said Quatermain. "Shields up! Screens up! Laser canon at the ready!" It began playing a male chorus singing an invigorating martial song.

Tarica and Donahue peered out through a suddenly-raised titanium grid that covered the windows. The daggerhorns continued their grazing, paying no attention to the approaching vehicle.

Suddenly Quatermain's voice blasted out at 300 decibels through the external speakers. "I warn you: I am fully armed and will not let any harm come to my passengers. Go about your business peacefully and make no attempt to molest them."

The second they heard the speakers, all grazing stopped, and the entire herd suddenly decided it had urgent business elsewhere. A moment later Quatermain and its passengers were all alone on the savanna.

"Invigorating, wasn't it?" said Quatermain in satisfied tones.

"I'm starting to understand why the corporation could afford this particular safari company," muttered Tarica.

"Tailswinger at nine o'clock," announced Quatermain.

"Where?" said Donahue, who was on the left side of the vehicle.

"Well, actually it's about 1,400 yards away and is totally obscured by branches, but my sensors detect its body heat."

"Well, let's go over and look at it."

"I can't, sir."

"Why not?"

"There is a female tailswinger in an adjacent tree, and she's nursing an infant."

"We're not going to steal it," said Donahue. "We're just going to look at it."

"I really can't disturb a nursing mother, sir," said Quatermain.

"But you had no problem disturbing twelve hundred razorhorns," complained Donahue.

"None of *them* were nursing, sir."

"Fine," muttered Donahue. He tested the door handle. "Oh, well, as long as you're stopped, unlock this thing."

"Why, sir?"

"We left the spaceport before I could stop by a bathroom and I've got to pee." He tried the door again. "What's the problem? Is the door stuck?"

"Certainly not, sir," said Quatermain. "I am in perfect repair."

"Then let me out."

"I can't, sir."

"Nothing's going to attack me," said Donahue. "You scared all the animals away, in case you don't remember."

"I agree, sir. There are no potentially dangerous animals within striking distance."

"So why won't you open the goddamned door?"

"Uric acid can do untold harm to any vegetation it comes in contact with, sir," said Quatermain. "We must keep the planet pristine for future adventurers. Surely you can see that, sir."

"Are you telling me that all those razorhorns we saw never take a piss?"

"Certainly they do, sir."

"Well, then?"

"Unlike yourself, *they* are part of the ecosystem."

"I don't believe this!" yelled Donahue. "Are you telling me no one you ever took out had to relieve himself?"

"If you will check the pouch just ahead of you, sir," said Quatermain, "you will find a small plastic bag."

"What if he needs a big one?" asked Tarica.

Another humming sound.

"I have just scanned his bladder, sir, and it contains only thirteen fluid ounces." A brief pause. "You really should cut down on your sugars and carbohydrates, Mr. Donahue."

Donahue muttered an obscenity and reached for the bag.

It was ten minutes later that Quatermain announced that they had come to a small herd of six-legged woolies.

"They look just like sheep," observed Tarica.

"They are identical to Earth sheep in almost every way," agreed Quatermain. "Except, of course, for the extra legs, and the heart, lungs, spleen, pancreas, kidneys, jaw structure, and genitalia."

"But besides that..." said Donahue sardonically.

"Note the billpecker perched on the nearest one's head," said Quatermain. "It forms a symbiosis with the wooly. It keeps the wooly's ears clean of parasites, and the wooly provides it with an endless supply of food." Suddenly the wooly bellowed and shook its head, sending the billpecker shooting off into the air before the shocked bird could spread its wings.

"Its ear is bleeding," noted Donahue.

"Very nearsighted billpecker," said Quatermain knowingly. "It is my opinion, not yet codified in the textbooks, that this is actually a triple symbiosis. The billpecker is a bird with notoriously poor vision, and the blood it inadvertently draws due to this shortcoming actually attracts bloodsucking parasites. Without the blood, no parasites. Without the parasites, no billpecker. It works out very neatly."

"Without the parasites there's no need for billpeckers," said Tarica.

"All the more reason for parasites," answered Quatermain, leaving Tarica certain that there was something missing from the equation but unable to put his finger on it.

"It will be dark in another 45 minutes," announced the vehicle. "I think it's time to choose a place to set up the tent."

"How about right here?" said Donahue.

"No," said Quatermain thoughtfully. "I think 75 feet to the left would be better."

"We're in the middle of an open plain. What the hell's the difference?"

"A meteor fragment landed there 120,427 years ago. One has never landed here. The odds of a second fragment landing in the very same spot are—"

"Never mind," said Donahue wearily. "Set it up where you want."

Quatermain drove 75 feet to the left, and the tent constructed itself as if by magic. "I will be the fourth wall," announced the vehicle. "That way I can continue seeing to your comfort."

The two men exited through the right-hand door and found themselves in a rustic but spotless tent that possessed two cots, plus a table and two chairs.

"Not bad," commented Tarica.

"There is also a portable bathroom just behind this door," said Quatermain as a small door began flashing.

"When's dinner?" asked Tarica. "I'm starving."

"I shall prepare a gourmet dinner, specially adjusted to your individual needs. It will be ready in approximately two minutes."

"Now *that's* service," said Donahue. "Maybe we misjudged you."

"Thank you, sir," said Quatermain. "I do my best."

"Yeah, it was probably just a matter of getting used to each other," added Tarica. "But what the hell—a gourmet dinner on our first night on the trail!"

"We are not on a trail, sir. We are on the Maraguni Plains."

"Same thing."

"No, sir," said Quatermain. "A trail is a—"

"Forget it," said Donahue.

"I'm sorry, sir, but it is embedded in my language banks. I cannot forget it."

"Then stop talking about it."

"Yes, sir." A brief pause. "Please take your seats at the table. Dinner is ready."

The two men sat down, and a moment later a long mechanical arm extended from the vehicle and deposited two plates.

Tarica looked at his dish. "That's an awfully big salad," he remarked. "I'll never have room for the main course."

"Not to worry, sir," said Quatermain soothingly. "This *is* your main course."

"I thought we were having a gourmet dinner!"

"You are, sir. On your plate is lettuce from Antares III, tomatoes from Greenveldt, radishes from far Draksa VII, mushrooms from—"

"There's no meat!" thundered Tarica.

"Your cholesterol reading is 243," answered Quatermain. "I would be ignoring my responsibilities if I were to prepare a meal that would add to it."

"Your responsibilities are to take us to animals, damn it!"

"No, sir. My contract stipulates a total experience. Clearly that includes nourishment."

"What about me?" said Donahue. "There's nothing wrong with *my* cholesterol."

"You are friends with Mr. Tarica, are you not?" asked Quatermain.

"So what?"

"Clearly you would not want to cause your friend emotional distress by consuming an 18-ounce steak smothered in caramelized onions while he was obligated to eat a salad with fat-free dressing."

"It wouldn't bother me a bit," said Donahue.

"This false bravado cannot fool me, sir," said Quatermain. "I know you do not want your friend to suffer."

Donahue saw that it was an unwinnable argument and took a bite of his salad.

"That washer and dryer is looking mighty good to me," said Tarica. "Hey, Quatermain—are there any animals around?"

"No, sir, not at this moment."

Tarica got to his feet. "I think I'll take a walk. Maybe I can work up an appetite for this junk." He walked to the doorway and fiddled with it for a moment. "How the hell do you open this thing?"

"I'm sorry, sir," said Quatermain. "But it is not safe for you to go out."

"I thought you said there weren't any animals in the vicinity."

"That is correct, sir. There are no animals in the vicinity."

"Then why isn't it safe?"

"There is a six percent chance of rain, sir."

"So what?"

"The last 94 times there was a six percent chance of rain, my clients left the tent and came back totally dry," explained Quatermain. "That means statistically you are almost certain to be rained on."

"I'll take my chances."

"I cannot permit that, sir. If you get rained upon, there is a 1.023% chance that a man of your age and with your physical liabilities could come down with pneumonia, and our company could be held legally culpable, since our contract states that we will protect your health and well-being to the best of our ability."

"So you won't let me out under any circumstances?" demanded Tarica.

"Certainly I will, sir," said Quatermain. "If the chance of rain drops to four percent, I will happily open the door to the tent."

"Happily?"

"Yes, sir."

"You have emotions?"

"I have been programmed to use that word, sir," responded Quatermain. "Actually, I don't believe that I have any emotions, hopes, fears, or perverse sexual desires, though of course I could be mistaken."

"Can you at least pull back the roof so we can enjoy the sounds and smells of the wild?" asked Donahue. "You can put it back up if it starts raining."

"I wish I could accommodate you, sir," said Quatermain.

"But?"

"But flocks of goldenbeaks are constantly flying overhead."

"So what?"

"You force me to be indelicate, sir," said the vehicle. "But when you stand beneath an avian...."

"Never mind."

The two men finished their salads in grumpy silence, and went to sleep shortly thereafter. Twice Quatermain woke Donahue and told him to turn over because his snoring was so loud it was likely to wake his friend, and once Tarica got up and trudged to the bathroom, which he used only after demanding that Quatermain avert its eyes or whatever it used to see inside itself.

Morning came, the two men had coffee (black) and low-calorie cheese Danishes (minus the cheese and the frosting), and then climbed back into the vehicle. The tent was disassembled and packed in less than twenty seconds, furniture included, and then they were driving across the plains toward a water hole where Quatermain assured them they were likely to encounter at least a dozen different species of game.

"We're in luck, sirs," announced Quatermain when it was still half a mile away.

"We are?"

"Yes, indeed," the vehicle assured them. "There are silverstripes, spiralhorns, six-legged woolies, Galler-Smith's gazelles, and even a pair of treetoppers, those fellows with the long necks."

"Can you get us any closer?" asked Tarica without much hope.

"Yes," answered Quatermain. "They are all on the far side of the water hole. I foresee no danger whatsoever. In fact, with no avians in the area, I feel I can finally accommodate your wishes and put my top down."

The vehicle drove closer, finally stopping about one hundred feet from the edge of the small water hole. The two men spent the next twenty minutes watching as a seemingly endless parade of exotic animals came down to drink.

Suddenly Quatermain shook slightly.

"Did you backfire or something?" asked Donahue.

"No," answered the vehicle. "I am in perfect working order."

"There it is again," noted Donahue.

"Yeah, I feel it too," said Tarica. "A kind of thump-thump-thump."

Suddenly there was an ear-shattering roar. Most of the animals raced away from the water hole. A few froze momentarily in terror.

"What is it?" asked Tarica nervously.

"This is your lucky day, sirs!" enthused Quatermain. "You are about to see a Gigantosaurus Selous."

As the vehicle spoke, a huge creature, twenty five feet at the shoulder, eighty feet in length, with canines as long as a tall man, raced up the water hole, killing two silverstripes with a swipe of its enormous foreleg, and biting a treetopper in half.

"My God, he's awesome!" breathed Donahue.

"Maybe we should put the top back up," said Tarica.

"Unnecessary," said Quatermain. "He's made his kill. Now he'll stop and eat it."

"What if he wants to eat *us*?" whispered Tarica.

"Calm yourself, sir. He is hardwired to attack his species' prey animals, into which category safari cars and humans from Earth do not fall."

The gigantosaur glared across the water hole with hate-filled red eyes, and emitted a frightening roar.

"I'd back up if I were you," urged Tarica.

"He's just warning us off his kill," explained Quatermain.

"He's not eating," said Donahue. "He's just looking at us."

"Hungrily," added Tarica.

"I assure you this is all in keeping with his behavior patterns," said Quatermain.

"Uh... he's just put his front feet in the water."

"He has no sweat glands," said the vehicle. "This is how he cools his blood."

"He's halfway across the water hole!" said Tarica.

"He has a long neck," answered Quatermain. "Wading into the water makes it easier for him to drink."

"He's not drinking!" said Donahue. "He's coming straight for us!"

"It's a bluff," said Quatermain.

The gigantosaur emitted a roar that was so loud the entire vehicle shook.

"What if it's not?" screamed Tarica.

"Just a moment while I compute the odds of your survival."

"We haven't *got* a moment!" yelled Donahue.

"Checking...." said Quatermain calmly. "Ah! I see. The shaking of the ground dislodged a small transistor in my data banks. Actually, the odds are 9,438 to 1 that he *is* attacking us. That's very strange. I've never had a transistor dislodged before. The odds of it happening are—"

"Shut up and get us out of here!" hollered Tarica as the gigantosaur reached their side of the water hole, leaned forward, and bared its fighting fangs.

"Shall I back up first or put up the top first?" mused Quatermain. "Ah, decisions, decisions!"

Tarica felt something hit the top of his head. He looked up and found himself staring into the hungry eyes of the gigantosaur, who was drooling on him. It opened its enormous mouth, lowered its head—

—and the top of the vehicle slammed shut. There was a bone-jarring shock as the gigantosaur's jaws closed on Quatermain. Three teeth were broken off, and the creature roared in rage, releasing its grip. Quatermain backed up quickly, spun around, and raced off in the opposite direction.

"Well, that's that!" said Tarica, pulling out a handkerchief and wiping the drool from his face and head.

"Not quite," noted Quatermain. "The gigantosaur is in full pursuit."

"You've already told us you won't run out of fuel for decades," said Donahue.

"That is true."

"Then there's no problem."

"Well, there is one little problem," said Quatermain. "My right rear tire is dangerously low, and of course if it goes flat I will have to stop to change it."

"Why did I work Super Bowl Sunday?" moaned Tarica. "I sold five units during the game. Why didn't I stay home and watch like any normal man?"

"I didn't have to sell at nights," added Donahue. "I could have sneaked off to the waterbed motel with that sexy little blonde from the billing department who was always giving me the eye. She was worth at least four sales."

"Relax, sirs," said Quatermain. "The gigantosaur has stopped to kill and devour a purplebeest. We are totally safe." There was an explosion as the tire burst. "Well, 13.27% safe, anyway."

"I'm starting to hate mathematics," said Tarica.

"I don't suppose one of you gentlemen would like to help?" suggested Quatermain.

"I thought you could change it yourself," said Tarica.

"I can. But when unassisted, it takes me 4 hours and 17 minutes. The gigantosaur, should he choose to take up the pursuit again, can reach us in 3 minutes and 22 seconds."

"Why would he?" asked Donahue. "I mean, he just made a kill, didn't he?"

"He made some kills at the water hole," said Tarica. "Maybe he's not hungry at all. Maybe he just likes killing things."

"Open the door and tell me where the jack, wrench, and spare are."

"Those are obsolete," said Quatermain. "Get outside and I will instruct you. My tool case is in the trunk."

Donahue and Tarica were outside, standing before the remains of the back tire, tool kit in hand, half a minute later.

"All ready?" asked Quatermain. "Good. Now, which of you is better versed in quantum mechanics?"

The two men exchanged looks.

"Neither of us."

"Oh, dear," said Quatermain. "You're quite sure?"

"Quite," said Tarica.

"How about non-Euclidian mathematics?"

"No."

"Are you certain? I don't mean to distress you, but the gigantosaur has finished his meal—I believe it took three bites, though there is a 14.2% chance that it took four, given his missing teeth—and he will be upon you in approximately 53 seconds."

"Oh, shit!" said Donahue. "Let us back in. At least you're armored."

"Please replace the tool kit first," said Quatermain. "We can't leave it here for some unsuspecting animal to injure itself on it."

Tarica raced to the back of the vehicle.

"Open the goddamned trunk!" he bellowed.

"Sorry," said Quatermain. The trunk opened, Tarica hurled the tool kit into it, and it slammed shut.

"You shouldn't have yelled so loud," said Quatermain, as the ground began to shake. "The sound of the human voice seems to enrage the gigantosaur. He will be here in 19 seconds."

"Let us in, damn it!" yelled Donahue, tugging at the door.

"I am afraid I can't, sir," said Quatermain. "I am obligated to protect the company's property, which is to say: myself. And the odds are 28.45 to 1 that you both can't enter me and close the door before he reaches us."

Tarica looked behind him. It seemed that the entire world consisted of one gaping gigantosaur mouth.

"I hate safaris!" he yelled, diving under the vehicle.

"I hate safari cars!" screamed Donahue, joining him as the gigantosaur's jaws snapped shut on empty air, sounding like a clap of thunder.

"What are we going to do?" whispered Tarica.

"I'll tell you what we're *not* going to do," replied Donahue. "We're not going to crawl out from under this thing."

They lay there, tense and silent, for half a minute. Then, suddenly, they became aware of a change in their surroundings.

"Do you notice it getting lighter?" asked Tarica.

"Yeah," said Donahue, frowning. "What's going on?"

"Do not worry about me, sirs," said a voice high above them. "I am virtually indestructible when my doors and trunk are locked. Well, 93.872% indestructable, anyway. Besides, it is a far better thing I do today than I have ever done."

They looked up and saw Quatermain sticking out of both sides of the monster's jaws. The gigantosaur tensed and tried to bring his jaws together with full force. Six more teeth broke, he dropped the vehicle (which missed Tarica and Donahue by less than two feet), and raced off, yelping like a puppy that had just encountered a porcupine.

"If you gentlemen will lift me off my side," said Quatermain, "I will change my tire and we will continue the safari as if nothing happened."

The men put their shoulders into the task, and a few moments later Quatermain was upright again.

"Thank you," said the vehicle. "Please re-enter me now, while I go to work on the tire."

They climbed into the car, and the door closed and locked behind them.

"Four hours and 17 minutes and I'll be as good as new," said Quartermain. "Then we'll travel to the Marisula Delta and explore an entirely different ecosystem."

"Let's just travel back to the safari office," said Tarica. "I've had enough."

"Me, too," added Donahue.

"You want to end your safari four days early?" asked Quatermain.

"You got it."

"I am afraid I cannot accommodate you, sirs," said Quatermain.

"What the hell are you talking about?"

"Your company paid for five full days," explained Quatermain. "If you do not experience all five days, we could be sued for breach of contract."

"We've experienced five days' worth," said Tarica. "We just want to go home."

"Clearly your travel has left you mentally confused, sir. You have actually experienced only 21 hours and 49 minutes. I am not aware of confusion taking this form before, but I suppose it can happen."

"I know how long we've been here, and I'm *not* confused," said Donahue. "Take us back."

"Yes, sir."

"Good."

"As soon as the safari is over. My tire will be ready in 4 hours and 13 minutes, and then we will proceed to the Marisula Delta."

Tarica tried the door. "Let me out!"

"I am afraid I cannot, sir," said Quatermain. "You might try to find your way back to the spaceport. If you do, there is a 97.328% likelihood that you will be killed and eaten, and should you make it back intact, there is a 95.673% chance that a breach of contract suit will be brought against my owners. Therefore, I feel I must fulfill our contract. Sit back and try to relax, sir."

"We'll starve."

"Not to worry, sir. I will be able to feed you right where you are."

"We can't sleep in this thing," complained Donahue.

"My understanding of human physiology, which I should note is encyclopedic, is that when you get tired enough, you can sleep anywhere." A brief pause. "All your needs will be provided for, sir. I even have a one-month supply of plastic bags."

IT WAS FIVE days later that Quatermain pulled up to the spaceport.

"Serving you has been a true pleasure, sirs," it intoned as Tarica and Donahue wearily opened the door, raced around to the back, and grabbed their luggage. "I hope to see you again in the near future."

"In your dreams!" growled Tarica.

"I do not dream, sir."

"I do," muttered Donahue. "And I'm going to have nightmares about this safari for the rest of my life."

A squat robot, looking for all the world like a fire hydrant on wheels, rolled up, took their bags from them, and led them to a small waiting spaceship.

"This isn't the same spaceliner we took here," said Tarica dubiously. "It looks like a small private ship."

"Your Stellar Voyages ship is not available, sir," said the robot, as it placed their luggage in the cargo hold "This ship was supplied, gratis, by the safari company as a sign of their appreciation."

"And to dissuade us from suing?" asked Donahue.

"That, too," agreed the robot.

The two men climbed into the ship and strapped themselves into the only two seats provided.

"Welcome, gentlemen," said the ship as the hatch closed and it began elevating. "I trust you enjoyed your once-in-a-lifetime safari experience on the planet Selous. I will be returning you to Earth. I come equipped with all creature comforts except sexual consorts"—it uttered an emotionless mechanical chuckle—"and have a gourmet kitchen at your disposal."

"What happened to the ship we were supposed to be on?" asked Tarica.

"I regret to inform you that it was destroyed in an ion storm just as it was entering the system," answered the ship.

"Uh... we're not going through that same storm on the way out, are we?" asked Donahue.

"Yes, sir," said the ship. "But there is no need for concern, sir. I am a new model, equipped with every conceivable safety device. I am far more maneuverable than a—" The ship shuddered for just an instant. "Just some minor space debris. Nothing to worry about. As I was saying, I am far more maneuverable than a spaceliner, and besides, this is my home system. Every ion storm during the past ten years has been charted and placed in my data banks."

"So you've flown through them before?" said Tarica.

"Actually, no," said the ship. "This is my first flight. But as I say, I am fully equipped and programmed. What *could* go wrong?"

Tarica cursed under his breath. Donahue merely checked to make sure there was a small paper bag near his seat.

"I am sure we're going to get along splendidly together," continued the ship. "You are Mr. Tarica and Mr. Donahue, am I correct?

"Right," said Tarica.

"And my name was clearly discernable in bold letters on my nose as you entered me," said the ship proudly.

"I must have missed it," said Tarica. "What was it?"

"I am the *Pequod*."

Donahue reached for the bag.

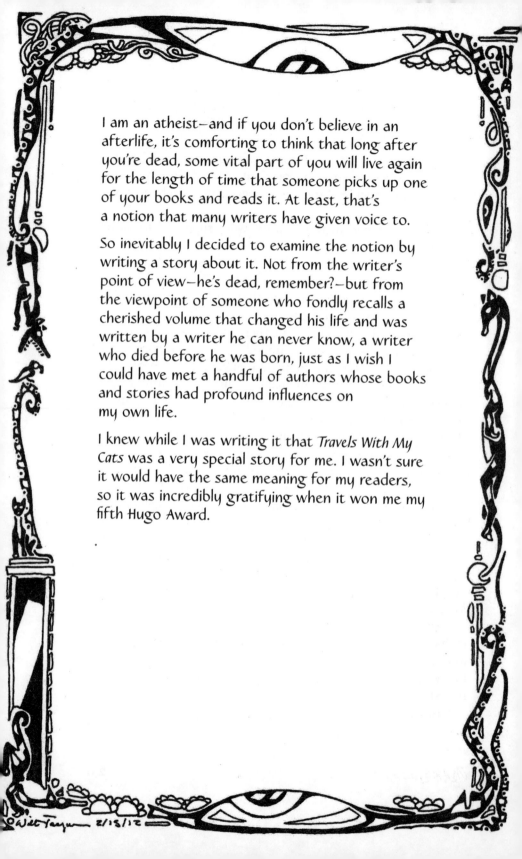

I am an atheist—and if you don't believe in an afterlife, it's comforting to think that long after you're dead, some vital part of you will live again for the length of time that someone picks up one of your books and reads it. At least, that's a notion that many writers have given voice to.

So inevitably I decided to examine the notion by writing a story about it. Not from the writer's point of view—he's dead, remember?—but from the viewpoint of someone who fondly recalls a cherished volume that changed his life and was written by a writer he can never know, a writer who died before he was born, just as I wish I could have met a handful of authors whose books and stories had profound influences on my own life.

I knew while I was writing it that *Travels With My Cats* was a very special story for me. I wasn't sure it would have the same meaning for my readers, so it was incredibly gratifying when it won me my fifth Hugo Award.

Travels With My Cats

I found it in the back of a neighbor's garage. They were re-
tiring and moving to Florida, and they'd put most of their
stuff up for sale rather than pay to ship it south.

I was eleven years old, and I was looking for a Tarzan
book, or maybe one of Clarence Mulford's Hopalong Cassidy
epics, or perhaps (if my mother was looking the other way) a
forbidden Mickey Spillane novel. I found them, too—and then
the real world intruded. They were 50 cents each (and a whole
dollar for *Kiss Me Deadly*), and all I had was a nickel.

So I rummaged some more, and finally found the only book
that was in my price range. It was called *Travels With My Cats*,
and the author was Miss Priscilla Wallace. Not Priscilla, but
Miss Priscilla. For years I thought Miss was her first name.

I thumbed through it, hoping it at least had some photos
of half-naked native girls hidden in its pages. There weren't
any pictures at all, just words. I wasn't surprised; somehow I
had known that an author called Miss wasn't going to plaster
naked women all over her book.

I decided that the book itself felt too fancy and feminine

for a boy who was trying out for the Little League later in the day—the letters on the cover were somehow raised above the rest of the surface, the endpapers were an elegant satin, the boards were covered with a russet, velvet-like cloth, and it even had a bookmark which was a satin ribbon attached to the binding. I was about to put it back when it fell open to a page that said that this was Number 121 of a Limited Printing of 200.

That put a whole new light on things. My very own limited edition for a nickel—how could I say No? I brought it to the front of the garage, dutifully paid my nickel, and waited for my mother to finish looking (she always looked, never shopped—shopping implies parting with money, and she and my father were Depression kids who never bought what they could rent cheaper or, better yet, borrow for free).

That night I was faced with a major decision. I didn't want to read a book called *Travels With My Cats* by a woman called Miss, but I'd spent my last nickel on it—well, the last until my allowance came due again next week—and I'd read all my other books so often you could almost see the eyetracks all over them.

So I picked it up without much enthusiasm, and read the first page, and then the next—and suddenly I was transported to Kenya Colony and Siam and the Amazon. Miss Priscilla Wallace had a way of describing things that made me wish I was there, and when I finished a section, I felt like I'd *been* there.

There were cities I'd never heard of before, cities with exotic names like Maracaibo and Samarkand and Addis Ababa, some with names like Constantinople that I couldn't even find on the map.

Her father had been an explorer, back in the days when there still *were* explorers. She had taken her first few trips abroad with him, and he had undoubtedly given her a taste for distant lands. (My own father was a typesetter. How I envied her!)

I had half-hoped the African section would be filled with rampaging elephants and man-eating lions, and maybe it was—but that wasn't the way she saw it. Africa may have been red of tooth and claw, but to her it reflected the gold of the morning sun, and the dark, shadowy places were filled with wonder, not terror.

She could find beauty anywhere. She would describe two hundred flower sellers lined up along the Seine on a Sunday morning in Paris, or a single frail blossom in the middle of the Gobi Desert, and somehow you knew that each was as wondrous as she said.

And suddenly I jumped as the alarm clock started buzzing. It was the first time I'd ever stayed up for the entire night. I put the book away, got dressed for school, and hurried home after school so that I could finish it.

I must have read it six or seven more times that year. I got to the point where I could almost recite parts of it word-for-word. I was in love with those exotic faraway places, and maybe a little bit in love with the author, too. I even wrote her a fan letter addressed to "Miss Priscilla Wallace, Somewhere," but of course it came back.

Then, in the fall, I discovered Robert A. Heinlein and Louis L'Amour, and a friend saw *Travels With My Cats* and teased me about its fancy cover and the fact that it was written by a woman, so I put it on a shelf and over the years I forgot about it.

I never saw all those wonderful, mysterious places she wrote about. I never did a lot of things. I never made a name for myself. I never got rich and famous. I never married.

By the time I was forty, I was finally ready to admit that nothing unusual or exciting was ever likely to happen to me. I'd written half of a novel that I was never going to finish or sell, and I'd spent twenty years looking fruitlessly for someone I could love. (That was Step One; Step Two—finding someone who could love me—would probably have been even more difficult, but I never got around to it.)

I was tired of the city, and of rubbing shoulders with

people who had latched onto the happiness and success that had somehow eluded me. I was Midwestern born and bred, and eventually I moved to Wisconsin's North Woods, where the most exotic cities were small towns like Manitowoc and Minnaqua and Wausau—a far cry from Macau and Marrakech and the other glittering capitals of Priscilla Wallace's book.

I worked as a copy editor for one of the local weekly newspapers—the kind where getting the restaurant and real estate ads right was more important than spelling the names in the news stories correctly. It wasn't the most challenging job in the world, but it was pleasant enough, and I wasn't looking for any challenges. Youthful dreams of triumph had gone the way of youthful dreams of love and passion; at this late date, I'd settled for tranquility.

I rented a small house on a little nameless lake, some fifteen miles out of town. It wasn't without its share of charm: it had an old-fashioned veranda, with a porch swing that was almost as old as the house. A pier for the boat I didn't own jutted out into the lake, and there was even a water trough for the original owner's horses. There was no air-conditioning, but I didn't really need it—and in the winter I'd sit by the fire, reading the latest paperback thriller.

It was on a late summer's night, with just a bit of a Wisconsin chill in the air, as I sat next to the empty fireplace, reading about a rip-roaring gun-blazing car chase through Berlin or Prague or some other city I'll never see, that I found myself wondering if this was my future: a lonely old man, spending his evenings reading pop fiction by a fireplace, maybe with a blanket over his legs, his only companion a tabby cat....

And for some reason—probably the notion of the tabby—I remembered *Travels With My Cats*. I'd never owned a cat, but *she* had; there had been two of them, and they'd gone everywhere with her.

I hadn't thought of the book for years. I didn't even know if I still had it. But for some reason, I felt an urge to pick it up and look through it.

I went to the spare room, where I kept all the stuff I hadn't unpacked yet. There were maybe two dozen boxes of books. I opened the first of them, then the next. I rummaged through Bradburys and Asimovs and Chandlers and Hammetts, dug deep beneath Ludlums and Amblers and a pair of ancient Zane Greys—and suddenly there it was, as elegant as ever. My one and only Limited Numbered Edition.

So, for the first time in perhaps thirty years, I opened the book and began reading it. And found myself just as captivated as I had been the first time. It was every bit as wonderful as I remembered. And, as I had done three decades ago, I lost all track of the time and finished it just as the sun was rising.

I didn't get much work done that morning. All I could do was think about those exquisite descriptions and insights into worlds that no longer existed—and then I began wondering if Priscilla Wallace herself still existed. She'd probably be a very old lady, but maybe I could update that old fan letter and finally send it.

I stopped by the local library at lunchtime, determined to pick up everything else she had written. There was nothing on the shelves or in their card file. (They were a friendly old-fashioned rural library; computerizing their stock was still decades away.)

I went back to the office and had my computer run a search on her. There were thirty-seven distinct and different Priscilla Wallaces. One was an actress in low-budget movies. One taught at Georgetown University. One was a diplomat stationed in Bratislava. One was a wildly successful breeder of show poodles. One was the youthful mother of a set of sextuplets in South Carolina. One was an inker for a Sunday comic strip.

And then, just when I was sure the computer wouldn't be able to find her, the following came up on my screen:

"Wallace, Priscilla, b. 1892, d. 1926. Author of one book: *Travels With My Cats.*"

1926. So much for fan letters, then or now; she'd died

decades before I'd been born. Even so, I felt a sudden sense of loss, and of resentment—resentment that someone like that had died so young, and that all her unlived years had been taken by people who would never see the beauty that she found everywhere she went.

People like me.

There was also a photo. It looked like a reproduction of an old sepia-toned tintype, and it showed a slender, auburn-haired young woman with large dark eyes that seemed somehow sad to me. Or maybe the sadness was my own, because I knew she would die at thirty four and all that passion for life would die with her. I printed up a hard copy, put it in my desk drawer, and took it home with me at the end of the day. I don't know why. There were only two sentences on it. Somehow a life—any life—deserved more than that. Especially one that could reach out from the grave and touch me and make me feel, at least while I was reading her book, that maybe the world wasn't quite as dull and ordinary as it seemed to me.

That night, after I heated up a frozen dinner, I sat down by the fireplace and picked up *Travels With My Cats* again, just thumbing through it to read my favorite passages here and there. There was the one about the stately procession of elephants against the backdrop of snow-capped Kilimanjaro, and another about the overpowering perfume of the flowers as she walked through the gardens of Versailles on a May morning. And then, toward the end, there was what had become my favorite of all:

"There is so much yet to see, so much still to do, that on days like this I wish I could live forever. I take comfort in the heartfelt belief that long after I am gone, I will be alive again for as long as someone picks up a copy of this book and reads it."

It *was* a comforting belief, certainly more immortality than I ever aspired to. I'd made no mark, left no sign by which anyone would know I'd ever been here. Twenty years after my death, maybe thirty at most, no one would ever know that

I'd even existed, that a man named Ethan Owens—my name; you've never encountered it before, and you doubtless never will again—lived and worked and died here, that he tried to get through each day without doing anyone any harm, and that was the sum total of his accomplishments.

Not like her. Or maybe very much like her. She was no politician, no warrior queen. There were no monuments to her. She wrote a forgotten little travel book and died before she could write another. She'd been gone for more than three-quarters of a century. Who remembered Priscilla Wallace?

I poured myself a beer and began reading again. Somehow, the more she described each exotic city and primal jungle, the less exotic and primal they felt, the more they seemed like an extension of home. As often as I read it, I couldn't figure out how she managed to do that.

I was distracted by a clattering on the veranda. *Damned raccoons are getting bolder every night,* I thought—but then I heard a very distinct *meow.* My nearest neighbor was a mile away, and that seemed a long way for a cat to wander, but I figured the least I could do was go out and look, and if it had a collar and a tag, I'd call its owner. And if not, I'd shoo it away before it got into the wrong end of a disagreement with the local raccoons.

I opened the door and stepped out onto the veranda. Sure enough, there was a cat there, a small white one with a couple of tan markings on its head and body. I reached down to pick it up, and it backed away a couple of steps.

"I'm not going to hurt you," I said gently.

"He knows that," said a feminine voice. "He's just shy."

I turned—and there she was, sitting on my porch swing. She made a gesture, and the cat walked across the veranda and jumped up onto her lap.

I'd seen that face earlier in the day, staring at me in sepia tones. I'd studied it for hours, until I knew its every contour.

It was *her.*

"It's a beautiful night, isn't it?" she said as I kept gaping at her. "And quiet. Even the birds are asleep." She paused. "Only the cicadas are awake, serenading us with their symphonies."

I didn't know what to say, so I just watched her and waited for her to vanish.

"You look pale," she noted after a moment.

"You look real," I finally managed to croak.

"Of course I do," she replied with a smile. "I *am* real."

"You're Miss Priscilla Wallace, and I've spent so much time thinking about you that I've begun hallucinating."

"Do I look like a hallucination?"

"I don't know," I admitted. "I don't think I've ever had one before, so I don't know what they look like—except that obviously they look like you." I paused. "They could look a lot worse. You have a beautiful face."

She laughed at that. The cat jumped, startled, and she began stroking it gently. "I do believe you're trying to make me blush," she said.

"*Can* you blush?" I asked, and then of course wished I hadn't.

"Of course I can," she replied, "though I had my doubts after I got back from Tahiti. The things they *do* there!" Then, "You were reading *Travels With My Cats*, weren't you?"

"Yes, I was. It's been one of my most cherished possessions since I was a child."

"Was it a gift?" she asked.

"No, I bought it myself."

"That's very gratifying."

"It's very gratifying to finally meet the author who's given me so much pleasure," I said, feeling like an awkward kid all over again.

She looked puzzled, as if she was about to ask a question. Then she changed her mind and smiled again. It was a lovely smile, as I had known it would be.

"This is very pretty property," she said. "Is it yours all the way up to the lake?"

"Yes."

"Does anyone else live here?"

"Just me."

"You like your privacy," she said. It was a statement, not a question.

"Not especially," I answered. "That's just the way things worked out. People don't seem to like me very much."

Now why the hell did I tell you that? I thought. *I've never even admitted it to myself.*

"You seem like a very nice person," she said. "I find it difficult to believe that people don't like you."

"Maybe I overstated the case," I admitted. "Mostly they don't notice me." I shifted uncomfortably. "I didn't mean to unburden myself on you."

"You're all alone. You have to unburden yourself to *someone*," she replied. "I think you just need a little more self-confidence."

"Perhaps."

She stared at me for a long moment. "You keep looking like you're expecting something terrible to happen."

"I'm expecting you to disappear."

"Would that be so terrible?"

"Yes," I said promptly. "It would be."

"Then why don't you simply accept that I'm here? If you're wrong, you'll know it soon enough."

I nodded. "Yeah, you're Priscilla Wallace, all right. That's exactly the kind of answer she'd give."

"You know who *I* am. Perhaps you'll tell me who *you* are?"

"My name is Ethan Owens."

"Ethan," she repeated. "That's a nice name."

"You think so?"

"I wouldn't say so if I didn't." She paused. "Shall I call you Ethan, or Mr. Owens?"

"Ethan, by all means. I feel like I've known you all my life." I felt another embarrassing admission coming on. "I even wrote you a fan letter when I was a kid, but it came back."

"I would have liked that," she said. "I never once got a fan letter. Not from anyone."

"I'm sure hundreds of people wanted to write. Maybe they couldn't find your address either."

"Maybe," she said dubiously.

"In fact, just today I was thinking about sending it again."

"Whatever you wanted to say, you can tell me in person." The cat jumped back down onto the veranda. "You look very uncomfortable, perched on the railing like that, Ethan. Why don't you come and sit beside me?"

"I'd like that very much," I said, standing up. Then I thought it over. "No, I'd better not."

"I'm thirty-two years old," she said in amused tones. "I don't need a chaperone."

"Not with me, you don't," I assured her. "Besides, I don't think we have them anymore."

"Then what's the problem?"

"The truth?" I said. "If I sit next to you, at some point my hip will press against yours, or perhaps I'll inadvertently touch your hand. And...."

"And what?"

"And I don't want to find out that you're not really here."

"But I am."

"I hope so," I said. "But I can believe it a lot easier from where I am."

She shrugged. "As you wish."

"I've had my wish for the night," I said.

"Then why don't we just sit and enjoy the breeze and the scents of the Wisconsin night?"

"Whatever makes you happy," I said.

"Being here makes me happy. Knowing my book is still being read makes me happy." She was silent for a moment, staring off into the darkness. "What's the date, Ethan?"

"April 17."

"I mean the year."

"2004."

She looked surprised. "It's been that long?"

"Since...?" I said hesitantly.

"Since I died," she said. "Oh, I know I must have died a long time ago. I have no tomorrows, and my yesterdays are all so very long ago. But the new millennium? It seems"—she searched for the right word—"excessive."

"You were born in 1892, more than a century ago," I said.

"How did you know that?"

"I had the computer run a search on you."

"I don't know what a computer is," she said. Then, suddenly: "Do you also know when and how I died?"

"I know when, not how."

"Please don't tell me," she said. "I'm thirty-two, and I've just written the last page of my book. I don't know what comes next, and it would be wrong for you to tell me."

"All right," I said. Then, borrowing her expression, "As you wish."

"Promise me."

"I promise."

Suddenly the little white cat tensed and looked off across the yard.

"He sees his brother," said Priscilla.

"It's probably just the raccoons," I said. "They can be a nuisance."

"No," she insisted. "I know his body language. That's his brother out there."

And sure enough, I heard a distinct *meow* a moment later. The white cat leaped off the veranda and headed toward it.

"I'd better go get them before they become completely lost," said Priscilla, getting to her feet. "It happened once in Brazil, and I didn't find them for almost two days."

"I'll get a flashlight and come with you," I said.

"No, you might frighten them, and it wouldn't do to have them run away in strange surroundings." She stood up and stared at me. "You seem like a very nice man, Ethan Owens. I'm glad we finally met." She smiled sadly. "I just wish you weren't so lonely."

She climbed down to the yard and walked off into the darkness before I could lie and tell her I led a rich full life and wasn't lonely at all. Suddenly I had a premonition that she wasn't coming back. "Will we meet again?" I called after her as she vanished from sight.

"That depends on you, doesn't it?" came her answer out of the darkness.

I sat on the porch swing, waiting for her to reappear with the cats. Finally, despite the cold night air, I fell asleep. I woke up when the sun hit the swing in the morning.

I was alone.

IT TOOK ME almost half the day to convince myself that what had happened the night before was just a dream. It wasn't like any other dream I'd ever had, because I remembered every detail of it, every word she said, every gesture she made. Of course she hadn't really visited me, but just the same I couldn't get Priscilla Wallace out of my mind, so I finally stopped working and used my computer to try to learn more about her.

There was nothing more to be found under her name except for that single brief entry. I tried a search on *Travels With My Cats* and came up empty. I checked to see if her father had ever written a book about his explorations; he hadn't. I even contacted a few of the hotels she had stayed at, alone or with her father, but none of them kept records that far back.

I tried one line of pursuit after another, but none of them proved fruitful. History had swallowed her up almost as completely as it would someday swallow me. Other than the book, the only proof I had that she had ever lived was that one computer entry, consisting of ten words and two dates. Wanted criminals couldn't hide from the law any better than she'd hidden from posterity.

Finally I looked out the window and realized that night had fallen and everyone else had gone home. (There's no night shift on a weekly paper.) I stopped by a local diner, grabbed a ham sandwich and a cup of coffee, and headed back to the lake.

I watched the ten o'clock news on TV, then sat down and picked up her book again, just to convince myself that she really *had* lived once upon a time. After a couple of minutes, I got restless, put the book back on a table, and walked out for a breath of fresh air.

She was sitting on the porch swing, right where she had been the night before. There was a different cat next to her, a black one with white feet and white circles around its eyes.

She noticed me looking at the cat. "This is Goggle," she said. "I think he's exceptionally well-named, don't you?"

"I suppose," I said distractedly.

"The white one is Giggle, because he loves getting into all sorts of mischief." I didn't say anything. Finally she smiled. "Which of them has your tongue?"

"You're back," I said at last.

"Of course I am."

"I was reading your book again," I said. "I don't think I've ever encountered anyone who loved life so much."

"There's so much to love!"

"For some of us."

"It's all around you, Ethan," she said.

"I prefer seeing it through your eyes. It was like you were born again into a new world each morning," I said. "I suppose that's why I kept your book, and why I find myself re-reading it—to share what you see and feel."

"You can feel things yourself."

I shook my head. "I prefer what *you* feel."

"Poor Ethan," she said sincerely. "You've never loved anything, have you?"

"I've tried."

"That isn't what I said." She stared at me curiously. "Have you ever married?"

"No."

"Why not?"

"I don't know." I decided I might as well give her an honest answer. "Probably because none of them ever measured up to you."

"I'm not that special," she said.

"To me you are. You always have been."

She frowned. "I wanted my book to enrich your life, Ethan, not ruin it."

"You didn't ruin it," I said. "You made it a little more bearable."

"I wonder...." she mused.

"About what?"

"My being here. It's puzzling."

"Puzzling is an understatement," I said. "Unbelievable is more the word for it."

She shook her head distractedly. "You don't understand. I remember last night."

"So do I—every second of it."

"That's not what I meant." She stroked the cat absently. "I was never brought back before last night. I wasn't sure then. I thought perhaps I forgot after each episode. But today I remember last night."

"I'm not sure I follow you."

"You can't be the only person to read my book since I died. Or even if you were, I've never been called back before, not even by you." She stared at me for a long moment. "Maybe I was wrong."

"About what?"

"Maybe what brought me here wasn't the fact that I needed to be read. Maybe it's because you so desperately need someone."

"I—" I began heatedly, and then stopped. For a moment it seemed like the whole world had stopped with me. Then the moon came out from behind a cloud, and an owl hooted off to the left.

"What is it?"

"I was about to tell you that I'm not that lonely," I said. "But it would have been a lie."

"It's nothing to be ashamed of, Ethan."

"It's nothing to brag about, either." There was something about her that made me say things I'd never said to anyone else, including myself. "I had such high hopes when I was a boy. I was going to love my work, and I was going to be good at it. I was going to find a woman to love and spend the rest of my life with. I was going to see all the places you described. Over the years I saw each of those hopes die. Now I settle for paying my bills and getting regular check-ups at the doctor's." I sighed deeply. "I think my life can be described as a fully-realized diminished expectation."

"You have to take risks, Ethan," she said gently.

"I'm not like you," I said. "I wish I was, but I'm not. Besides, there aren't any wild places left."

She shook her head. "That's not what I meant. Love involves risk. You have to risk getting hurt."

"I've *been* hurt," I said. "It's nothing to write home about."

"Maybe that's why I'm here. You can't be hurt by a ghost."

The hell I can't, I thought. Aloud I said: *"Are* you a ghost?"

"I don't feel like one."

"You don't look like one."

"How *do* I look?" she asked.

"As lovely as I always knew you were."

"Fashions change."

"But beauty doesn't," I said.

"That's very kind of you to say, but I must look very old-fashioned. In fact, the world I knew must seem primitive to you." Her face brightened. "It's a new millennium. Tell me what's happened."

"We've walked on the moon—and we've landed ships on Mars and Venus."

She looked up into the night sky. "The moon!" she exclaimed. Then: "Why are you here when you could be there?"

"I'm not a risk-taker, remember?"

"What an exciting time to be alive!" she said enthusiastically. "I always wanted to see what lay beyond the next hill. But *you*—you get to see what's beyond the next star!"

"It's not that simple," I said.

"But it will be," she persisted.

"Someday," I agreed. "Not during my lifetime, but someday."

"Then you should die with the greatest reluctance," she said. "I'm sure I did." She looked up at the stars, as if envisioning herself flying to each of them. "Tell me more about the future."

"I don't know anything about the future," I said.

"*My* future. Your present."

I told her what I could. She seemed amazed that hundreds of millions of people now traveled by air, that I didn't know anyone who didn't own a car, and that train travel had almost disappeared in America. The thought of television fascinated her; I decided not to tell her what a vast wasteland it had been since its inception. Color movies, sound movies, computers—she wanted to know all about them. She was eager to learn if zoos had become more humane, if *people* had become more humane. She couldn't believe that heart transplants were actually routine.

I spoke for hours. Finally I just got so dry I told her I was going to have to take a break for a couple of minutes while I went into the kitchen and got us some drinks. She'd never heard of Fanta or Dr. Pepper, which is what I had, and she didn't like beer, so I made her an iced tea and popped open a Bud for me. When I brought them out to the porch, she and Goggle were gone.

I didn't even bother looking for her. I knew she had returned to the *somewhere* from which she had come.

SHE WAS BACK again the next three nights, sometimes with one cat, sometimes with both. She told me about her travels, about her overwhelming urge to see what there was to see in the little window of time allotted us humans, and I told her about the various wonders she would never see.

It was strange, conversing with a phantom every night. She kept assuring me she was real, and I believed it when she said it, but I was still afraid to touch her and discover that she was just a dream, after all. Somehow, as if they knew my fears, the cats kept their distance too; not once in all those evenings did either of them ever so much as brush against me.

"I wish I'd seen all the sights *they've* seen," I said on the third night, nodding toward the cats.

"Some people thought it was cruel to take them all over the world with me," replied Priscilla, absently running her hand over Goggle's back as he purred contentedly. "I think it would have been more cruel to leave them behind."

"None of the cats—these or the ones that came before—ever caused any problems?"

"Certainly they did," she said. "But when you love something, you put up with the problems."

"Yeah, I suppose you do."

"How do you know?" she asked. "I thought you said you'd never loved anything."

"Maybe I was wrong."

"Oh?"

"I don't know," I said. "Maybe I love someone who vanishes every night when I turn my back." She stared at me, and suddenly I felt very awkward. I shrugged uncomfortably. "Maybe."

"I'm touched, Ethan," she said. "But I'm not of this world, not the way you are."

"I haven't complained," I said. "I'll settle for the moments I can get." I tried to smile; it was a disaster. "Besides, I don't even know if you're real."

"I keep telling you I am."

"I know."

"What would you do if you *knew* I was?" she asked.

"Really?"

"Really."

I stared at her. "Try not to get mad," I began.

"I won't get mad."

"I've wanted to hold you and kiss you since the first instant I saw you on my veranda," I said.

"Then why haven't you?"

"I have this... this dread that if I try to touch you and you're not here, if I prove conclusively to myself that you don't exist, then I'll never see you again."

"Remember what I told you about love and risk?"

"I remember."

"And?"

"Maybe I'll try tomorrow," I said. "I just don't want to lose you yet. I'm not feeling that brave tonight."

She smiled, a rather sad smile I thought. "Maybe you'll get tired of reading me."

"Never!"

"But it's the same book all the time. How often can you read it?"

I looked at her, young, vibrant, maybe two years from death, certainly less than three. I knew what lay ahead for her; all she could see was a lifetime of wonderful experiences stretching out into the distance.

"Then I'll read one of your other books."

"I wrote others?" she asked.

"Dozens of them," I lied.

She couldn't stop smiling. "Really?"

"Really."

"Thank you, Ethan," she said. "You've made me very happy."

"Then we're even."

There was a noisy squabble down by the lake. She quickly looked around for her cats, but they were on the porch, their attention also attracted by the noise.

"Raccoons," I said.

"Why are they fighting?"

"Probably a dead fish washed up on the shore," I answered. "They're not much for sharing."

She laughed. "They remind me of some people I know." She paused. "Some people I *knew*," she amended.

"Do you miss them—your friends, I mean?"

"No. I had hundreds of acquaintances, but very few close friends. I was never in one place long enough to make them.

It's only when I'm with you that I realize they're gone." She paused. "I don't quite understand it. I know that I'm here with you, in the new millennium—but I feel like I just celebrated my thirty-second birthday. Tomorrow I'll put flowers on my father's grave, and next week I set sail for Madrid."

"Madrid?" I repeated. "Will you watch them fight the brave bulls in the arena?"

An odd expression crossed her face. "Isn't that curious?" she said.

"Isn't what curious?"

"I have no idea what I'll do in Spain... but you've read all my books, so *you* know."

"You don't want me to tell you," I said.

"No, that would spoil it."

"I'll miss you when you leave."

"You'll pick up one of my books and I'll be right back here," she said. "Besides, I went more than seventy-five years ago."

"It gets confusing," I said.

"Don't look so depressed. We'll be together again."

"It's only been a week, but I can't remember what I did with my evenings before I started talking to you."

The squabbling at the lake got louder, and Giggle and Goggle began huddling together.

"They're frightening my cats," said Priscilla.

"I'll go break it up," I said, climbing down from the veranda and heading off to where the raccoons were battling. "And when I get back," I added, feeling bolder the farther I got from her, "maybe I'll find out just how real you are, after all."

By the time I reached the lake, the fight was all but over. One large raccoon, half a fish in its mouth, glared at me, totally unafraid. Two others, not quite as large, stood about ten feet away. All three were bleeding from numerous gashes, but it didn't look like any of them had suffered a disabling injury.

"Serves you right," I muttered.

I turned and started trudging back up to the house from the lake. The cats were still on the veranda, but Priscilla wasn't. I figured she'd stepped inside to get another iced tea, or perhaps use the bathroom—one more factor in favor of her not being a ghost—but when she didn't come out in a couple of minutes, I searched the house for her.

She wasn't there. She wasn't anywhere in the yard, or in the old empty barn. Finally, I went back and sat down on the porch swing to wait.

A couple of minutes later, Goggle jumped up on my lap. I'd been idly petting him for a couple of minutes before I realized that he was real.

I BOUGHT SOME cat food in the morning. I didn't want to set it out on the veranda, because I was sure the raccoons would get wind of it and drive Giggle and Goggle off, so I put it in a soup bowl and placed it on the counter next to the kitchen sink. I didn't have a litter box, so I left the kitchen window open enough for them to come and go as they pleased.

I resisted the urge to find out any more about Priscilla with the computer. All that was really left to learn was how she died, and I didn't want to know. How does a beautiful, healthy, world-traveling woman die at thirty four? Torn apart by lions? Sacrificed by savages? Victim of a disfiguring tropical disease? Mugged, raped, and killed in New York? Whatever it was, it had robbed her of half a century. I didn't want to think of the books she could have written in that time, but rather of the joy she could have felt as she traveled from one new destination to another. No, I very definitely didn't want to know how she died.

I worked distractedly for a few hours, then knocked off in midafternoon and hurried home. To her.

I knew something was wrong the moment I got out of my car. The porch swing was empty. Giggle and Goggle jumped off the veranda, raced up to me, and began rubbing against my legs as if for comfort.

I yelled her name, but there was no response. Then I heard a rustling inside the house. I raced to the door, and saw a raccoon climbing out through the kitchen window just as I entered.

The place was a mess. Evidently he had been hunting for food, and since all I had were cans and frozen meals, he just started ripping the house apart, looking for anything he could eat.

And then I saw it: *Travels With My Cats* lay in tatters, as if the raccoon had had a temper tantrum at the lack of food and had taken it out on the book, which I'd left on the kitchen table. Pages were ripped to shreds, the cover was in pieces, and he had even urinated on what was left.

I worked feverishly on it for hours, tears streaming down my face for the first time since I was a kid, but there was no salvaging it—and that meant there would be no Priscilla tonight, or any night until I found another copy of the book.

In a blind fury, I grabbed my rifle and a powerful flashlight and killed the first six raccoons I could find. It didn't make me feel any better—especially when I calmed down enough to consider what she would have thought of my bloodlust.

I felt like morning would never come. When it did, I raced to the office, activated my computer, and tried to find a copy of Priscilla's book at *www.abebooks.com* and *www.bookfinder.com,* the two biggest computerized clusters of used book dealers. There wasn't a single copy for sale.

I contacted some of the other book dealers I'd used in the past. None of them had ever heard of it.

I called the copyright division at the Library of Congress, figuring they might be able to help me. No luck: *Travels With My Cats* was never officially copyrighted; there was no copy on file. I began to wonder if I hadn't dreamed the whole thing, the book as well as the woman.

Finally I called Charlie Grimmis, who advertises himself as The Book Detective. He does most of his work for anthologists seeking rights and permissions to obscure, long-out-of-print books and stories, but he didn't care who he worked for, as long as he got his money.

It took him nine days and cost me $600, but finally I got a definitive answer:

Dear Ethan:

You led me a merry chase. I'd have bet halfway through it that the book didn't exist, but you were right: evidently you did own a copy of a limited, numbered edition.

Travels With My Cats was self-published by one Priscilla Wallace (d. 1926), in a limited, numbered edition of 200. The printer was the long-defunct Adelman Press of Bridgeport, Connecticut. The book was never copyrighted or registered with the Library of Congress.

Now we get into the conjecture part. As near as I can tell, this Wallace woman gave about 150 copies away to friends and relatives, and the final 50 were probably trashed after her death. I've checked back, and there hasn't been a copy for sale anywhere in the past dozen years. It's hard to get trustworthy records farther back than that. Given that she was an unknown, that the book was a vanity press job, and that it went only to people who knew her, the likelihood is that no more than 15 or 20 copies still exist, if that many.

Best,
Charlie

WHEN IT'S FINALLY time to start taking risks, you don't think about it—you just do it. I quit my job that afternoon, and for the past year I've been crisscrossing the country, hunting for a copy of *Travels With My Cats*. I haven't found one yet, but I'll keep looking, no matter how long it takes. I get lonely, but I don't get discouraged.

Was it a dream? Was she a hallucination? A couple of acquaintances I confided in think so. Hell, I'd think so too—except that I'm not traveling alone. I've got two feline companions, and they're as real and substantial as cats get to be.

So the man with no goal except to get through another day finally has a mission in life, an important one. The woman I love died half a century too soon. I'm the only one who can give her back those years; if not all at once, then an evening and a weekend at a time—but one way or another she's going to get them. I've spent all my yesterdays and haven't got a thing to show for them; now I'm going to start stockpiling her tomorrows.

Anyway, that's the story. My job is gone, and so is most of my money. I haven't slept in the same bed twice in close to four hundred days. I've lost a lot of weight, and I've been living in these clothes for longer than I care to think. It doesn't matter. All that matters is that I find a copy of that book, and someday I know I will.

Do I have any regrets?

Just one.

I never touched her. Not even once.

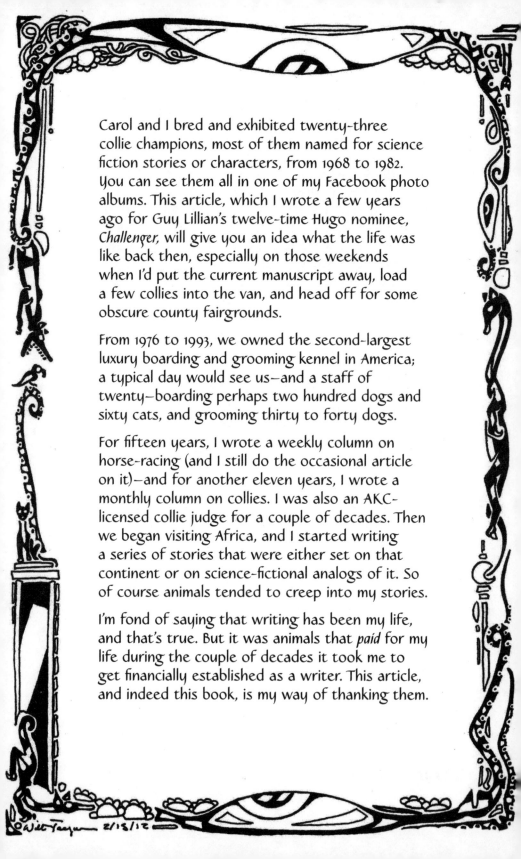

Carol and I bred and exhibited twenty-three
collie champions, most of them named for science
fiction stories or characters, from 1968 to 1982.
You can see them all in one of my Facebook photo
albums. This article, which I wrote a few years
ago for Guy Lillian's twelve-time Hugo nominee,
Challenger, will give you an idea what the life was
like back then, especially on those weekends
when I'd put the current manuscript away, load
a few collies into the van, and head off for some
obscure county fairgrounds.

From 1976 to 1993, we owned the second-largest
luxury boarding and grooming kennel in America;
a typical day would see us—and a staff of
twenty—boarding perhaps two hundred dogs and
sixty cats, and grooming thirty to forty dogs.

For fifteen years, I wrote a weekly column on
horse-racing (and I still do the occasional article
on it)—and for another eleven years, I wrote a
monthly column on collies. I was also an AKC-
licensed collie judge for a couple of decades. Then
we began visiting Africa, and I started writing
a series of stories that were either set on that
continent or on science-fictional analogs of it. So
of course animals tended to creep into my stories.

I'm fond of saying that writing has been my life,
and that's true. But it was animals that *paid* for my
life during the couple of decades it took me to
get financially established as a writer. This article,
and indeed this book, is my way of thanking them.

Appendix

Lord of the
(Show) Rings

Now that so many dog shows are turning up on product-hungry cable TV, I figured that *Challenger's* animal issue was a good place to explain just what a dog show is all about and how it works.

To begin with, a dog show is nothing more than a gigantic elimination contest. At the beginning of the day, there may be up to three thuosand dogs in competition; each continues going into the ring until he is defeated; and when only one is left, the show is over.

Now, the notion of having three thousand dogs walk into a single ring at the same time is just a little far-fetched, so the competition is initially divided into breeds, and each breed is subdivided into various classes.

In collies (which are what Carol and I bred and exhibited for over a dozen years)—and indeed in all other breeds—the sexes are divided for all but the final class. Males are judged first, then bitches, and finally there is an intersex competition for Best of Breed Award.

The classes are as follows: 6-to-9-month-old puppies,

9-to-12-month-old puppies, novice (for dogs who haven't ever won a class), bred-by-exhibitor (which should be self-explanatory), American-bred (also self-explanatory), and finally the open class (for which all dogs six months and older are eligible).

Where there are color differences, the open class is frequently divided. Thus, in collies, there is an open sable class (sable being the "Lassie," color which can vary from lemon-yellow to rich mahogany), open blue merle (the gray or mottled collie that we had inadvertently specialized in), open tricolor (the basically black collies, with white collars and legs and tan facial markings), and the very rare open white (for collies which have colored heads but predominantly white bodies).

Thus, after the judging of the various classes in males, only the class winners are still unbeaten. They in turn come back into the ring for what is known as the Winners class, from which the judge will select one male as the best of the dogs he has seen thus far, an award known as Winners Dog. As a rather meaningless honorarium, he will select the second-best dog as well, an award known as Reserve Dog and not at all unlike first runner-up in the Miss America pageant.

Of all the males entered in the breed on a given day, only Winners Dog will receive points toward his championship. Based on the number of dogs he defeats, he will win from one to five championship points in a day, and he requires fifteen points to become a champion.

And as if that is not hard enough, the American Kennel Club has placed two further stipulations on the attainment of a championship: first, a dog must win at least two "major" shows, which by definition are shows that are worth three, four, or five points (which prevents him from beating a pair of stinkers fifteen times in a row); and second, he must win his two majors under two different judges and must have won some of his remaining points under a third judge (which prevents him from following one judge who happens to like him all over the country and showing under no one else). The point scale varies from breed to breed and area to area; in the Midwest, where our collies did most of their campaigning from 1968 to 1983, a male had to defeat 2 other collies in order to win one point, 10 to win two points, 19 to win three points, 31 to win four points, and 53 or more dogs to win five points. The magic number is 19, since a dog cannot complete a championship without beating 19 or more dogs at least twice. The point scale was usually a little higher for bitches.

Once the points are awarded to Winners Dog, the same procedure is repeated in bitches. Then Winners Dog and Winners Bitch, representing the best non-champion in the breed that day, enter Best of Breed competition against the champions, who compete only in this class since they have already amassed their fifteen points and have no use for any more. One dog, usually but not always one of the champions, is chosen as Best of Breed, and a dog of the opposite sex is chosen as Best of Opposite Sex. If a male is Best of Breed, a bitch will be Best of Opposite Sex, and vice versa.

Finally, the judge chooses between Winners Dog and Winners Bitch and awards one of them Best of Winners. Best of Winners is occasionally a very important award, for it represents a way of picking up extra points without working very hard for them. Let us say that Winners Dog has won three points and Winners Bitch has won only two points. If Winners Bitch is selected as Best of Winners, she has, by proxy, defeated all males and is hence awarded that extra point that Winners Dog had won.

Once Best of Breed Award has been given out in one hundred or more breeds, the original three thousand dogs have been whittled down to a hundred or so who are as yet undefeated on that day. These breeds are then divided into six groups—Sporting, Hound, Working, Terrier, Toy, and the catch-all Non-Sporting Group—and very shortly only six dogs still remain undefeated. These six Group winners now enter the ring for the top prize of the day: Best in Show. Once that

Since we retired from the game, they split the Working group into Working an Herding, so ther are now seven groups.

is awarded, the show is over, everyone packs up their dogs and grooming equipment, and the whole pageant moves on to the next day's show site.

Why do people who lose on a Saturday go right back against the same competition twenty miles away on Sunday?

Simple.

The judging of a dog show is entirely subjective. If Secretariat wins a race by twenty lengths and sets a track record in the process, no one can deny he was the best horse in the race; there is an official photograph of the finish that proves he was first across the wire, there is an automatic timer that proves he ran the distance four seconds faster than the second-place horse, and there are tens of thousands of spectators, each and every one of them ready to testify that he did indeed finish ahead of all the other horses. But a dog show depends on a judge's subjective taste. He may have an innate prejudice against the color of the dog you are exhibiting, or his own kennel may have been plagued by the very fault your animal possesses, or he may simply have gotten up on the wrong side of the bed. Or, in altogether too many cases, he may be licensed to judge fifty or sixty breeds, and is the equivalent to a man who is a jack of all trades and master of none.

On what does a judge base his decision?

Each breed has a written Standard, a verbalization of the ideal dog, and theoretically the judge selects those dogs that most closely approximate their Standards. To do this, he will have the handlers trot their dogs around the ring so he can evaluate their soundness, he will examine each dog's head and body individually so that he can determine its structure, and he will have each dog strike an alert pose so that he can stand back and evaluate the animal as a whole.

Dog shows are held almost every weekend of the year, all across the country, at sights ranging from Madison Square Garden (infrequently) to out-of-the-way fairgrounds that can be reached only by the most circuitous of back roads (altogether too frequently). The only stipulation placed on them by the American Kennel Club is that shows being held on the same day must be at least 250 miles apart.

Okay, you've got the basics. Now let me give you a typical day in the life of a show kennel—ours. And let me take a show from May, which is Desperation Month for collies, because once they shed their coats, they can't be shown until the hair grows back five or six months later. This particular show occurred in May of 1974 and was a little more memorable than most.

On a chilly Saturday morning, I packed three collies into my trusty Dodge minivan and headed north from Libertyville, Illinois to a pair of Wisconsin shows.

One of the three was Ch. (for "Champion") Gully Foyle. (Recognize the name?) Gully, a burly, big-coated blue merle, was the Eddie Stanky of the collie world. Leo Durocher used to say of Stanky: "He can't hit, he can't field, and he can't run. All he can do is beat you." The same was true of Gully. There were dogs with better heads, dogs with better bodies, even a few dogs with better coats—but Gully was the consummate show machine. He loved traveling (and a top show dog will log 30,000 miles a year or more), he loved strange surroundings, and he never relaxed in the ring. He knew exactly what was expected of him and always did the job to perfection.

Around the house, Gully was a little on the dull side. All of his personality was channeled into his stomach (not necessarily a bad thing in a show dog, since they are "baited" with liver in the ring to make them look alert). The best example came in 1973, during the final days of the seventeen-year locust infestation. We had heard stories that 1973 was to be the "year of the locust" but laughed it off as merely leftover dialogue from an old Charlton Heston film—until the spring day the sky became black with them. They didn't exactly harm anyone, but for the better part of a month they were an incredible nuisance. Then, in midsummer, they began dying off by the millions. Every day I would go out to the dog runs, each of which was 50 feet by 15 feet, with my shovel, prepared to get rid of another ten thousand or so of the little insects—and never once did I find a single locust corpse in Gully's run. He was motivated entirely by his appetite, which was exactly what was needed in a show dog. It was enough to make a man quietly proud—once he finished retching.

When Gully wasn't eating—and his diet consisted of anything smaller than himself (or larger, if it was cut into pieces)—he spent his days and nights lying atop his dog house, very much like Charlie Brown's Snoopy. Once, after hearing one joke too many from a visitor, I decided to break Gully of the habit by erecting an A-frame dog house. The next morning, when I went out to clean the runs, I found Gully on the roof, his front feet wrapped over the top of the A-frame, his back legs suspended in space. At this point I gave up and gave Gully his old roof to lie on.

The second of the three dogs was Elf, a tricolor bitch who was fast closing in on her championship. Elf was an unusual case, the kind of dog Albert Payson Terhune would have loved to write about. Some dogs, like some people, try very hard to live; Elf, in her happy but empty-headed way, tried just as hard not to. She was one of the few collies on the grounds that we had bought rather than bred, and when she stepped out of the fibreglass airplane crate that brought her, she was just about the prettiest puppy either of us had ever seen. She remained that way for almost three days. Then she got progressively uglier, and progressively bouncier, until it reached the point where she was offered as a pet, first for $100, then for $75, and finally for free. There were no takers.

So we decided to train her for the show ring, on the unlikely chance that she might some day look like a show dog again. Training Elf was not like training other dogs. She bounced. And bounced. And then bounced some more. At one point I recall suggesting, only half in jest, that we nail her feet to the floor until she learned what was expected of her. We never got around to it, and she never quite learned what was expected, either.

Finally, when she was seven months old, and bearing the official name of Nightwings (which made her Bob Silverberg's favorite dog), she was entered in a huge show in Cincinnati—and lost about as badly as a dog can lose. We decided that the competition might be easier further away from home, and she was sent to a handler in Texas. She was perfectly healthy when she boarded the airplane, and just about dead when she got off. No one knew what had happened during the flight. It took a veterinarian in Texas some two weeks to save her life, and she was then returned home.

She was entered in a show in mid-April of 1971, at which time she would be ten months of age, but two weeks earlier, while Carol and I were away, she was the victim of the only serious dog fight the kennel had ever seen. (We never found out quite what happened, but we knew it had to be her fault. She just naturally got on people's—and collies'—nerves.) When we came home, we found her lying on the ground in a state of shock. I immediately raced her to the vet's, where her front legs required forty-seven stitches—and while her legs were being sewn up, she began wagging her tail and finally jumped around so playfully that the vet was forced to anesthetize her.

Convinced by this time that the God of Dog Shows simply didn't want Elf to get into the ring as a puppy, we decided to breed her—just in time to discover a mild vaginal infection that made breeding her impossible at that time. Unbothered by all of this, Elf bounced her way to her first birthday, managing to sprain a leg while jumping up to visit Gully on his roof.

She was entered in another show in September, but when Carol was brushing her coat out prior to putting her in the car, Elf suddenly yelped—and blood began pouring down her leg. It turned out that she had done so much playful thrashing around while getting her stitches that one tuft of hair had been inadvertently stitched into a wound, and the brush had pulled it out, opening up the wound as well.

Elf bounced along for another three or four months, and was then bred. She whelped eight puppies, three of them of unquestioned show quality. As each of the five pets was sold, Elf was offered to the prospective purchaser at the same price. There were no takers, and so the little tricolor bitch, still addle-pated and undaunted, remained in Libertyville.

In late August of 1972, we were preparing to go to California for a science fiction convention when we received a phone call from Stan Flowers, a professional handler who occasionally exhibited our dogs when we couldn't get to the ring ourselves.

"I've got a couple of nice judges coming up on Labor Day weekend," said Stan.

"Forget it," I said. "Everything is out of coat."

"Are you sure?" urged Stan. "These two have put your dogs up before. They like what you breed."

"No," I said. "The only thing I've got in coat is a pet bitch that nobody wants."

"Let me take a look at her."

So I packed Elf into the car, drove the five miles to Stan's house, and unloaded her.

Stan looked at her and grinned. "You think this is a pet, huh?"

"Yeah," I said. "Don't you?"

"I think she's the best collie in your kennel, including all your champions."

I did a double-take and looked at Elf again. Yes, she had a nice coat, and yes, she wasn't quite so ugly any more, but it was hard to think of her as anything but the resident kook. This was the bitch who, three days before whelping her litter, had climbed onto the kitchen counter, waited until I walked by, and then jumped into my arms, thereby causing me to slip a disk in my back. This was the bitch who, when singing, could reach K above high Q, usually at three in the morning. She had a lot of talents, but winning dog shows would never be numbered among them.

"I'm not going to pay you to take a pet in the ring," I said at last. "I could enjoy my money more by burning it on cold winter nights."

"Double or nothing," said Stan. "Pay me twice my fee if I win, nothing if I lose."

"Sold," I said.

A week later we returned home and found out that we owed Stan double his fee. Elf had won four points, two at each show.

"Luck," I said.

Two weeks later, at her next show, Elf not only won the points but went Best of Breed over the champions.

She showed four more times in October, going Winners Bitch at two of the shows for four more points and Reserve Bitch at the other two.

Then, as cold weather returned to the Midwest, she perversely began losing her coat, and we drove 500 miles to Nebraska with her, hoping to find a major before she was shed out completely. The Nebraska Collie Club, held the day after Thanksgiving, drew an entry of more than forty collie bitches, quite enough for a major, and the judge was an old friend, Noel Denton, who usually liked our dogs.

Carol spent two hours grooming what was left of Elf's coat, applying chalk to the huge white collar to make it even brighter and then brushing it out, trimming feet and whiskers, making each hair on her body stand out proudly and beautifully.

"This is it," Carol announced when she was finished. "We won't be able to get her into another show for months." She pointed to the pile of hair, more than enough to fill a 50-pound grocery bag, that lay on the floor near Elf's grooming table.

I walked into the ring with her, and evaluated the competition. There'd be no sweat winning the class; all I had to do was keep her calm enough to take the Winner's Class as well.

Noel began walking around the ring, looking at each dog in turn, and I decided it was time for Elf to strike a pose and hold stock-still, displaying her body, neck, legs, and expression to best advantage.

Look at me, boss! said Elf. *I'll bet I can touch the ceiling!*

The ceiling was sixty feet overhead. Elf made a valiant attempt to reach it.

When she landed, Noel was staring at her. "Okay, pose her later," he said. "Let's see her move now."

I began trotting across the ring, praying that Elf would run in a reasonably straight line.

You're O.J. Simpson and I'm Dick Butkus and I've got to stop you from scoring a touchdown, said Elf. She hurled herself happily against the back of my legs.

I finally made it around the ring and wound up in front of Noel again. He bent down to examine her head, checking to see if the sides of it were properly smooth and the teeth formed a scissors bite. Elf decided it was mountain-climbing time and just about got her back feet up to Noel's shoulders before she fell off. The crowd at ringside loved her. I began trying to remember any old recipes I might have seen for boiled dogmeat, while Carol covered her eyes with her hands and began walking, trancelike, back to the grooming table.

Elf was given a second-place ribbon and, having time of her life, bounced all the way back to the grooming area. When the show was over, an outraged Noel Denton sought me out.

"Who taught you to handle a dog?" he demanded furiously. "You ought to be ashamed of yourself! This bitch might have won the points today if she had behaved!"

I handed the leash to Noel. "Show me how," I said, trying to hide a malicious grin of anticipation.

"I certainly will," said Noel. As he was speaking, Elf did a back flip.

Noel blinked once, handed the leash back, and walked away without another word.

She was bred to Gully a month later, aborted the litter with her usual good luck, and never coated up in time to find a major entry. Thus, when she came into season in the summer of 1973, she was bred to Gully again and produced a litter of five puppies. Once a bitch weans a litter, she sheds down almost to the skin; with her usual over-enthusiasm, Elf had

This is Elf. You can find Kim on page 43 and Gully on page 57. From the personal photo collection of Mike Resnick.

lost so much hair that she had once again been out of coat for most of the winter and spring shows. And now she was going up to Oshkosh with me, hoping to win one of those elusive majors before the size of the entries dropped off and she had to wait until autumn again.

The third of the dogs I packed into the van was Kim, Gully and Elf's seven-month-old blue son Kim, officially The Gray Lensman, had been something special from the moment he was born. Very rarely can a breeder look at a litter of still-wet newborn puppies and spot a top-notcher, but Kim was one of those exceptions. He was simply the best male we had ever produced, and we knew it the second he popped out.

So much for beauty. Emotionally, he was even more scatterbrained than his mother. Physically, he was stronger and bouncier. He outweighed her by a good 25 pounds, and was capable of doing far more damage with only half the effort.

Take, for example, dog crates. Almost all show dogs ride to and from shows in metal crates, and for a very good reason: if the car should have an accident, the crate will protect the dog and you won't have to spend the next few days scraping his remains off one of the windows. (And, in the case of Gully, it kept him from sitting on your lap and helping you read the traffic signs.)

Kim didn't like dog crates. Since his strength, even as a puppy, was measured in megatons rather than foot-pounds, getting him through the tiny door of a crate was usually a ten-minute undertaking. Once he was inside, however, the door was locked and he could be driven safely to his destination—until the day he became the first collie on record to break out of a locked crate. It occurred on the way to a handling class when Kim was five months old. There was a huge crash, and a moment later Kim trotted to the front of the van, proudly carrying a horribly misshapen metal door in his mouth.

The Oshkosh Kennel Club was Kim's first dog show and he acquitted himself well, winning a large puppy class. When three bitches didn't show up, the entry fell below the level of a three-point show, and I withdrew Elf, who didn't need any more minor points. Gully went Best of Breed again, for the tenth of some twenty-two such awards he was to win during the year.

Gully didn't win the Working Group, a loss which carried no disgrace with it, since there were some thirty Best of Breed winners competing, almost all of them champions, rather than the vast numbers of non-champion dogs involved in the individual breed competition, and I packed up the dogs and headed for the Oshkosh Holiday Inn. (Dog people soon become experts an the best motel chains, as well as individual motels within those chains: this one has enough room to set up three crates and a grooming table next to the bed, that one doesn't have enough grass to walk the dogs,, another one has good food but lousy water, and so forth.)

The next morning I prepared to drive to Appleton, some thirty miles north of Oshkosh, for the Sunday show. I opened the door to the van, took Gully's leash off, snapped my fingers, and the big blue dog jumped into his crate. I repeated the procedure with Elf.

Then I brought Kim out to the van, absentmindedly unhooked the leash, and gestured to a crate.

I HATE CRATES! screamed Kim and ran off in the general direction of the highway. He had gone about fifty yards when he spotted a puli practicing his obedience routine with his owner and ran over to see if this was some game he could join.

The puli took one look at the 85-pound instrument of destruction bearing down upon him and didn't wait to find out whether or not it was a playful puppy. He took off like a bat out of hell, with Kim in hot and happy pursuit, and me and the puli's owner racing after the pair of them.

Around and around the Holiday Inn we raced, through pass-throughs and under playground equipment. Then, as I was turning a corner, I stepped into a fresh pile of dog stool, slipped, and crashed foot-first into a glass wall with a bone-jarring thud. Thinking that I had invented a new sport, Kim raced up, tail a-wag, ready to participate. I grabbed him by the neck, limped painfully to the van, threw him bodily into a crate, and drove to Appleton.

By the time we reached the show site, my foot was swollen to almost twice its normal size from the collision, and I paid a group of helpful boy scouts to unload the dogs and grooming equipment and place them right next to the show ring. I then went around borrowing pain-killers from my competitors.

When asked why I didn't go home, I replied doggedly that Bernard Esporite was judging, and that Esporite had given Elf a Reserve three weeks earlier, and that the bitch that went Winners on that day had finished her championship in the interim and wouldn't be competing and that no goddamned little bruise was going to keep me out of the ring

(Well, nobody ever said dog breeders had to be smart.)

Kim was the first dog in the ring, and I hobbled around painfully, praying that we would be second so as not to have to return for the Winners class. Esporite fell in love with Kim, giving him the first-place blue ribbon and gaiting him around the ring half a dozen times in the Winners class before finally giving the points to a more mature sable dog.

At this point, I considered taking my shoe off to relieve the pressure, but decided I'd never be able to get it on again over the swelling. An hour later, I walked into the ring with Elf, who was bouncier than usual. She won her class, and returned a moment later in the Winners class. Esporite had narrowed down his choice to two bitches, Elf and a lovely locally-owned sable. He decided to base his decision on proper movement.

We went around the ring once, then twice more. Then we ran in an L-shaped pattern, then a T-pattern. Then, just so he would be sure he was making the proper selection, Esporite ran the entire class around the ring twice more. Just as I was sure my foot wouldn't hold up for another step, Esporite pointed to Elf, and the little black bitch celebrated winning her first major by jumping on me and knocking me down.

"Thank God, that's over!" I grated as I hobbled out of the ring.

"What about Gully?" someone asked.

So it wasn't over, after all. I sought out Jean Greenwood, a friend who had bought a number of dogs from us when starting her kennel, and asked her to take Elf into the ring.

"And remember," I said. "It wasn't a major in males, so do everything you can do to let the male beat you for Best of Winners. Don't take any liver into the ring, don't let her stand right, the whole bit."

"But why?" she asked.

"It's a common courtesy," I replied. "She can't win any more points today, but the male can get a major if he beats her—and maybe someday, when we have to go Best of Winners for the extra point, somebody will do the same for us."

Then I was in the ring again. Gully tried his very best, but I simply couldn't keep up with him as we gaited around the ring. As for Elf, she evidently had decided to make a good impression on her new-found friend; everything that she usually did wrong for me she did right for Jean. A few moments later, Esporite awarded her Best of Breed over Gully, who was Best of Opposite Sex. Best of Breed, of course, made her Best of Winners as well; I gave an apologetic look across the ring to the owner of the Winner's Dog, decided that I couldn't stay on my foot long enough to pose for victory photos with Elf and Gully, and hopped off to a telephone to tell Carol the news. Carol was properly overjoyed about the major, but a little too busy to celebrate. The milk had gone bad on the bitch who had whelped a few weeks earlier—the reason she had stayed at home—and she was being forced to wean the puppies earlier than usual.

I hunted up another batch of boy scouts, had them load the van, and stayed just long enough to watch Jean handle

Elf in the Working Group. Elf was back to emulating a rubber ball again, and while the spectators loved it, the judge had scant use for such antics and ignored her throughout the class.

Then came the four-hour drive home. I had borrowed a knife, cut my canvas shoe off, and wrapped my bare foot in my coat. Since the temperature was about 70 degrees, I opened all the windows and pointed the van toward Illinois.

By the time we reached Milwaukee, it was 35 degrees out, and since I was driving in a short-sleeved shirt, I was damned near frozen. I pulled the car over to the side of the road in order to close the windows—and discovered that I couldn't walk. So I shivered for the final ninety minutes and at long last pulled into the driveway. I turned off the motor and began honking the horn, waiting for Carol to come out and help me make it to the door—but Carol was in one of the back rooms, teaching toothless puppies to eat raw hamburger, and didn't hear. Finally, I got out of the van, hopped to the front door, and opened it, yelling for help.

Carol unloaded the dogs, put them in runs, and drove me right to the hospital, where the injury was diagnosed as a badly torn ligament complicated by gross stupidity, and I was fitted with a pair of crutches.

"That's about the dumbest thing I ever heard of," said the doctor as he finished applying an elastic bandage to the foot. "Why didn't you come home the minute it happened—or at least get someone else to show your dogs?"

"It was a major," I said, as if that explained everything.

"What the hell does that mean?" asked the doctor.

"Let me put it this way," I said. "If you were on the eighteenth tee, five under par, and you sprained an ankle, would you quit?"

"Hell, no!" came the explosive reply.

"This is the same thing."

Now that it had been explained in medical terms, the doctor's expression softened.

"Did you break par?" he asked.

"Yes."

"I guess it was worth it, at that," said the doctor.

And, strangely enough, it was.

About the Author

Mike Resnick is the winner of five Hugo Awards (from a record thirty-five nominations), a Nebula Award, and numerous other major awards in the USA, France, Poland, Spain, Croatia, and Japan. According to *Locus Magazine*, he is the all-time leading award winner, living or dead, for short fiction. He is the author of 68 novels, over 250 stories, and 2 screenplays, and the editor of more than 40 anthologies. He has served stints as the science fiction consultant for BenBella Books and the co-editor of *Jim Baen's Universe*, and is currently editing the Stellar Guild line of books for Arc Manor. His work has been translated into twenty-five languages, and he has been named Guest of Honor for the 2012 World Science Fiction Convention. He lives in Cincinnati, Ohio. His website is *MikeResnick.com*.

About the Artists

Borislav "Guddah" Varadinov is a Bulgarian-born artist living near Brussels, Belgium, where he teaches art at the St. John's International School. He works in many styles and genres, from fine art to book illustrations to web design. His fine art was exhibited in Brussels and New York. An avid fan of science fiction, he delights in illustrating science fiction books. His other work for Silverberry Press includes the cover art and interior illustrations for *Pink Noise: A Posthuman Tale* by Leonid Korogodski. He is a finalist of the *AntiMotion: FUTR WRLD* digital art contest. You can find out more about him at *Guddah.com*.

Will Jacques is a product of the Hippie/Psychedelic Movement of Boulder, Colorado during the late 1970s. A strict pen-and-ink traditionalist, Jacques produces his intricate drawings with only a pen. He starts with his signature and goes on from there, often with no plan at all. A life-long fan of Sci-Fi/Horror fiction and imagery, Jacques maintains his own small-press magazine, *GhastlyDoor.com*. Jacques is also an avid ghost hunter with an extensive collection of Real Ghost Photographs. He currently lives with his wife, children, and dogs, in a house built on his great great grandfather's land in southeastern Georgia.

Colophon

The principal font used in this book is Alisal™, one of the best but undeservedly underused creation by Matthew Carter, a 2010 MacArthur Fellow and the founder of Bitstream Inc., the first digital type foundry in the United States. Classified as an Italian old style design, Alisal combines the open fluidity of Renaissance with some slight quirkiness, while remaining eminently readable—as does Mike Resnick's work in general. Moreover, the name of the font means "grove of sycamores" in the Chumash language (also, the name of a guest ranch in California), which makes it a good match in spirit to Mike's animal-themed collection of short stories.

Caterina is a calligraphic sans serif by Paul Veres. Close enough to handwriting to feel informal, but not so much as to be difficult to read, Caterina is used here mainly in the author's introductions to each tale. It shares certain qualities with Alisal.

The titling fonts are *Jaguar*™ by Georg Trump and **Jungle Bones** by Phat Fonts Design.

The book is typeset in Adobe® InDesign® CS4.
The dust jacket art is by Borislav Varadinov.
The interior illustrations are by Will Jacques.
The book is designed by Leonid Korogodski.

The sidenotes (few as they are) are set in Agilita® Condensed, a contemporary humanist sans serif by Jürgen Weltin.

PINK NOISE

A POSTHUMAN TALE

Leonid Korogodski

"PINK NOISE is daring in all the ways that science fiction is supposed to be daring... the most thorough-going exploration of the posthuman condition that I have read."
—KARL SCHROEDER

ALSO FROM SILVERBERRY PPRESS

O ne of the best brain doctors of his time, Nathi lost his own brain five centuries ago when he became a posthuman.

He is called upon to save a comatose girl. The damage is extensive, so he decides to map his own mind into her brain in order to replace the badly damaged part.

But something unexpected waits for him within the Girl's brain. She is a carrier of a Wish Fairy, an enigmatic sentient cyber being whose only purpose is to kill the Wish, a virus used by the ruling cyber Wizard Orders to enslave all posthuman minds—including Nathi's.

Liberated, Nathi forms a symbiotic union—the Dancer—with the Girl, discovers the true cause of her brain injury, and finds a way to break out of the Castle, their high-tech prison, and into the Martian polar night.

But once outside, the real chase begins.

They must resist the cyber wizards who are trying to remotely regain control of their minds while also sending a force in pursuit. This battle must be fought both in the physical world and that of the mind.

"*Pink Noise* is daring in all the ways that science fiction is supposed to be daring. Not only is it great fun to read, filled with moments of touching grace and emotional power, but *Pink Noise* is also the most thorough-going exploration of the posthuman condition that I have read. Korogodski succeeds in giving us a very human story of loneliness and loves lost that's also a mind-bending exploration of all the ways that technology could change what it means to be human. He's raised the bar for the rest of us."
—*Karl Schroeder*

"Korogodski's solution is to garland the tale with a kind of scientific poesie—a super-dense rush of technical explanations for the atomic structure of the human—and posthuman—mind, written with the kind of passion that a pornographer might reserve for a detailed description of someone's reproductive organs, and the kind of lyricism that a poet might use to describe the same parts (albeit by allegory). [...] sucks you in and spits you out again some 120 pages later, having somehow convinced your mind to care about the trials and tribulations of people who can't properly die and who are mostly made from computation." —*Cory Doctorow, BoingBoing.net*

"*Pink Noise* grabs you with the opening paragraph and doesn't let go until you've finished your roller-coaster ride through its fascinating world. Leonid Korogodski has crafted a riveting story in a fully realized future that is as alien as any you're likely to find."
—*Mike Resnick*

"*Pink Noise* [...] combines the force of a parable with a sense of what Wordsworth called 'something more deeply interfused,' that strange, almost mystical effect of the whole being far more than the sum of its parts. It's the sense that we get in *The Great Gatsby* and *Heart of Darkness*." —*SF Site, Top Ten Books of 2010*

Chopin
in the
Attic

Elisabeth Bell Carroll

"A dazzling spiral of passions. A thrilling book."
—*John Casey*, Author of National
Book Award winner *Spartina*